RUSH

THE GAME BOOK ONE

Eve Silver

KATHERINE TEGEN BOOKS
An Imprint of HarperCollins Publishers

Katherine Tegen Books is an imprint of HarperCollins Publishers.

Rush: The Game Book One

Library of Congress Cataloging-in-Publication Data
Silver, Eve.
    Rush / Eve Silver. — 1st ed.
        p.   cm. — (The game ; bk. 1)
    Summary: Rochester, New York, high schooler Miki Jones is pulled
into a sort of a game in which she and other teens battle real-life aliens and
the consequences of each battle could be deadly.
    ISBN 978-0-06-219213-4 (hardcover bdg.)
    [1. Science fiction.   2. Combat—Fiction.   3. Extraterrestrial beings—
Fiction.   4. Interpersonal relations—Fiction.]   I. Title.
PZ7.S58566Rus 2013   2012025496
[Fic]—dc23   CIP
                                         AC

13 14 15 16 17   CG/RRDH   10 9 8 7 6 5 4 3 2 1
❖
First Edition

TO DYLAN, MY LIGHT;
SHERIDAN, MY JOY;
AND
HENNING, MY FOREVER LOVE

CHAPTER**ONE**

MIKI.

My head jerks up. My attention narrows. I push off the chain-link fence that marks the limit of school property. My friends are sitting cross-legged on the grass a few feet away under the massive oak tree we've claimed as our little corner of the field.

Actually, Glenbrook High has a ton of fields: two softball, two baseball, five tennis courts, track and field, the discus/hammer throw, four general-purpose fields, and the football turf with the thousand-seat bleachers. Our spot is at the edge of an all-purpose field, chosen by my friends for the excellent view of the track and the tennis courts. They like to watch boys in shorts.

We're here pretty much every day after school.

Definitely days when there's track. No track today, just a lone boy running laps.

Miki.

There it is again, a boy saying my name. Like he knows me. Like he expects me to listen when he speaks.

I can't place the voice and I can't see the speaker. Last year, a girl in my class had this creeper guy following her home. I hope I haven't acquired a shadow of my own. The possibility sends a chill crawling up my spine despite the late-afternoon sun that's warm on my face.

I take a couple of steps toward the path that runs from the school fence to the street—one of several that fan out from the school like the spokes of a wheel. The path's more of a small park that sits between two houses, a narrow strip of asphalt bounded by wide strips of grass. Trees rise on either side, their branches forming a green canopy. It's not quite fall yet; the leaves won't change color for a few weeks.

I wander to the edge of the small park and stop half a dozen yards from my friends, a dozen yards from the street.

There's no one on the path.

But *someone* said my name.

From where I'm standing, I can see a handful of little kids being ushered across the street by the crossing guard in front of Oakview Elementary a block away. I watch for a few minutes, until no more little kids wait by the side of the road and the crossing guard gets ready to leave.

"Miki!" This time, it's my best friend, Carly Conner, calling my name. She's stretched out on the grass, her long legs crossed at the ankles. The weight of her torso rests on her bent elbow, her #11 Extra Light Blond hair falling in a sleek curtain just past her shoulders. I like it better than last month's #100 Bleach Blond.

At five feet six, I'm a shade taller than Carly. My hair's as dark as hers is pale. My features reflect the fact that my mom's dad was Nisei—second-generation Japanese-American—but my eyes are my dad's mom's unique shade of indigo blue. Every time people tell me I look "exotic," I have to resist the urge to kick them in the shin.

Carly's brows lift. Her unspoken question hangs between us: *Why are you over there instead of over here?*

I open my mouth, but before I can say a word, Deepti Singh asks, "Did you see him?"

"See who?" I ask, too sharp, thinking she knows something about the boy who was calling my name.

"What bug crawled up your ass?" Dee snaps back at the same time as Carly pushes upright and says, "New guy."

Then Kelley Zimmer chimes in with, "Incredibly hot new guy," and I realize we're talking about completely different things.

Dee crosses her arms over her chest and presses her lips together. Hurt feelings. I sigh. Carly gives me her *make nice* look. She's a middle child. Always the peacemaker.

"How do you know he's hot?" I ask, more to mollify Dee than from genuine interest.

Success. She perks up and says, "We heard from Sarah. She saw him. Sort of. His profile, anyway."

"I got to see more than his profile." Carly draws out every word, playing Dee and Kelley like the keys of a piano. "I took the attendance sheet to the office for Ms. Smith during last period, and he walked in just as I was walking out. We were practically chest to chest."

I know Carly might be exaggerating just a little. She probably saw him from across the office, but her modified version makes a far better story.

"And?" Dee asks.

"Let's just say his guns"—Carly strokes her fingertips along her biceps—"ought to be *licensed*."

I snort at the outdated expression. Carly shoots me a look and waggles her eyebrows. Of course, she's pushing all Dee's buttons, and Dee plays right into her hands.

"Oh. My. Gawd." Dee's eyes widen, and she claps her palms together.

"Describe him. Every detail," Kelley demands.

Carly reaches into her backpack, pulls out a lighter, and flicks it. The tip of her cigarette glows red. My gut clenches at the too-familiar sight. A white curl of smoke drifts from between her lips, and I look away before I say something I'll regret.

She knows my history, but she's smoking anyway. Preaching won't make her do anything differently. It'd probably just make her dig in her heels. Been there, tried that when she went through her emo phase, then her multiple piercing phase, then her drinking phase—which ended in a puddle of puke right in front of Principal

Murray's office, a one-week suspension, and a monthlong grounding.

I stood by her through all of it.

She stood by me through worse.

Miki.

With a gasp, I spin around to find empty space behind me. The only boy anywhere near me is the one running laps on the track, and he's too far away to be the one saying my name. I watch him for a bit, watch his arms and legs pumping, and I know what he's feeling: endorphins racing through him. Runner's high. Crack of dawn five days a week I'm there, in my zone, alone with my music and the rush I get as my feet slap the ground.

The boy on the track slows. Stops. Walks over to the grass and grabs his water bottle. He's tall, dark haired. The distance between us is enough that I can't be sure, but I think he's looking at me. Then I *know* he is because he offers a terse nod.

Luka Vujic. We were friends about a million years ago, until . . . when? The middle of fourth grade? He wasn't at Glenbrook last year as a sophomore—I think his dad was transferred somewhere out west. Now he's back, and he's changed. It isn't just that he's taller and leaner. There's something in his eyes that wasn't there before.

Now those eyes are fixed on me. I bob my head in reply and turn back to my friends.

"Oh. My. Gawd," Dee says. She's an equal-opportunity oh-my-gawder. "Is that Luka?"

They all turn their heads and stare.

"He is so cute," Kelley says.

"So cute," Dee agrees. "And so much more mature than his friends."

"You think?" Carly asks.

Dee shrugs. "He doesn't burp and make fart jokes. Not in the caf, anyway."

Now there's a recommendation of maturity if ever I heard one. But I do think Dee's right. Despite the fact that he's easygoing and friendly, Luka always seems to hold himself apart somehow, even in a crowd.

Carly watches Luka for a moment, and then she says, "He's not just gorgeous. He's smart, too."

We all stare at her. That isn't something that usually impresses her. She's more of a solely-interested-in-cute-face-and-lots-of-muscles, all-the-better-if-he-has-a-car kind of girl.

"What?" she asks, eyes wide. "It's hard to miss. He's in my chem class and he pretty much skates through every question without a hitch." She smirks. "He sits next to me and doesn't seem to mind explaining stuff."

"But you're good at chem," I point out. "Why do you need him to explain stuff?"

All three of them look at me like I've grown a second head. Then I get it. "Right. It isn't a question of need—"

"It's a question of want," Carly finishes for me with a grin. "So far, I have Luka helping me in chem, Darnell helping me in Spanish, and Shey helping me in geometry."

"Shey," Kelley says on a sigh.

"You don't need help in any of those classes," I say.

All three of them roll their eyes at me.

"I do," Carly says, with a lift of her brows. "I really do."

"I hope the new guy's in *all* my classes," Kelley says. "Was he in any of yours today?"

"I don't think he started classes yet," Carly says. "I think he was just meeting with Principal Murray when I saw him in the office this afternoon."

"I guess it's a paperwork thing." Kelley sighs again. "Now we have to wait till Monday to see what classes he has."

And they're off, talking about him again, speculating on how his schedule might overlap with theirs. My attention wanders, but I catch the words *hot* and *old-school aviator sunglasses*. They jump to the next topic: the Halloween dance. It's still weeks away, but it takes time to plan a good costume.

I haven't yet put much thought into mine.

I wish I could. I wish I thought it mattered. My friends all get so excited about things like movies and dances and shopping; they *feel* things so intensely. I go through the motions and bluff extremely well, but I'm not like them. I haven't been for almost two years. And that kills me. I just want to be . . . normal again.

I stand by the fence, watching them, far enough away that I'm part of their group, but not.

This time, the chill crawls up my spine *before* I hear the words.

Miki Jones.

Better and better. He knows my last name, too.

"What?" I ask under my breath, scanning the trees, the garbage can, the fence. I'm annoyed now. Someone's hiding somewhere. Voices don't just materialize in a person's head. But my friends are focused on one another, not one of them noticing that someone's calling my name, and I have the horrible thought that maybe I *am* hearing voices, like that guy in the movie about the beautiful mind.

Not liking that possibility, I decide it's a prank. "Having fun?" I mutter as I spin a slow circle and end up facing the street again. The crossing guard's gone. There's no one else around. Except—

There's a girl, a little girl. She's squatting in the road in the middle of the crosswalk. Doing what? Picking something up? I expect her to stand up and move along, and when she doesn't, wariness shoots through me.

A memory hits: me walking across that same crosswalk when I was a kid, and my mother waiting on the far side of the street with a hug and a cookie. I hit back, burying the image because it hurts too much to think about it. Pain's one of the two things I *do* still feel with a razor's edge. Anger's the other. Everything else is muted and distant, like I know I *ought* to feel things even when I don't.

Right now, I choose anger instead of pain. That little girl shouldn't be there. Someone should have picked her up after school. Her head's bowed, and she doesn't look up when I yell, "Hey," and again, louder, "Hey!"

There's something familiar about her. . . .

Crap. She's Janice Harper's little sister. She's deaf. And Janice isn't here to get her because she's in detention.

Miki! Now!

The words reverberate in my thoughts, but I'm already moving before the unseen boy finishes barking the order. Because there's a truck—old, rusted, going too fast—just moving into the blind curve, picking up speed and weaving side to side. The driver's head is down; there's a phone in his hand. I can't be sure, but I think he's texting.

My heart slams against my ribs.

I don't think. I just run. My feet hit the ground, but I feel dull, sluggish, like I'm running through waist-deep water and everything in the world—including me—has slowed down to a crawl except that truck.

I'm too far away.

Faster. I need to move faster.

The truck is coming out of the curve now, doing at least double the speed limit, music blaring from the open windows.

I'm screaming at the top of my lungs, my throat already raw. The kid can't hear me. She can't hear me.

I run full tilt, chest heaving, terror driving me. And something else. All the anger and fear and grief I've been bottling up for two years bubbles to the surface, finding its release in the slim hope that I can control the outcome here, that I can reach her in time.

I'm at the sidewalk now. A single leap carries me over the grass and the curb onto the road.

My shadow falls across the girl and she looks up, her eyes going wide and her mouth rounding a perfect little O. She starts to rise. There's a terrible shriek of tires on asphalt as the driver sees us and hits the brakes. The truck skids sideways to come at us broadside.

I dive, hands outstretched. My palms connect with the girl's chest, and I shove her as hard as I can.

She goes flying back with a cry.

I see everything with abnormally sharp clarity, like a series of perfect snapshots capturing each millisecond. I see the girl. I see her tears. I see the blur of motion from the corner of my eye as my friends run along the sidewalk toward us. And someone else shooting past them . . . Luka.

I see the truck spinning again to come at me head-on—so close I can make out the chunks of rust on the grille—and the pavement, flat and gray, coming up to meet me. I hit hard and slide along the rough surface, layers of cloth and skin scraping away.

There's the endless screech of the brakes and the smell of burning rubber. My head jerks up and I try to scramble out of the way. I can't find my footing.

Terror clogs my throat.

Then there's a hand on my arm, tight as a vise, yanking me to my feet.

Luka.

He pulls. I pull. Opposite directions. Our dance is all wrong.

The truck slams us both.

I shouldn't be able to define each sensation, each event. But I can. I double over forward with the force of the blow. Then I'm lifted. I'm flying. Screaming. Until I hit the ground and my breath is forced out in an obscene rush.

There's no pain. Not yet. Only shock and the cold knife of my fear.

Sound hurts my ears. My name. People are screaming my name, over and over. I want to tell them I'm okay, but my mouth won't work, and I have no breath to lend sound to my words.

Turning my head, I see the little girl standing at the side of the road, her face streaked with tears. My friends are standing beside her, screaming, pushing at the air. I don't understand what they're trying to do. The roaring in my ears drowns out whatever they're saying.

The lights flicker like someone flipped a switch, except we're outside and there's no switch to flip. Everything goes dark. Then light again. The truck's right in front of me, the rusted chrome bumper stained red, like finger paint or smears of cherry juice.

I turn my head to the opposite side and see Luka, his body twisted and broken, a puddle of blood forming beneath him on the road. His eyes are open. They're dark blue, bright and clear as an arctic lake. Like mine. I never noticed that before; I thought his eyes were brown. His lips move. I can't hear, but I think he's saying, "Okay."

He's wrong. This definitely is not okay.

I look down and feel a sort of distant horror as I see a body that is mine but not mine. My limbs are bent at odd angles. Shards of bone poke out through my skin. When I try to move, I realize that I feel no pain because I feel *nothing*. Nothing at all. And no matter how hard I try, I can't move anything but my head.

I'm broken, like Luka. Broken and bloody.

The thought feels hazy, as though it ought to mean more to me than it does.

I smell cotton candy and cookies. I smell metal and raw steak.

Then I hear it again. The screaming. But it's far away, growing fainter. It fades until I hear only the sound of my own heartbeat, growing ever slower. Slower.

Slower.

Stay still. Let it pass, the boy says in my head.

Sounds like a plan.

I wait for the next heartbeat, but it doesn't come.

CHAPTER **TWO**

I OPEN MY EYES TO SEE THE BLURRED OUTLINES OF LEAVES and branches and a sky so blue it hurts. As the world tilts and drops, I curl my fingers into the long grass and hang on. The world's still spinning, but at least if I hold on, I won't fall off.

The grass . . . it feels wrong, but I can't say why. Confusion rides me as I try to sit up.

"Wait. Let it pass." A boy's voice. Cool. Authoritative. Familiar?

I feel like I should recognize it. I think there are all sorts of things I ought to know—*would* know—if the knowledge would just stop dancing away from me. But I can't quite grab hold of it. The thoughts drift away as my vision clicks into sharp focus.

The colors here are too bright. Too blue. Too green. They burn my eyes, straight through to my brain, a deep, agonizing pain. I close my eyes against the glare.

"Just lie still."

Definitely sounds like a plan. The ground feels like it's going to fall away, and my head feels like it's about to explode. Carly gets migraines. I've never had one before, but I wonder now if they feel like this. If so, I need to be a lot more sympathetic to her in the future.

Carly. My best friend. I remember *her* . . . but I can't remember where I am or how I got here.

Fear uncoils in my gut. I know from experience that fear can easily tip down the slippery slope to full-on panic.

Eyes closed, I concentrate on visualizing a sandy beach and slowing my breathing—in through my nose, hold, out through my mouth—the way Dr. Andrews, my grief counselor, taught me. I've done this often enough to know it works. I've used it to numb the panic and sorrow for the past two years. Problem is, I've also succeeded in dulling pretty much every other emotion. There's always a price.

". . . scores . . . ," a girl says, her voice tinny and distant.

"Nice . . . multi-hit bonus . . . ," a boy says a few seconds later. Neither voice is familiar. Their words fade in and out.

I want to open my eyes and see who's talking, but my lids are heavy. I feel like I'm being sucked into a murky lake, hearing the words through water. I lose track of their conversation, then the girl says, ". . . didn't make it back . . ."

". . . selfish jerk . . . ," the boy answers. "Put all of us at risk so many times. Hanging back and stealing the hit points . . . all he cared about was himself and getting out. . . ."

"Doesn't mean he deserved to . . ."

"He put *you* at risk. As far as I'm concerned, that means he deserved . . ."

The girl's voice changes, becomes softer. ". . . Ty . . ."

The conversation fades until all I can hear is my own heartbeat. I focus on that, only that. But there's something about my heartbeat, something I *should* know. My thoughts are sludgy. I try to sift through the mess. I'm—

In a sickening burst, I remember. The little girl. The truck. The blood. That's why the grass feels wrong. Because last thing I remember I was lying in the road.

—I'm dead.

My eyes snap open again. With a gasp I try to push upright, but there's a hand flat on the middle of my chest, holding me down.

"I told you to wait. Lie still." *This* voice I recognize. It's the boy, the voice in my head. Except now he's not in my head. He's hunkered down next to me with the heel of his palm on my breastbone and his fingers splayed toward my throat.

"Is this heaven?" The words slide free before I can think them through. I wish I could call them back.

"Hardly." He sounds amused.

My gaze lifts to his face. Whatever I mean to say shrivels on my lips and all I can do is stare.

Of all the things I ought to notice at this precise

moment, his appearance should be the last on my list. But I notice anyway. Not because he's beautiful, though he definitely is that. He's about my age, with the sort of wide-shouldered, lean build that makes girls look. His hair is light brown, shot with gold and honey, worn in long, messy layers that fall to frame high, chiseled cheekbones. But the part I most want to see—his eyes—are hidden by mirrored, old-school aviator sunglasses.

That's why I stare. Because of those glasses. I'm afraid they aren't real, that none of this is real.

I remember Carly's description of the hot new guy and his aviator shades, just like the ones this boy is wearing. I shiver. What if I'm not here, lying on the ground under a too-blue sky? What if I'm unconscious in a hospital bed attached to tubes and wires and all of this is conjured by my imagination and wispy memories of Carly's words?

"It's real," he says, his tone flat. I watch his mouth shape the words. He has beautiful lips, the lower slightly fuller than the upper.

"What—" The word comes out as a croak. I roll my lips inward and swipe them with my tongue, then try again. "You can read my mind?" Not a possibility I'd normally even consider, but today's shaping up to be a day that's anything but normal.

He smiles, a faint curve of his lips that reveals the barest hint of a long dimple carved in his right cheek. "No, but I can read your expression. And I've been doing this long enough that I know what most people tend to think when they first open their eyes."

"Doing *what* long enough?"

"This," he says, and nothing more.

A second of silence stretches into two. Though I can't see behind his glasses, I have the feeling he's not looking at me anymore, that he's scanning the area, looking for . . . something. But as I stare at him, *I* see me—tiny distorted reflections of me in the shiny, convex lenses. He leans a little closer and my image sharpens, my skin too pale, my hair too dark. The contrast makes me look like a goth.

This time he smiles with a flash of white teeth, and the dimple carves a little deeper. "A goth," he echoes.

"I said that out loud."

"Yeah. Happens to all the new arrivals. Hard to separate thought from speech at first." He tips his head a bit to the side, studying me. "It'll pass."

"I heard you," I whisper.

"That's a good thing. Your hearing's fine."

"No, I mean I heard you earlier, inside my head."

"Did you now?" He doesn't sound surprised, or even curious.

I wait, and when he doesn't say anything more, I sift through the bunch of questions that are clamoring for release and pick the simplest one. "Where am I?"

"The lobby."

I glance around at the wide patch of long grass bounded by trees. "Lobbies have marble tiles."

"Not this one."

So maybe that wasn't the simplest question. Or was it just the answer that was complicated? "Who are you?"

"Jackson Tate." He says only his name, with no elaboration and no follow-up question of his own.

I jump in and offer, "I'm Miki. Miki Jones."

"I know."

Right. He knows my name. He's been calling it all afternoon. In my head.

I'm about to ask how he did that when I register what he said earlier about all the new arrivals. Put that together with his assertion that this is a lobby, and I'm forced to revisit the impression I had when I first woke up. I blurt out, "Am I—"

I can't finish the question. Not out loud. It's like if I say it out loud, it'll make it true. I struggle to sit up.

"No," he says, but I'm not sure if he's answering my unspoken question—telling me I'm not dead—or telling me not to move.

With a bit of effort I manage to sit up. He doesn't help, but he doesn't stop me, either. Then he touches my wrist. I glance down to see that I'm wearing a bracelet with a black strap and a rectangular screen that's filled by a shimmering, swirling pattern.

I frown. "That's not mine."

"It is now." His fingertips play across the screen.

"What are you doing?" A sensation of warmth flows from my wrist to my elbow. It isn't unpleasant, just unexpected.

"Activating it."

"Uh . . . no you're not." I jerk my hand away. "You're not activating anything until I get some answers."

"Yeah, I am. If I don't activate it, it explodes." He sounds dead serious.

"For real?"

He doesn't answer, and that pisses me off. But I can't be certain it isn't for real, and since I'm fond of having a hand at the end of my arm, I offer my wrist. He finishes running his fingers over the screen. I notice that he's wearing a bracelet, too. The pattern on mine is silver; the one on his is forest green.

Except . . . now the one I'm wearing isn't silver anymore. Whatever he did, he turned mine green, too.

"What is it?" I ask, feeling like I'm parroting myself . . . what, what, what? But I can't seem to make my brain come up with anything better.

"Health."

My gaze flashes to his. Sort of. I can't see his eyes; he's still wearing those opaque glasses. His expression gives me nothing. "Can you be a little less cryptic?" I snap, and then regret my tone. Biting his head off isn't likely to get me any answers. The whole catch-more-flies-with-honey thing. But then, I've been perfectly polite up till now, and that hasn't gained me any ground, either.

I shake my head, and as I do, I realize the headache's gone. That's one good thing, at least. Never let it be said that I'm not an optimist. With effort, I modulate my tone. "So . . . the bracelet? You said it's . . . *health*?"

One brow arches, and he dips his chin toward my wrist. "The bracelet's your con. The color's your health. Don't let it turn red."

For a long moment, I stare at him, waiting for the rest of the explanation. It never comes. "Am I supposed to know what that means?"

"Not a gamer, huh?" He sighs. "It means exactly what I said."

When I was a kid, my grandfather used to do that: answer my questions with nonanswers or riddles. I doubt Jackson Tate plays that game better than Sofu.

I change direction and ask, "Would the bracelet really have exploded if you didn't activate it?"

There's a slight pause that makes me think I've surprised him by shifting topics. Good. Better that I have him on his toes than he have me on mine.

"No," he says, and I think the corners of his mouth twitch in the hint of a smile. I'm hit with a weird sense of déjà vu, like I've been in this moment before, seen his face, the sun on his hair, that smile. I smell the ocean, hear the waves breaking. Before I can figure it out, he rises and walks away, and the feeling's gone.

"Good to know," I mutter under my breath, sort of getting the last word, but he's too far away to hear me, so maybe that doesn't count.

Pushing up on all fours, I wait for the dizziness to hit. I'm surprised when it doesn't. I feel fine. Better than fine. Everything's in perfect working order. I run my palms along my jeans-clad thighs, then tug at the hem of my T-shirt. Even my clothes are intact, as though I never scraped away cloth and skin on the pavement, never cracked my bones into pieces and watched the jagged edges tear through muscle and flesh.

A shudder crawls across my skin, and my stomach does an unpleasant roll. Better not to think about my injuries.

The injuries that were there and now aren't there.

Yeah, better not to think about *that*, either.

Carefully, I get to my feet, then glance at my wrist. The screen's a dark forest green, swirling with shades of lighter green and turquoise and blue. I slide my index finger under the band. It's tight, but not tight enough to be uncomfortable. It doesn't yield as I try to pull it off, and I can't find the clasp to undo it.

"Don't bother. It's on there until our mission's complete."

My head jerks up. "Luka!" I feel a surge of relief at seeing him standing in front of me, whole, unhurt, unbloodied. I take a step forward, my hands coming up on instinct to hug him, my smile stretching into a grin. Then I see the look on his face and I freeze. He looks decidedly uncomfortable. Maybe even . . . guilty. Of what?

"You're okay," I say, and drop my hands back to my sides, feeling lame.

"Yeah. For now." He rakes his fingers back through his dark, wavy hair. He's wearing a black wristband identical to mine, but he's not tugging at his.

My thoughts rewind. "Wait . . . what . . ." I shake my

head. "What mission?"

"Listen—" He exhales in a rush. "I need to tell you—"

I wait, but he says nothing more, and I'm getting a little tired of boys who talk in cryptic spurts or don't talk at all. So I take the lead. "Telling me sounds like a great plan." He doesn't take the bait, so I prompt him. "What mission?"

He just stares at me.

Okay. New approach. "What happened back there on the road?"

The change of topic makes him blink. "We died. I mean, *you* died. On the road. *I* died last year." He grimaces. "I'm making a mess of this."

You died on the road. I feel like I've been punched in the gut. A part of me suspected it, but actually having it acknowledged as fact . . .

My first thought is for my dad. If I'm dead, he's alone. If I'm dead, it'll kill him. And Carly and Kelley and Dee and Sarah and all my other friends . . . I know what it feels like to mourn, to have a film of gray settle over every moment of every day, a fog that coats everything, leaching out color and joy. I don't want that for them. My heart gives a hard thump in my chest. And that stops me cold.

My heart is *beating.* That means Luka's wrong. I'm alive.

"You're not making sense," I whisper. "You died last year, but you're still going to school? Still on the track team? Still going to classes?" My voice rises with each word until I'm practically screaming. "What, you're a zombie? One of the living dead?"

22

I take a step forward. He takes a step back.

"No." He shakes his head. "I'm not saying this right."

"No shit, Sherlock." I'm shaking with fear and anger. "This isn't funny, Luka."

"No, I know. Listen, I understand how you feel. I remember waking up right where you did. I remember what I thought. That I was dead. That I was in a coma. That I was dreaming the whole thing." He touches my shoulder, and then jerks his hand away, his fist clenching as he drops it to his side. "Those same thoughts went through your head, right?"

They had. Every single one of them.

I slap my palm against his chest, over his heart. I feel the steady drum of his heartbeat. "You're lying. You're alive. I can feel it. Dead. People. Don't. Have. Heartbeats." I punctuate each word with a tap against his chest, and then let my hand fall to my side.

He shakes his head. "I am. You are. Alive, I mean." He lifts his hand like he's going to touch my shoulder again, but he only holds it there for a second, then drops it. "We're mostly alive. Most of the time. But for the mission, we're not. Not really. We're here, and we get to go back when we're done."

"Start making sense, Luka, because so far, everything you've said just sounds crazy." I feel sick, woozy, adrenaline slamming my pulse into overdrive and making me want to run, scream, hit something. "Just tell me what's going on." I enunciate each word, slow and careful. "In plain, simple terms. Just tell me what the hell is going on."

Luka glances around like he's looking for an escape route. I follow his gaze. We're in a clearing surrounded by trees. There's nothing familiar. No street. No crosswalk. No schools. No landmarks I recognize. And for the first time, I notice that there are more than three of us here.

About ten feet away are two large boulders. A boy is sitting on one, a girl on the other. I don't recognize either one of them. The boy's a little older, maybe twenty or so. His blue eyes are a stunning contrast to his dark skin and black lashes. His curly hair is trimmed close to his skull. He looks like a model in a J.Crew ad, and he's watching me with an expression that I can only read as sympathetic. The girl's red haired and pale, blue eyed, too—what's with that?—very pretty, with a figure that's all curves. She's wearing a cheer uniform. The only things missing are the pom-poms. They're both wearing the wristbands.

After a minute, the girl pushes off the boulder and walks over. She approaches me warily, like I'm some wild animal that's going to pounce on her and tear her throat out.

"Listen . . . um . . ." Her brows shoot up and she looks at me expectantly, waiting for me to tell her my name.

"Miki Jones."

"Richelle Kirkman." She gestures back toward the boy on the boulder. "That's Tyrone Walker." I recognize her voice. She's the girl who was speaking when I first woke up, and I'm guessing Tyrone is the guy she was talking to. "You already had the pleasure"—she rolls her eyes—"of meeting Jackson." At the mention of his name, I glance over to where he's standing on the far side of the boulders. "And from the looks of things, you already know Luka," Richelle continues, then frowns. "Which is odd because we've never had anyone go through who knew each other from . . . before. You go to the same school or something?"

"Yeah. Glenbrook, in Rochester," Luka says.

"Minnesota? Michigan?"

"What are you, a geography teacher?"

"It's a hobby," Richelle says.

Luka purses his lips and nods. "Rochester, New York. But I was living in Seattle when I was pulled. My dad was only transferred back to Rochester a couple of weeks ago. Right before school started. So we weren't actually pulled from the same geographic area. But I wouldn't say it's never happened."

Richelle nods like that means something to her. She and Luka seem to know each other, so I wonder why she doesn't know where he goes to school or that he used to live in Seattle. But I have more important questions to ask.

"Pulled?" I glance at Luka.

"Pulled from real life," he says.

His answer makes me shiver. I wrap my arms around my waist, holding myself together.

Richelle shoots a hard look his way and jumps in with, "Don't listen to him. We still have real lives. They just get temporarily interrupted every now and then."

CHAPTER**THREE**

PULLED FROM REAL LIFE. I HEAR THE WORDS THEY'RE SAYING, but there's a lag between my ears and my brain. Hearing and understanding are two completely different things. "Real lives?" I ask.

"Sure. I'm meeting my girls at Franklin Mills for some major shopping when we're done here." Richelle glances down at her cheer uniform and offers a wry grin. "I do plan to change first."

"Franklin Mills?"

"Big mall in Philadelphia," she clarifies.

"But . . . we're in Rochester. . . ."

"You aren't in Rochester anymore, Toto. We're in the lobby, and in a few minutes we'll be"—she makes a sweeping gesture—"somewhere else." She pauses. "Listen, Miki.

Here's the deal. We get a mission. We kill—"

"Terminate." Luka cuts her off. "We don't kill anything."

"That's a relief." I don't even try to temper the sarcasm.

"Prettying it up doesn't change it at all," Richelle says to Luka, her tone prim.

"And that's even less of a relief," I mutter, feeling like Alice down the rabbit hole.

Richelle turns back to me. I read commiseration in her expression. She doesn't need to tell me that she gets it, that she knows how freaked out I am and that my questions and sarcasm are my only defense.

"We terminate whatever it is we're sent to terminate," she continues. "Sometimes we're sent to destroy a facility or a nest. It's free-for-all scoring. There's an individual score tally for each player. No team score. But really, the score that matters the most is survival." She pauses, and her tone takes on a note of urgency. "Don't let one of them get you before you're pulled back. When you finish the mission, when you manage to make it through? Then you respawn, you know . . . rematerialize miraculously healed and you get to go back to your regularly scheduled life. Until the next time. Got it?"

I don't get it, not even a little. I cut a glance at Luka. He shrugs and says, "What she said."

"I don't understand." I mean, I understand the words— *team, score, mission, respawn*—but the concepts make no sense. "Is this a game? Are we LARPing?"

Richelle frowns. "LARPing?"

"Live action role playing? Like *Dungeons and Dragons*?" I ask, even though I already know the answer.

"No," Luka says. "How do you know about LARPing?"

"Terry Chen."

He nods.

I look at Richelle. "Is this cosplay?" Costume play. Before Luka can ask, I explain, "Kelley dragged all of us to an anime fan convention last year, and tons of people were dressed up and carrying weapons that looked real. Actually, a lot of them seemed to believe their costumes *were* real." But I don't really think we're playing dress-up here.

"Think of it like a video game. One we don't play on a screen," Luka says at the same time as Jackson says from behind me, "It isn't a game."

I spin to find Jackson standing just a couple of feet away. He's still wearing the khaki green pants and T-shirt that I saw him in when I first woke up, but now he looks different. It takes me a second to realize that he's wearing a sheath tied against his thigh, the handle of what I suspect is a knife sticking out the top. There's a leather band crossing his shoulder and a second one riding low on his hips with the butt of a weapon protruding from the holster.

"This isn't a game," he repeats. "It's real. What you do here determines your survival." He pauses. "And the survival of every other person on this planet."

I laugh.

He doesn't.

And that tells me he's either serious or seriously crazy. *Please let him be crazy.*

As I stare at him, something flickers at the edge of my vision. I turn my head. Nothing's there. But as I turn back to Jackson, something flickers again. People. Trees. Boulders.

When I was little, Gram had this powder room that was all done in mirrors. I'd stand there and wash my hands and see a million Mikis washing their hands at a million sinks in a million bathrooms. That's what this feels like. The images I catch from the corner of my eye are like the reflections I used to see in those mirrors; if I turned my head, the reflections would change. If I turn my head now, the reflections disappear.

I stare at Jackson, and in my peripheral vision, I see other clearings filled with people, on and on ad infinitum.

"Who are they?" I ask softly, my question aimed at Jackson, but it's Luka who answers, "Who?"

I shift my attention to him, and at the edges of my vision are the others. "Them."

"Them who?" Luka's brows draw together, and he pulls his head back. "You okay, Miki? We're the only people here." He makes a big show of looking around the clearing and spreading his hands. "You see anyone else?"

So Luka doesn't see them. But I do. And Jackson does; he knows exactly what I'm talking about. I can feel him watching me, even though I can't see his eyes. Before I can question him, he says, "Gear up," talking to the others even though he's still facing me. They move off, out of my line of sight, and I'm left alone with him, almost as confused as I was when I first woke up.

He reaches toward me. I jump back.

Again, that barely there hint of a smile that I saw earlier. Not a nice smile; not warm or friendly. Dark and feral and inexplicably appealing. I feel it all the way down to my toes. "Good reflexes," he says. "That's a bonus."

"Eight years of kendo."

"The way of the sword." His tone is speculative. "Are you any good?"

"Yes." I was taught by a master—my grandfather. "Mess with me and I'll mess right back." I can't believe I just said that.

Jackson's brows shoot up.

"Good to know," he says, echoing what I muttered after him earlier. I hadn't thought he heard, but now I think he must have.

I glance over at where the others are gearing up. They're on the far side of the boulders, strapping on holsters like Jackson's. "Who are the others?"

"Tyrone and Richelle already introduced themselves."

He knows I wasn't asking about them. Annoyance surges, but I tamp it down. I need to redirect, come at the problem from a different angle. So instead of pursuing that line of attack, I ask, "Where'd the weapons come from?"

This time, Jackson's smile is wider. Obviously he approves of my approach. Like I care what he thinks.

"They're here waiting for us whenever we arrive," he says.

"Right-handed?" he asks.

"Yes, why?"

"Now lift your arm. I'll show you how the holster works. Next time, you do it for yourself."

I lift my arm and he slides the straps over my shoulder. It's a complicated layout, with a strap going diagonally across my chest and a second loop resting on my hips. I pay attention to the way he settles the buckles and snaps down the holster. If there is a next time, I definitely want to be doing this myself. I don't like feeling like a toddler who needs help putting on her coat.

"You want your weapon on your dominant side. You don't want to cross reach. It'll slow you down."

Jackson holds out a metal cylinder that's about eight inches long. It looks like the handle of the toy light saber I used to play with as a kid.

"Please tell me a glowing blade doesn't leap out of the end of this." I hear a snicker to my left. I glance over and catch Richelle's wink, then turn back to Jackson.

He's not smiling. "You point this and you fire at anything that comes at you."

"Anything?" I ask. "Bees? Wasps? Lost puppies?"

His lips thin, confirming what I already suspected. "You have no sense of humor," I point out.

He ignores my observation. "Anything non-terrestrial."

"Non-terrestrial? As in . . . *extra*terrestrial?"

He gives a short nod.

"Of course. I died today, and now I'm going to fight aliens with a light saber. Maybe after that we can look for mermaids. Or unicorns."

"No," he says. "Just aliens."

Was that the barest hint of humor in his tone? I narrow my eyes. "What if I don't want to go on this alien-hunting mission?"

"What makes you think you get a choice?" The words are harsh, but his tone is oddly gentle, like he knows I've been pushed almost as far as I can go. It's the gentleness that undoes me.

Words flow like water before I can muster the will to turn off the tap. "I don't want to be here. I don't want to do this. I woke up this morning and I was just a normal girl," I say softly, my sarcasm deserting me.

Jackson goes very still. After a long second, he says, "No, you weren't. You were never just a normal girl."

I gasp, his words cutting me like a scalpel.

"None of us were ever normal," he continues, either oblivious to my pain or purposely ignoring it. "That's why we're here. We're anything but normal." One side of his mouth curls in a dark smile. "Some of us being less normal than others."

I open my mouth to protest, to ask—

"Don't ask," he cuts me off before I can say a word. "We don't have time for the answer."

I can almost hear the clock ticking.

His tone turns fierce. "Make it through this, Miki Jones, and I'll give you all the answers you want."

"Now, there's incentive," I murmur. *Make it through this.* The only thing that keeps me from freezing in terror is what Luka and Richelle said about being miraculously healed at the end of whatever it is we're about to face. As impossible as their assurance seems, I believe them because I *know* what happened to me when the truck hit, but I woke up here with all my injuries gone. Is that the respawn Richelle was talking about?

Jackson tucks the cylinder in my holster like I'm some sort of rebel gunslinger.

I brush my fingers over the end of it. "How do I fire it?" I ask.

"You point it and you think it."

"Think it. Right. And how do I use—" I hold up the black band on my wrist and turn it back and forth. "What did you call it? My con?"

He nods.

"Um . . . what does that mean? Con?"

His brows rise, and then he shrugs. "Connection. Conversation. Contact. Connectedness. Take your pick. They all apply equally."

"You don't actually know, do you?" When he doesn't answer, I ask, "Who decided to call it a con?"

Again, that dark half smile. "You could say the name was chosen by committee."

"So how do I use it?"

"You don't need to use it. It's activated. It'll do what it needs to do."

Before this moment, I never understood just how thin my patience could stretch. I hold on to it by a thread. "Which is what?" I ask, syrup sweet.

His expression doesn't change, but for some reason, I think he's almost as frustrated as I am, that he *wants* me to understand; he just doesn't know how to explain. Or maybe that's just wishful thinking. He takes a step away from me.

Suddenly, I've had enough. I grab his wrist as tight as I can. His face turns toward me, and I have to fight the urge to rip the sunglasses off, to get a look at the emotions reflected in his eyes. His tendons are taut beneath my fingers. It hits me that he's all lean muscle and strength, that he could jerk away with ease but he's choosing not to.

"Just give me something to help me understand," I whisper. "Tell me *something*."

He juts his chin toward the others. "They already told you. *I* already told you. What we're saying makes no sense to you because you refuse to believe. The only way you'll believe is if you see it. It's always that way." He looks away, then back toward me. "You know the story of Medusa?"

I nod.

"The things we're after won't turn you to stone, but what they will do is just as bad. Maybe worse. Whatever you do, don't look in their eyes."

"Whose eyes?"

"The Drau."

He holds up one finger in the universal symbol for *wait*. He looks like he's listening to something I can't hear. "We've got thirty seconds," he barks, and I figure he's talking to all of us. Then to me, he says, low and intense, "You stay close to me, Miki Jones. Close enough that I can hear you breathe. Got it?"

Something in his tone makes my breath catch. Aiming for sassy with a nice dose of bravado, I ask, "You always take care of the new recruits?"

He clenches his jaw and seconds tick past before he answers. "Never." He sounds anything but happy.

Never.

But this time is different.

Before I can process that, an agonizing pain starts in the center of my skull and pulses outward until it blows me apart.

CHAPTER **FOUR**

THE NOISE HITS ME FIRST. CARS. LOTS OF THEM. HORNS.
People. Voices and laughter. Guess my head didn't blow up
after all.

My palms are braced on my thighs and I'm bent forward at the waist, feeling disoriented and woozy. I've
always been the girl with the cast-iron stomach, but nausea
seems to be my new normal.

The glare of the lights hits me next. I straighten, and
everywhere I look there are brightly lit signs against a
backdrop of night sky. *Casino. Pick your numbers. Girls!* To
my right are Richelle and Tyrone, to my left Jackson and
Luka. None of them appear to be affected by whatever it is
we just lived through. I wonder how many times they've
done this. And how often.

Where are we? There's a giant pirate ship to one side and two mirrored buildings to the other. Overhead is a bridge and, beyond that, what appears to be a mall. The signs and scenery make me think Las Vegas. I've never been here before, but I've seen it in movies. I don't even try to figure out how we got here. At this point, I'm just going along for the ride.

When are we? It's night, but last thing I remember, it was late afternoon. In Rochester. Which is ahead of Vegas. "We've lost . . . like . . . ten hours," I say to no one in particular.

"They've been banked," Richelle replies. "We'll get them back."

I almost ask if they're in Bank of America or Chase, but the way Luka's mouth compresses in a tight line stops me. A chill crawls up my spine on creepy little centipede legs.

He catches me watching him and offers a weak imitation of a reassuring smile.

"Move," Jackson says, already striding forward. As he passes me, he shoots me a look. At least, I think he's looking at me. He's still wearing those shades, even though it's night, the smooth lenses reflecting all the bright signs in miniature.

I remember his tone when he told me to stick close enough for him to hear me breathing. I jog a couple of steps to catch up, aware of the others right behind us, forming a tight little group.

Luka falls into step beside me. "Magic," he says, and

when I glance at him, he explains, "I know you're wondering how we got here. I said *magic*. I'm trying to be funny. . . ." He shakes his head. "Never mind."

"We got pulled," Tyrone says from Luka's far side.

Jackson picks up the pace, so we all pick up the pace, now more of a slow jog than a walk.

"Pulled," I repeat, remembering them using that word back in the clearing. The *lobby*. Luka and Richelle used it in the context of getting pulled from our real lives.

"We get pulled through time and space," Tyrone says, and he must have read the disbelief in my expression, because he laughs and says, "Just go with it."

Advice I decide to take, mostly for lack of alternatives. "So we can get pulled anywhere, at any time?"

"Pretty much." He shrugs. "When we finish the job, we get pulled back again."

His explanation only makes me want to ask about a billion more questions, like who pulls us, and how. Every time they try to clarify something, I end up more confused. Maybe Jackson was right when he told me that explanations wouldn't cut it, that I'd have to see things for myself.

"You're not arguing in disbelief," Luka observes.

"Finding myself on a crowded street in Vegas is definitely going a long way toward making me a believer."

Tyrone snorts. "You a gamer?" he asks.

I frown at the non sequitur and shake my head. "I've played." Sometimes. With Carly's brothers. But I'm no expert.

"Being a gamer helps with being a believer," he says. "Anyway, here's the crash course. You get points for every hit. There's a bonus for timeliness. It starts out as triple points and decays by increments of point five."

"We've yet to earn the time bonus," Richelle says. She nudges Tyrone's side with her elbow. "Some of us talk too much, which slows everyone down."

"That'd be Jackson. He's all chatty-chat," Tyrone says, and he and Richelle exchange an amused glance. Then he looks back at me and continues. "Target at least three Drau in less than two seconds and you get multi-hit bonus points. Get them in the head? Bonus points. Get a stealth hit? Bonus points. Penalty points for injuries. Cost points for weapons." He glances at Luka. "That pretty much covers it, right?"

"Tyrone's our resident expert," Luka says unnecessarily.

"Yeah. I get that," I say.

Richelle laughs. "If you can actually understand what he's talking about." She cuts him a sidelong look through her lashes. "He has this idea that someday he's going to turn all of this into a game and sell it for the big bucks." The way she says it tells me she doesn't think that's such a crazy plan. She sounds proud.

We keep moving. People flow around us like water, not looking at us, but parting to let us pass.

I follow Jackson right through the center of a group of women who are laughing and talking about girls' night and some guy's abs. We've cut through a few large groups, but this time it hits me. "They don't see us," I blurt.

He slows just long enough for me to catch up. "No, but somewhere in their subconscious, they sense our presence."

"Wow. You strung more than ten words together and offered information voluntarily." I don't know why I say it. There's just something that makes me want to needle him. Maybe because it distracts me from being afraid. But I regret the lost opportunity to ask more questions when he clips out, "I'm already regretting it."

He doesn't look at me when I mutter, "Dish it out but can't take it."

"Ten," he says.

"What?"

"You said I strung more than ten words together. But I didn't. I strung together precisely ten."

My jaw goes slack and I can't think of a single snappy comeback.

I jog in silence for a few seconds before I hear, "Give me a *j*." I glance over to see Richelle beside me, doing a high V, moving her hands like she's holding pom-poms. She repeats the movement and trills, "Give me a *k*." Her brows lift. "I'll let you fill in the two letters in between. Try *e* and *r*."

I mentally add the letters and huff out a laugh.

"That's our Jackson," she says with a wink.

"You're on the squad."

"What gave it away?" She gestures at her outfit and grins. "My mom wanted me to be at the top like she was, but I'm a base. That means I'm the one on the bottom, lifting the flyer into her stunt. Which is actually fine with me. I wouldn't want to be the one at the top. I'm scared of heights." She looks me over, then asks, "You?"

I shake my head. "No squad for me. I run."

There's a surreal quality to this conversation. It's so ordinary. And our situation . . . isn't. We're jogging along the Vegas strip on a mission to hunt aliens. It hits me then that I've accepted that fact. I know I'm not dreaming or fantasizing. This is *real*.

"Track team?" Richelle asks.

"No." I shake my head. "I'm not much of a team player. That's Luka's thing. I run just for me."

She laughs, but there's an edge to it. "Good for you. Sometimes I think I'm so busy trying to make my mom proud, doing everything exactly as she wants me to do, I forget to do anything for me."

"What would you want to do?"

"That's the question, isn't it? I guess I need to figure out where Mom's ideas end and mine begin."

We turn onto a quieter street. Richelle's jogging along beside me, and I shock the hell out of myself when I say in a rush, "My mom's dead. SCLC. Small cell lung cancer." On my fourteenth birthday, she was laughing and chasing me into the waves at Atlantic Beach. We'd been going to North Carolina, renting the same oceanfront cottage my whole life. But that birthday everything changed. I remember the wave taking her under. I remember her coming up coughing. And coughing. I don't think she ever stopped coughing after that. Four months later, she was dead. *Four months.* Chemo and radiation didn't help worth shit. "I made my father put a pack of cigarettes and a lighter in her coffin along with the photos he chose of me and him and all of us together." I pause, remembering that, remembering all the times my parents sat watching TV or reading the paper, a cloud of smoke hanging over them. "I was that angry."

"Maybe you still are," Richelle says.

I stop dead, because I can't believe I've told her all this—I never talk about it. Not even with Carly. *Never*— and because I can't believe a girl I've only just met hit the nail so precisely on the head.

I turned sixteen last month, and it was just me and Dad at Atlantic Beach, running into the ocean with our memories. I pretended the salty streaks on my face were from the waves.

So did he.

I pretended my bathing suit didn't reveal the small eagle I'd had tattooed over my heart—a symbol of courage: Mom's as she faced the horror of her disease. Mine as I continue to cling to the edge of the dark pit by my fingernails, trying to move forward, my memories of her slowly curling up at the edges and growing hazier with each passing day.

Dad pretended he didn't see my ink, because he'd already told me not till I was eighteen.

We get by that way, Dad and me. Mostly honest, but sometimes not.

I stare at Richelle. Maybe she's right; maybe I am that angry.

Tyrone nudges me on the shoulder. "Focus," he says softly. I follow his gaze to see Jackson stalking back toward us.

"This isn't social time," Jackson says. *I told you stay close enough that I could hear you breathe,* he doesn't say. But I swear I hear it anyway.

His words are a reminder that closes around my heart like a fist. For an instant, I'd been lulled into a sense of complacency, pushing aside the confusion and fear and questions about the bizarre turn my life has taken. Instead, I'd focused only on Richelle and the fact that she seems nice, easy to talk to. She seems like someone I want to know.

But this *isn't* social time.

Jackson's already told me that he can't read my mind, but he might as well be able to because he says, "We aren't here to make friends."

"You're such an asshole."

"Keeps me alive."

"You love getting the last word," I grouse as he turns away.

"True enough," he tosses over his shoulder, and if it were anyone but him, I'd swear he was smiling as he said it.

▲▼▲

We must have been jogging for an hour or so when Jackson holds up a hand, and we slow to a walk. I'm barely winded. I'd like to chalk that up to my excellent physical condition, but the truth is, after a jog like that, I'd usually be drenched and breathing hard.

"You're not even sweating," I whisper to Luka.

He nods. "Being on a mission does that. We're stronger, faster. We don't need to eat or drink. I think it has something to do with this." He holds up his wrist to show me his con. "You're still feeling it a bit because you're so new. Next time will be easier."

Next time. "Yay." I roll my shoulders, then ask, "Why weren't we just dropped in exactly where we need to be? Why make us run for an hour?"

Even though my questions are aimed at Luka, it's Tyrone who answers. "Reason one: We need to acclimate to the shift. The time it takes us to get to the objective is the time it takes our bodies and minds to reach optimum performance. Endorphins and adrenaline stimulated by the run aid the transition. Reason two: When a rift is created so we can get dropped, it alerts our targets. The farther away we are, the less likely that they can pinpoint exactly where we were dropped or how long it'll take for us to reach them. If we're dropped in a city, the masses of people can help mask us, so we're dropped fairly close. If we're somewhere isolated, like a desert, we get dropped farther away. Our cons scramble our signal once we're here, and that makes it even tougher for them."

"You know a lot about this," I say.

"Been in it awhile." He pauses. "When I first got pulled, I asked a lot of questions, too."

"So you can apply the info to the game you plan to sell."

"Damn right." He grins. "Dollars are in the details."

"Got any more urgent questions?" Jackson asks.

"I'll let you know if I think of any."

"Fair enough."

We follow as Jackson leads us away from the lights and the people, down streets that look dingy to an alley that looks downright scary. There's a line of garbage bags up against a brick wall. At the far end of the alley is a single vertical sign with only one letter lit up: a *p*. There's a Dumpster to the left. Jackson leads us around it, into a narrower alley bordered by buildings that look deserted.

The smell of rotting garbage slaps me, but more than that, the air *feels* wrong. Too thick. Too heavy.

My pulse is pounding. My mouth is dry. My palms are slick. And I don't even know why I feel so afraid.

"There," Jackson whispers. He points first at Tyrone, then at Luka, then at a shadowy doorway.

Tyrone moves up so that he and Jackson flank the doorway. Luka turns his back to us, keeping an eye on the alley. Richelle looks ready for . . . *something*. They've done this before. Everyone seems to know their place. Except me.

As if he senses my uncertainty, Jackson turns his face toward me and gives his head a tiny jerk, beckoning me closer.

My fear ramps up as I will myself to take the few steps to close the distance between us. There's something here, behind that door. Something I don't want to be anywhere near. I can feel it on my skin, taste it on my tongue.

Enemy.

That certainty burns in some primitive part of my soul.

"Weapons," Jackson says, so low I almost miss it. From the corner of my eye, I see Luka pull out his cylinder from the holster at his hip. I do the same, mostly because I don't know what else to do. I don't know what's coming, but I know that I'm terrified. More scared than I was when I jumped in front of that truck. More scared than I was when I woke up thinking I was dead.

My fingers don't quite reach all the way around the cylinder, which is cool and hard in my hand. Pointing and firing this thing is going to be awkward. I'm used to holding the hilt of my kendo sword, but that's a whole different motion.

No sooner do I process that thought than the cylinder changes. It shifts and melds, taking on finger ridges, forming to my hand, as if it's an extension of my body. I can *feel* it there, like it's just part of me. I gasp and my gaze jerks up, searching for the others. But of course, this isn't the time to chat about the wonder of my new discovery.

Luka gives a last scan of the alley, then moves closer. Richelle inches forward and stretches her fingers toward the door while the others raise their weapons and cover her.

The feeling of horror in my gut curdles into an icy mass. I can't let her go in there. I can't let any of us go in there. If she goes through that door, we all die. I don't know how I know that, I just do.

I slam my palm against her shoulder blade, shoving her out of the way. She stumbles a couple of steps to the side. I dance back, away from the door and the horrific fear it drags from my soul.

Luka rests his hand on my arm and leans in. "We all feel it." His voice is low and reassuring. "You get used to it."

"I'll take care of this." Jackson's tone is terse. I read surprise in Luka's expression, then a hint of mutiny. He wants to argue. I can see it. A silent undercurrent I can't decipher passes between them. Finally, Luka nods and steps away.

Jackson's so close that the length of his arm presses against mine. We're lined up like a T, with my body at ninety degrees to his. "You're doing great, Miki," he says, very soft. "Better than great. You're focusing on the task and saving your confusion and questions for later, and that's exactly what you need to do. When you get in there, you'll fight. You'll win. And the world will survive."

"I'm afraid," I whisper, the words too small for what I feel. Not afraid. Terrified. Petrified. Bone-numbingly scared.

And Jackson gets it.

"That feeling inside you, it's inside all of us," he says, his voice calm, soothing, luring me to trust what he's saying. "It's in your cells. It's in your DNA. You were born knowing them"—he juts his chin toward the door, and I know he's talking about whatever's inside there—"knowing what they're capable of, knowing that they are the enemy."

Yes.

"They hunted our ancestors. They were the predators. We were the prey. They chased our ancestors from their home world. They turned it into a barren, frozen mass. Now, they're here, looking to conquer another planet. Earth. This planet. *Our* planet. That feeling of fear inside you is justified. It's been bred into your genes. Into all our genes." He gestures toward the others, who stand ready and alert. "But you have to master it. Beat it down. We're not the prey anymore."

His explanation is so far beyond believable that I want to discount it out of hand. But I don't. For the first time, his cryptic assertions actually make perfect sense to me. *But you have to master it. Beat it down.* It's a conundrum I know well: the need to stay when every instinct is screaming for you to go. I faced it every time I went to the hospital with Mom. I wanted to run as fast and as far as I could. From the tubes. From the machines. From the smiling nurses who hooked up bags of poison that drip, drip, dripped into my mother's veins in an effort to kill the thing growing out of control inside her. But for her, for Mom, I stayed.

"My instinct is to run, but you're telling me I can't. And you're telling me that somewhere inside of me, I know what's waiting in there. Genetic memory." At his raised brows, I clarify, "We talked about it in bio."

"Genetic memory." His lips shape that barely-there smile. "Yeah, that about sums it up."

"But why me? How am I supposed to do this? I'm not trained. Shouldn't there have been boot camp or something?"

"Or something. This is it. You have your genetic memory, your instincts. Trust them. Besides, you are trained, more than most who get pulled. Kendo, right?"

I swallow and nod. He's just added about a million questions to the billion already buzzing around in my brain. "You owe me answers when we're done," I say, reminding him of his earlier promise.

"When we're done." Jackson brushes the backs of his fingers against the backs of mine, the touch so fleeting I almost think I've imagined it. I *feel* his approval, his admiration, even though his expression doesn't change.

"Here's what you need to know right now. The things that are in there—"

"The Drau." That's what both he and Tyrone called them.

He nods. "They're day walkers. The planet they come from is in an S-type binary star system. Their planet has two suns. That means that they live in daylight almost all the time. And that means that at night, they're groggy and slower."

"Like bears hibernating in winter," Luka supplies.

Jackson doesn't acknowledge the interruption. "By going in at night," he continues, "we stand a better chance that all of us will walk out of here."

"With our health still green," I say, holding up my wrist.

"That's the plan." He pauses, and it's clear that he's battling over whether or not to say more. "I heard what you said earlier, about not being a team player—"

"I—"

"No." He cuts off my attempt to cut him off. "Listen to me. Not being a team player is good. I don't want you to be one. This *isn't* a team thing, Miki. Not really. If push comes to shove, you need to be all about you. You need to make sure *your* health stays green. Forget about everyone else. Take care of you, because no one else can do it for you."

And here I'd just started feeling a little warm and fuzzy toward him.

But he's just voiced aloud my darkest suspicion, the belief that started the day Mom died: You can't really count on anyone but yourself. Everyone leaves. "Is that what you do? Take care of *you*?" My cynicism leaks into the words.

"In the end, it's what we all do."

My mouth goes dry. "So despite what you said before, you're not actually going to watch out for this recruit." Why does that bother me? I've been relying on myself for a long time.

He huffs a short laugh, but it has a hard, ugly edge. "See, that's the thing. I shouldn't. But I'm going to. I just hope it doesn't get me killed."

I narrow my eyes. "Eight years of kendo," I toss back

the reminder that he tossed at me earlier. "I won't let you get killed." I think we're both startled by my vehemence.

"You ought to just take my advice and watch your own ass."

"I'll keep that in mind." For a second, I think I've done it, that I've had the last word.

"You do that," he says, and grins. White teeth and that killer dimple carved in his cheek. He's not afraid to go in there, to face the Drau, and that makes me a tiny bit less afraid.

As he walks around me, back toward the door, I catch Richelle watching me with a frown.

Everyone gets back in formation, Richelle reaching for the door while the others cover her. She pushes it open. The feeling of wrongness oozes out from the dark interior, weaving through my cells. Everything inside me screams for me to run. But I force myself to step forward. This is just a game of some sort. Richelle and Luka said we get to go back when we're done. And if their word isn't enough, I've already seen it in action: I got hit by a truck and survived that. Whatever happens in here can't be any worse.

CHAPTER **FIVE**

RICHELLE GOES IN FIRST. HER HAND SHOOTS BACK AND SHE gives a little *come on* curl of her fingers. Tyrone follows, then Luka. Jackson points to me, then to the open door. In I go, forcing my feet to move one in front of the other. With each step I feel colder, more desperate to get away. A rush of terror crashes over me. It's like I'm underwater and my lungs are screaming and I have to hold myself back from the surface, from the air.

Nearly choking on my fear, I fight it back and follow the others deeper inside, which only makes it worse. I need to run, hide—

Richelle reaches over and closes her hand on mine, just for a second, but it's enough. Her touch reminds me that I'm not alone, and that offers a weird sort of comfort.

It's dark. After a minute, my eyes adjust, and I realize there's a little light leaking through thin cracks in the boards covering the windows set high in the wall. Even so, I can't see much more than vague, shadowy outlines. There are some huge cardboard boxes in the corner, and some more stacked in a towering pyramid against the far wall.

Jackson prowls forward. I don't hear him move, and I can barely see him; he's just a shadow among shadows. I follow, trying to keep my movements as silent as his. He stops. I stop. After a second, I make out the shape of another door, directly ahead.

The terror that grabbed me outside digs deeper, grows bigger, and I feel like it's going to burst outward like a bomb.

Richelle's beside me. Shoulder to shoulder, we edge toward the door.

"Close your eyes," Jackson barks.

Confused, I freeze.

There's a flash of light, blindingly bright. I blink, wishing I had done as Jackson said as colored halos obscure my vision. They dance and flicker and then disappear, leaving only a rectangle of light boxed in by the dark doorframe.

I see then that the door's gone and in front of me are people. No . . . they aren't people. They have limbs, hair, faces, but they aren't human. After the first glance, they don't look even remotely human. They're pure, painful white, so bright they throw off a glare. They look like they've been dipped in glass, smooth and polished, but fluid. And their eyes . . . they're a silvery color, like the mercury in the antique thermometer that my mom used to have at the side of the front porch.

When I was ten, I knocked that thermometer off with my wooden kendo sword, shattering the glass. The little blobs of mercury went all over the porch. I was a kid. I didn't know better. I touched them, prodding the little balls until they joined the bigger blob. My mom swooped down on me and snatched me away, telling me it was poison. It could kill me.

I stare at the things in front of me: the Drau. I can't look away.

Somewhere in the back of my mind, I remember Jackson talking about Medusa. *Don't look at their eyes.*

Their mercury eyes.

They're poison.

They will kill me.

I want to move. I want to blink. But my will is not my own. I'm drowning in a silver lake. Drowning . . .

Something tangles in my hair and yanks my head so my face turns to the side. I gasp. Jackson lets go, his fingers sliding through my hair.

"Don't. Look," he snarls, and I realize that he just saved my ass and that what had felt like hours had been only seconds.

The aliens pour through the open doorway, fluid and terrifying. I can't tell how many there are. They're everywhere, moving wraithlike and impossibly fast between us: divide and conquer. My pulse races. I spin, and spin again, backpedaling, tripping, almost falling, trying to keep them in sight. I point my weapon, but have no clue what to do with it.

Jackson leaps in front of me, the metal cylinder in one hand, a long-bladed, black knife in the other. Why don't I have a knife? At least *that* I might be able to use. Light streaks toward us. Jackson slashes down and misses as the light retreats. Then it comes at us again. He slashes at it again. Misses.

I know nothing about the Drau, but instinct tells me they're toying with us.

My chest moves with shallow, panting breaths. I want to help. I want to fight. I have no idea what to do. Tiny bursts of blinding light come at us. Jackson jumps in front of me again, spinning in midair, taking the brunt of those lights full on his back. Taking the hit for me. His face twists with pain.

I grab the front of his shirt and yank him aside. I'm still pointing my weapon. I'm still wishing it would work.

A weird, high-pitched hum hits my ears. Something surges from Jackson's weapon like black oil forced out under immense pressure. Time seems to slow as I watch. I know the battle is unfolding in fractions of seconds, but I feel like I can see everything in freeze-frame clarity. As I watch, that darkness becomes a black mass that swells and contracts, oily and slick, moving with speed and power that defies my understanding.

The mass exerts an incredible pull. I feel drawn to it, sucked toward it, like matter to a black hole.

The streak of light stops abruptly and flickers in and out of human form so fast I can barely see the transitions. It cringes back, away from the dark surge, even as it is dragged inexorably along the floor. Then the light is snuffed out; the human form is gone, just gone, and the darkness retracts into Jackson's metal cylinder. The whole thing makes me think of a frog flicking out its tongue to snatch a fly and drag it into its waiting maw.

For an instant, I can't breathe. And then I can. A sharp inhalation that inflates my lungs and sends my blood zipping through my veins.

Jackson killed it.

And I stood beside him and watched.

I don't get the chance to figure out how that makes me feel. All around me, there's chaos. These things—the Drau—are fast, like blurs of light zipping throughout the room. Behind me, beside me, there are sounds and movements and surges of darkness that tell me the others are shooting. Hunting.

Something comes at me, light and speed, and then it's solid, taking the shape of a man directly in front of me. I can't help it. I look at it, right in its eyes, mercury smooth and silvery and bright. Terrifying and beautiful.

Pain explodes, eating my organs, my limbs, my brain. I feel like my insides are being ripped away, pulled out through my eyes. My legs turn to rubber. I fall to my knees.

The Drau's lips peel back, revealing rows of jagged teeth. Not human at all.

In my terror, I can't force myself to look away.

The need to fight, to defend myself, is overwhelming, stronger even than the magnetism of those eyes.

I raise my hand, the one holding my weapon.

Fire. Shoot. Do something.

Please.

My hand shakes. My pulse races. But my will isn't strong enough to get the stupid cylinder to spray out a black acid cloud. There's a sick feeling of helplessness and terror sitting like lead in the pit of my gut.

Again I will the weapon to fire.

Nothing happens.

The Drau lifts his hand. He's holding something metallic and smooth. It doesn't look solid. It appears fluid, jellylike. It's some sort of weapon. A million lights come at me, like the lights that made Jackson snarl in pain. Then all I know is agony, bright and deep.

I'm locked in the horrific compulsion of the alien's stare. I need to look away. I can't look away.

More shards of light disgorge from its shimmering weapon. As they hit, pain bursts on my skin, piercing me like the stingers of a hundred hornets. An invisible band tightens around my torso, constricting my ribs. *Crack.* The sensation of my rib snapping is sharp and pure and agonizing. I can't catch my breath. My vision goes gray at the edges. The bitter taste of my fear scrapes my tongue.

I think I cry out. Then I think that maybe my scream is locked in my mind. It takes me a second to realize that the sound I hear is actually coming from behind me, an inhuman cry followed by a human one, desperate and terrified.

"Tyrone!" Richelle's voice. There's a beat of silence, then a high, tortured scream.

Someone's hit. Someone's hurt. I want to look. I want to help. I can't. The alien holds my gaze, a predator mesmerizing its prey.

Miki! Jackson's voice is inside my head, shooting past the pain, both sharpening and shredding my focus.

From the corner of my eye I catch a flash of movement: a black-booted foot at the end of a khaki-clad leg. Then the alien's weapon flies up in an arc, spinning end over end, and the devastating pressure on my lungs eases. Dragging in a breath, I wrench my gaze away.

I'm shaking. My teeth are chattering. My fingers feel numb and prickly, like I've been out in a blizzard without gloves. It takes enormous effort to stay up on my knees and keep my grip on my weapon cylinder. I still haven't figured out how to use it, but I'm not willing to let it go.

The alien in front of me takes a step closer. Just one. It doesn't dart in for the kill . . . because it's *toying* with me.

Predator. Prey. It likes this game.

I will the cylinder to fire, but it sits smooth and inert in my grasp. So I chase the only option left to me and dive for the jellylike gun that Jackson kicked from the Drau's hand.

The alien's a beat faster. It has its weapon. I have mine—which is a boatload of useless because I still haven't figured out how to make it work. My heart gives an ugly lurch in my chest.

To my left there's another cry, high and short, even more disturbing than the one I heard before. The sound chills me. I don't dare look around to try to see who's been hit. I don't dare look anywhere but at the creature stalking me. We're separated by only a few feet now.

Sofu taught me to mask any fear and uncertainty because seeing it would give my opponent the edge. *Aim to intimidate, Miki, even when you don't feel it.* I remember his words as I huddle here facing an impossible foe, and I snarl, "You're going down," mostly because I can't dredge up anything better. Maybe if I say it, I'll actually believe it.

The Drau moves closer. Its face—almost human— looms larger and larger, filling my vision and my thoughts. I try to avoid its eyes, but in the end, I fail. Pain sears me, stronger than before. Unbearable.

I stumble and scream, my cry of agony reverberating through the room, echoing inside my head.

The pain, my fear—they piss me off. This is *not* the way I plan to make my exit from this life, kneeling on the floor, shaking and gasping. If I'm checking out, it'll be on my terms—just like my mom. Near the end, every doctor agreed that there was no hope and every test confirmed it, so she signed herself out of the hospital, declined heroic measures. For the longest time, I've been angry with her about that, too. But maybe, in this second, I understand her motivation just a little. She couldn't change the destination. All she could do was pick the route. When she closed her eyes for the last time, she was in hospice with my dad and me by her side and AC/DC rocking on. *Her* terms. Yeah, so maybe I get it now. What a time to have a revelation.

A fresh wave of pain assaults me. This time when I scream, it's the way my grandfather taught me, loud and true, a *kiai* shout that focuses my energy and my will into the attack and the weapon cylinder in my hand. The metal chills until it's like ice against my palm. A high-pitched hum starts, and vibrations run up my arm. Darkness arrows from the cylinder's open end, instantaneous and forceful, packed with power, like water shooting from the end of a fire hose. My arm jerks back with the recoil.

It worked. The weapon worked—

The Drau zips aside. My shot wavers and then disappears.

—I missed.

It's as if I hear my grandfather's voice in my head: *Mamoru.* Defend. Protect.

I won't just defend, because I have a feeling that won't be enough to keep me alive. I'll attack. I need to hit this thing where it has no defense.

I move on instinct, diving forward, belly to the floor, because I know my legs are too rubbery to hold my weight if I try to stand. I go sliding through the alien's spread legs, roll onto my back, and shoot directly up.

For a frozen millisecond, nothing happens.

The Drau reaches down, glowing fingers curled and clawlike, smooth and reflective as glass. My heart slams against my ribs.

Then the black hole spurting from the muzzle of my weapon sucks in the alien's hips . . . legs folding up alongside its torso . . . shoulders . . . arms. Gone. Its light is gone. Extinguished.

I did that. I killed it.

Bile burns the back of my throat.

I have no chance to puke. Or to celebrate. Another bright form comes at me. But I've learned from my mistakes. I don't look at its eyes, and I don't hesitate. I push to my knees and shoot. The hum starts; I realize now that it's the sound of the cylinder powering up. My weapon's darkness sucks out the Drau's light. I have a handful of seconds to lurch to my feet before another zooms at me. They don't just want me dead. They want to make me suffer. They want to enjoy it. Somehow, I *know* that, and it horrifies me.

Adrenaline surges. I spin. Shoot. Spin again. Shoot. I don't know how many there are or how long we fight, but then I'm spinning and aiming and there are no more targets.

I'm panting, gasping, feeling like the whole world is out of control. It takes me a second to orient myself. When I do, I see Luka by the far wall.

"I thought you guys said they're slower at night." The words that come out are not the ones I mean to say.

"That was slow," Luka answers, his voice tight. "You

don't want to see them during the day."

He's right. I don't. I don't want to ever see anything like them again.

Luka sags back against the wall. He's holding his arm across his abdomen, supported by his opposite hand. There's blood dripping from a ragged gash in his forearm. "I'm going to lose points for this," he says wanly.

I stagger toward him, barely able to stay upright, but the look of sheer horror that creeps across his features stops me cold.

"How many times were you hit?" he asks, trying to push off the wall and failing.

"I don't know." I glance down. I see nothing to justify his expression. And then I do. First, I see my thigh. My jeans are sliced clean through, and the cloth is wet, saturated with my blood. I don't remember getting cut.

Then I see my wrist. The screen on my black band's no longer green. It's an orangey red.

Don't let it turn red. That's what Jackson said to me back in the lobby.

"It's not red," I say to Luka, though I don't know if I'm reassuring him or myself. "It's orange, not red." I've barely finished saying that when my legs drop out from under me and I slump to the floor. Fatigue hits me like a truck. I'm tired, so tired, and colder than I've ever been. And every inch of my body screams in pain.

"You looked in their eyes," Luka says, every word dripping horror.

I look at Luka's con. It isn't the dark green we started with, either. It's more of a greenish yellow. *ROY G BIV. Red, orange, yellow, green, blue, indigo, violet.* I can almost hear Mr. Clement's voice droning out the spectrum over and over again as he handed out the prisms back in eighth-grade science class. I don't know why, but thinking about it now makes me want to laugh.

Then it makes me want to cry.

I'm so tired.

I force my eyes to stay open even though they want to close. Luka tells me to hang on, his voice tinny, echoing like it's coming to me through a very long tube. I see him try to move toward me, but his leg buckles. He's hurt. There's blood. The uneven shards of his arm bones are poking through his skin, so white against the red, red, red.

There's a low, keening moan beside me. I turn my head and see Tyrone crouched on the ground. There's some-thing in front of him. No . . . not some*thing*. Some*one*.

"Richelle," Tyrone rasps, and holds out his hand toward her. But he doesn't touch her. Why doesn't he touch her? Why doesn't he help her?

She's not moving. She's just lying there, her limbs at awkward angles.

Pushing my hands against the floor, I try to leverage myself up. But I can't. I'm too weak. The screen on my con's a very dark orange, and the skin of my arm looks gray. My gaze shoots back to Richelle. I can see her legs, though Tyrone's back blocks the rest of her from my view.

The skin of her legs looks gray, too.

"Why don't we make the jump?" Luka asks, his tone edged with panic.

"Luka," I whisper. He's slumped to one side, barely upright. The smile he sends me is a shadow of itself. His lips are bloodless, his skin chalk pale. I know he means to reassure me, but that smile scares me.

"I don't know," Tyrone says, his voice dull. "They're terminated. We did the job. We should jump. I don't know why we don't jump." He moves a little to the left, and I see Richelle's arm stretched across the cold floor. Her con's red. Completely red.

My stomach drops.

"Hang on, baby. Hang on," Tyrone says, and lays his palm against Richelle's cheek. Then he snarls, "Where the hell is Jackson?" Even as he finishes the question, the light in the doorway flickers out, then returns, but dimmer than it was before. A dark silhouette fills the rectangle of light. It's Jackson.

"There was a problem," he says. I'm guessing he means there was another alien or two. "It's taken care of. We'll be pulled in thirty."

In three strides, he's beside Richelle, but he's looking at me. He's still wearing those shades. I can't see his eyes, but I feel his gaze.

Tyrone's breathing too fast, and I can hear each breath catch on a sob.

Jackson squats down beside Richelle. His lips draw

thin, his head bows, and a tiny shiver shakes his shoulders. His head lifts, his expression blank. He's every inch the aloof, arrogant asshole he's been since the first second I met him, but something in his posture makes me want to lay my hand on his shoulder.

Then he rises. "Ten seconds."

"No." Tyrone shakes his head back and forth, very fast. "No. We can't leave her."

"We can't take her," Jackson says, his tone flat. "You know that."

"No. We can't leave her!" Luka pushes to his feet.

One side of Jackson's mouth twists. "What makes you think we have a choice?"

CHAPTER**SIX**

THE PAIN IN MY HEAD IS BACK, BUT NOT AS BAD AS BEFORE. Three headaches in one day. I've hit a milestone.

Last thing I remember, it was night, but now the late-afternoon sun shines down, hurting my eyes. So I close them. Carly screams my name, the sound shrill and panicked, but *off* somehow.

Snap. My eyes open. My focus sharpens. I'm falling, and there's no way to stop it. I see the truck, so close I can make out the chunks of rust on the grille. I see the pavement, flat and gray, coming up to meet me. I hit hard and slide along the rough surface, layers of cloth and skin scraping away.

There's the endless screech of the brakes and the smell of burning rubber. My head jerks up and I try to scramble out of the way. I can't find my footing.

Terror clogs my throat.

Then there's a hand on my arm, tight as a vise, yanking me to my feet.

Luka.

He pulls. I pull. Opposite directions. Our dance is all wrong.

He lets go abruptly. Stored momentum propels us away from each other. I tumble back and land hard on my ass and my elbows.

Music blares. Brakes scream. I feel a rush of air as the old pickup truck surges through the space between Luka and me. It comes to a screeching stop about five feet away.

Sprawled on the ground, I stare at the truck, my elbows stinging where they scraped along the pavement. A quick inventory tells me I'm not seriously hurt. My gaze jerks to Luka. He's on the ground, limbs splayed. The sight makes me think of Richelle, lying so still just before we got pulled.

Luka pushes to his feet. His arms are whole and smooth—no blood, no shattered bone, no torn skin. Other than a fresh scrape on his knee and another on his hand, he's all in one piece. And I'm in one piece, not broken and bloody. There's no gash on my thigh. Even my jeans are in one piece—no rip in the fabric, no bloodstain.

Luka and I are both fine. Just like Richelle said, we respawned: rematerialized miraculously healed. That must mean that wherever she got pulled to, Richelle is okay, too. And Tyrone. And Jackson. I exhale a breath I hadn't realized I was holding.

I stare at Luka. "The others—"

He slices the air with the edge of his hand and stalks toward me. "Not a word," he insists, low and intense, as he hunkers down beside me. "We don't talk to each other about it outside the game. And we don't talk to anyone else about it. Not ever. Not if we want to live."

The game. He's going to keep calling it that? The Drau, the fight—they felt real to me. If it's a game, it's one I don't want to play again. But Jackson was pretty adamant when he said it wasn't a game, and even if I wasn't willing to take his word for it, what I've seen today was pretty convincing.

I rub my forehead. I'm so confused.

"They'll know if we talk about it," Luka continues. "And they'll terminate us."

Our eyes lock. I can see that he believes everything he's saying, and he's afraid. I shiver. "Who are *they*?"

"Not a word," he snarls.

I nod. I know how to pick my battles. Defer. Distract. Wait it out. Right now, Luka won't spill. But some other time, when he's more relaxed, when his guard's down . . .

His lips compress in a tight line. His eyes are dark and fathomless.

Wait. What? His eyes are *dark*? They're not blue; they're the rich black-coffee brown I always thought they were until that moment when we were both lying broken on the ground after the truck hit us.

Except it never did hit us.

I glance at the truck, and then squint up at the late-afternoon sky. We're in exactly the same place—and time—as we were before everything happened. Before the lobby and the weapons and the aliens and the battle. Richelle said the hours were banked. I guess we just made a withdrawal.

"What do we do now?" I ask.

"We live our lives." There's an edge to Luka's answer, a tinge of bitterness.

We live our lives. That's what Richelle said in the lobby . . . something about getting to go back to our regularly scheduled lives. Until next time.

Carly screams my name again, the syllables dragged out, ridiculously slow. I turn my head and see her running toward me, but her movements are almost comical, like she's part of a film moving in slow motion. It takes me a second to realize that *everything* is in slow motion, except Luka and me.

I have so many questions, and none of them get answers because Luka clearly isn't willing to offer any and because I never get the chance to ask. The pain in my head grows until it pushes against the backs of my eyes and makes the joints in my jaw ache. My ears pop, and the pain is gone.

"*Bam*. We're back," Luka murmurs a millisecond before something changes and the world speeds up. Carly's no longer in slo-mo. She's running at me full tilt.

"Miki! Oh my gawd, Miki! Are you okay?" Carly skids to a stop and drops to a squat by my side. She runs her hands along my legs, then my arms. I glance down, expecting to see the con on my wrist. It's gone, just like the pain in my head and the pain in my ribs and the blood that should have been all over the ground.

Kelley and Dee are right behind her. I'm enveloped by my friends, who ask over and over if I'm okay. I tell them I am. I'm lying. I'm so far from okay, it's laughable.

I mutter reassurances and glance around for Luka. He's on his feet, backing away.

Janice Harper's standing on the curb, signing back and forth with her little sister. She lifts her head and looks at me. Her eyes are wide, her face pale. She squats down and pulls her sister into a tight hug, her gaze locked on mine. "Thank you." I can't hear her over the chatter of my friends, but I see her lips shape the words.

I did it. I saved her. Chaos under control. My brain pats me on the back, tells me to feel good, job well done. But I can't quite get there.

The metallic clang of a door slamming snags my attention. The driver of the truck leans against the hood, phone in hand. He talks, his fingers running repeatedly through his thinning hair, his face furrowed in concern. A moment later, sirens wail in the distance.

He takes one look at me surrounded by my friends and heads toward Luka. He stops and says something I can't hear. Luka nods and answers.

"Miki!" Carly snaps her fingers. "Talk to me. You seem kind of spacey."

That's one way of putting it. "I'm fine. Really."

Hands grasp my upper arms, helping me to my feet.

I'm surprisingly steady, no dizziness, no pain other than the twinge of my scraped elbows. I hold on to Carly's hand while Dee rubs my back and Kelley stares at me and presses her palms together and holds her fingers to her lips.

"Should you be standing? Should you be moving?" Kelley's hands flutter out to the sides now like butterflies. "I'm a lifeguard. I took first aid. I don't think you should be moving."

"I'm fine," I say.

"Maybe Kelley's right," Dee says. "Maybe you shouldn't be moving. You could have a concussion. Or a fractured neck. I saw this show where this guy was tackled during football practice and he thought he was okay and then a couple of days later he died because some bone at the top of his neck was actually broken and he"—her voice trails away as the others turn to stare at her—"died."

"I'm fine," I say again, and glance over at Luka. He's on the far side of the road, his expression anything but happy, his arms crossed over his chest. I'm confused. We're alive. We made it. What's he so pissed about? I take a step toward him. "I just need to—" *ask Luka something.* I don't get to finish my sentence because the police pull up, followed by an ambulance.

"You're not normal," Kelley says.

I wince. Carly glares at her. Dee gasps.

Cardinal sin—publicly calling me out on one of my issues. I have to bite my tongue to keep from hurling one of Kelley's own back in her face. I'm not usually quite that

71

vindictive, but at the moment, my defenses are pretty shredded.

"Don't do it," Carly says. "She didn't mean it that way." And that's enough to ground me. I know that if I snarl at Kelley, I'll just regret it later.

"I mean, you're so calm," Kelley rushes on, flushing. "If I was almost hit by a truck, I wouldn't be so calm. That's all I mean. I don't really mean that *you're not normal*; I just mean—"

"I know." I cut her off because the look on her face tells me that she feels like crap for saying the wrong thing, and right now, I don't want to feel like crap because she feels like crap because she's worried about my hurt feelings. Right now, the only person I want to talk to is Luka. He's right there, maybe twenty feet away. Twenty feet that might as well be a thousand, because it's painfully apparent that Luka doesn't want to talk to *me*.

And the fact that Luka isn't talking makes me think of Jackson. He promised that once we were done, he'd give me all the answers. An easy promise to make when he knew he wouldn't be here to hear the questions. I laugh darkly. My friends stare, but I'm saved from offering explanations as one of the EMTs strides over.

The next half hour passes in a blur. The EMTs check me out. The police take my statement. I think they write the driver a ticket, but I'm not sure.

They're done with Luka before they're done with me. With his back to me, he lifts his hand in a farewell wave, then walks away without even a glance, leaving me sitting in the open back of the ambulance while an EMT finishes bandaging my elbows.

I feel like crying; I feel like curling in a ball. I feel like punching something so hard that the skin on my knuckles splits. I feel like running for miles. Running away.

I can still see Luka in the distance when they're finally done with me. I'm about to bound after him when a dark blue Ford Escape pulls up, blocking *my* escape. Dad jumps out, his dark hair disheveled like he's run his fingers through it again and again. His mouth is tight, bracketed by lines of worry. He stands perfectly still, only his dark eyes moving until they light on me, and then he's moving, his strides eating the distance between us.

"You would have done exactly what I did," I say the second his arms close around me. I take a deep breath. He smells like fabric softener and spicy shaving cream. He smells like Dad and memories of childhood. He smells safe. And I'm incredibly grateful that right now, he doesn't smell like booze.

He tightens his embrace for a second and then releases me. "Yeah," he says, his voice like gravel. "But it doesn't mean that my blood didn't turn to ice when I got Carly's call."

"She didn't need to call you." I shoot her a dark look where she's standing on the sidewalk with Dee and Kelley, but she isn't looking my way.

"*You* should have called me."

"I'm fine." It's my day to do the parrot thing. First I kept squawking *what, what, what* and now it's *I'm fine.*

Dad gives me a stern look, and I press my lips together and say nothing. The truth is, I'm glad Carly called him. I'm glad he's here.

He walks me to the car and holds the front passenger door open for me while Carly and Kelley and Dee pile into the back.

"You want company?" he asks softly before I get in.

I shake my head. I love my friends, but right now, I just want my music and my privacy.

"I'll take them home, then."

I start to climb into the car, then pause with one foot inside and my hand on the roof as a cold wind touches the back of my neck. Except there is no wind.

I stare first up, then down the street.

Luka's not gone after all. He's there in the distance, watching me, as if he wants to make sure that I'm okay. Or to make sure I don't say anything I shouldn't.

But I still don't get in the car. I take my time looking around because I can't shake the feeling that he's not the only one watching me.

CHAPTER**SEVEN**

THE ALIEN IS REACHING FOR ME, SMOOTH, GLOWING LIMBS AND clawed fingers. Jackson is there, beside me. I wait for him to shoot. Why doesn't he shoot? His booted foot slams into the alien's hand, sending its weapon flying through the air, turning end over end.

There's a loud bang as the weapon hits the floor, then another and another. *Bang. Bang.*

I jerk awake, heart pounding, muscles twitching. My curtains are drawn, a sliver of early September sunlight leaking through the narrow crack where they meet. Someone's outside, banging on the door. Jackson. The second his name surfaces, I realize how unlikely the possibility is. He might be part of my nightmares—the one I lived yesterday and the ones I relived throughout the night—but he isn't part of my world.

With a groan, I roll to my side, get a look at the clock, and lurch to a sitting position. I missed my run. I missed the bell. Hell, I missed half my classes. Then I remember it's Saturday. No run, no bell, no classes, no school. That's both a relief—because I don't really want to face stares, whispers, or a bunch of questions about what went down yesterday—and a disappointment—because school means Luka, and Luka's my one hope for answers.

The person outside applies fist to door once more. Give them the prize for persistence.

I roll out of bed and head for the window, pull it open, and stick my head out. "Hey!"

Carly steps out from under the overhang that covers the front porch. I'm not surprised to see her; anyone else would probably have used the bell. But Carly started knocking at my door when she was so little that she couldn't reach the bell, and she kept knocking even as she grew.

"Hey, yourself." Her hair has a new bright pink streak on the right side. She's carrying a cardboard tray with two coffees, and she holds it to the side as she squints up at me. "I have told at least twenty people my eyewitness account of your heroics. Mostly because you aren't answering your phone, so you can't tell them yourself." She tips her head to the side. "For someone who slept in, you look like crap."

"Thanks. I feel like crap." I might have slept in, but I don't feel rested. No surprise. Despite being exhausted, I had trouble falling asleep last night, and once I did, I had trouble staying asleep. Too many dreams, none of them sweet.

"I've been calling and calling," Carly says. "Why didn't you answer? Never mind. Come down and let me in."

"Coming. By the way, nice hair," I mumble. Carly disappears back under the porch roof. I'm about to draw back from the window when the fine hairs at my nape prickle and rise. I freeze, scanning the empty street, feeling like someone's out there, watching me. But no one is. The only person in sight is the neighbor three doors down. She has her back to me and she's hunched over her garden, digging. I pull the window shut as I duck back inside.

I snatch my phone. Someone turned it off. There's a note on my nightstand that suggests that someone was Dad. I feel a moment's panic because he made that decision for me rather than letting me choose to sleep in. A couple of deep breaths, and the panic eases. Silly. I know it's silly to try and control every little thing, but silly or not, it's been my instinct ever since . . . Mom.

I pick up Dad's note.

GONE FISHING. THE SALMON'LL BE BITING. THOUGHT
YOU COULD USE SOME EXTRA REST. CALL ME IF YOU
NEED ME.
    DAD

He'll text anyone and everyone else, but he leaves me handwritten notes with smiley faces at the bottom. I ought to find it annoying. Sometimes I do. But after yesterday,

I appreciate the fact that even though my world's upside down, some things don't change. And I'm glad he's gone fishing. He asked me if I really was okay with it so many times last night, I felt like he'd set the question on Replay. I guess he finally believed me when I told him I was fine. In the past few months, he's been ignoring even his favorite hobbies like fly tying and fishing and bowling. Maybe this is a sign of change for the better. A girl can hope.

I turn my phone back on to find about a billion texts from people I know and people I barely know, all wanting to find out about how I saved Janice's sister. I turn my phone off again and drag on a pair of plaid flannels and a ratty sweatshirt, then head down to let Carly in.

She kicks off her shoes, follows me to the kitchen, and sets the coffees on the counter, right beside the neat line of empty beer bottles. They're perfectly aligned, labels pointing forward. She stares at them, saying nothing. I stare at them, trying to remember if they were there when I went up to bed last night. They weren't. Which means Dad polished them off, all seven of them, after I went up.

He quit smoking as soon as Mom got her diagnosis. He started drinking the day we buried her. Or maybe he drank before that, and I just never noticed. Funny how so much about the way I saw my parents shriveled away right along with my mom.

Carly opens the fridge and peers inside, then runs her index finger along the tops of the bottles on the door. "Seventeen," she says after a quick count. The number makes the tension in my shoulders ease. All bottles present and accounted for; Dad didn't take any beer with him. I touch the rim of each empty bottle on the counter in turn. Dry. So it's unlikely he drank them this morning. Dad pretends he doesn't have a problem because he steers clear of hard liquor. And he swears that he'll never drink and drive. I want to believe him, and it looks as if today I can.

Leaning one hip against the counter, Carly watches me as I put the empties in the cardboard box under the sink then wipe the counter even though it isn't dirty. She's waiting to see if I want to talk about it. I don't.

But I *do* wish I could talk about what happened yesterday; I want to, so badly that the words feel like they're clogging my throat. I usually tell Carly pretty much everything, and what I don't tell her, she figures out for herself. Keeping something this big from her feels wrong, but Luka's warning haunts me, and I don't dare say a thing. Besides, how could she possibly believe me even if I did tell her? I can barely believe it, and I lived it.

"What flavor?" I ask, dipping my chin at the coffees.

"Full-fat double-shot peppermint mocha for me, plain old decaf skinny latte for you."

I grab a couple of chocolate Pop-Tarts, keep one for myself and hand the other to Carly.

"Pop-Tarts?" she asks, one brow shooting up. I remember back to when we were like . . . nine, she practiced that look in the mirror until she felt she had it right. She's only gotten better at it since then.

That look makes everything feel like it always does, like nothing's different. I stare at her for a second, wishing that it were all a dream. A nightmare. A psychotic break. No such luck. Everything's different.

I force myself to shrug and take a bite. "Saturday morning breakfast of champions."

"Oh, right," she says. "It's Saturday."

Saturday's the one day I allow myself to break my healthy-eating rule—a habit that started when Mom was sick. She tried every treatment the doctors suggested, and some they didn't. Naturopath. Homeopath. Vitamins. Yoga. Dad and I tried a lot of stuff right along with her. For me, the healthy eating stuck. I like being in control of what goes into my body. What I eat, how often I run, how high my grades are, how neat I keep the house—all of that's my purview, and mine alone.

That's one of the things that made the dreams—nightmares—so terrible last night. I couldn't control what I saw in my sleep and, worse, I couldn't control what happened in my life yesterday. Thinking about it makes my skin prickle.

Carly licks foam from her upper lip. "Soooo . . . did you talk to him yet?"

"Him?" My heart stutters. How does she know about Jackson?

"Him," Carly repeats. "Luka." There's something weird about the way she says his name, kind of slow and soft.

"Luka." I press my lips together. "Right."

"He's got that whole dark-eyed, I'm-a-loner-even-in-a-crowd, just-try-and-get-my-attention thing going on," she says with a sigh. "It's hot."

"So maybe *you* should call him."

She taps her finger against her chin, genuinely considering it. An expression I can't read flits across her features, sort of regretful, sort of sad. Then she shakes her head. "No, you should. I saw the way he looked at you yesterday, right after he *almost got killed* running in front of that truck to save you. And you're obviously losing sleep over him. You should call. Just to see if he's feeling okay after yesterday, you know?" She grins. "It's the perfect excuse."

I stare at her. I don't remember Luka looking at me with any emotion other than panic when he was trying to tell me not to talk about the game. And I didn't lose sleep over him. The only person dancing through my nightmares along with me was Jackson.

Nightmares, not dreams. I've never dreamed about a guy, not the way Carly means. But if I were going to, I suppose it would be someone more like Luka than Jackson, someone who didn't boss me around and answer in riddles. Someone who didn't make every cell in my body edgy and nervous.

"I don't have Luka's cell number," I mumble around a mouthful of Pop-Tart.

"What about his landline? That ought to be listed."

I shake my head. "I checked last night—"

"Oh-ho! So you *did* try to call him."

I ignore her blatant glee, refusing to feed the beast. "I

didn't try to call him. I tried to find his number. There's a difference. Anyway, I couldn't find it. He and his dad just moved back recently. So maybe it isn't listed yet, or maybe they didn't bother with a landline."

"And he's not online?"

"Not that I could find. Maybe social media isn't his thing."

"Then you two definitely ought to be dating." Carly smirks at me. I have a page. Doesn't everyone? The difference is, I've updated mine maybe three times in the past three weeks while everyone else updates theirs at least three times an hour.

I ignore the bait and keep my tone casual. "Who's talking about dating? All I did was try to find his number."

"You should have called the specialist." Carly whips out her phone. "Give me a few seconds."

It doesn't actually take seconds, but close enough. Ten texts, three calls, and five minutes later, Carly has Luka's cell number. Between her and Dee and Sarah, they can pretty much ferret out anything.

"Thanks." I stare at the number Carly jotted down. She stares at me expectantly.

"I, um, have to think about what I want to say." I hedge. I don't want to call Luka right now, not with Carly here listening to every word. The things I want to ask him demand privacy.

"You are not getting off that easy." Carly waggles her index finger at me.

"Fine, I'll send a text." I keep it innocuous—just asking if he's okay—because Carly insists on checking it over. Once it's sent, she breaks into a grin, throws her arms around me, and holds on tight.

"I'm so glad you're finally feeling better," she whispers.

Her words stop me cold. She thinks I'm crushing on Luka. She thinks I'm going to be able to laugh without trying again. She thinks I'll be back to the way I was before. I feel sick because she couldn't be further from the truth and because I can't tell her that. I can't tell her anything. If Luka's right, her life might depend on my silence. All I can do is hug her back.

Carly fishes the remote from between the couch cushions and we sprawl out under the ancient afghan my mom knit when she was pregnant with me. While we watch TV, I text people back, directing them to Carly's page, where she's posted her eyewitness account of what went down.

An hour and a couple of cartoons later, I head to the bathroom to text Luka again. This time my message is a bit more insistent. An hour later, I do it again. Rinse and repeat as the day wears on. He doesn't reply.

Carly snorts as I head to the bathroom for the fifth time. "Bladder infection?" she asks, all sweetly innocent.

"Yup. Caught it from *your* toilet seat."

She throws a pillow at my head.

When my phone rings at five-thirty, I nearly jump out of my skin. But it's only Kelley, telling us to meet her at Mark's Texas Hots on Monroe for dinner.

It isn't until after midnight—once Dad's gone to bed and the house is quiet—that I build up the nerve to actually phone Luka. He doesn't answer, and I don't leave a message.

I'm drifting off when I get a text:

> dont ask any Qs. cant ansr. told u that. trying 2 protect u.

Frustration surges and I text back:

> Not buying that. Will u call me?

CHAPTER**EIGHT**

"PANCAKES?" I ASK DAD THE FOLLOWING MORNING, AIMING for bright and cheery even though last night's dreams were again populated by aliens and cries of pain.

And Jackson. I kept seeing him. The way he jumped in front of me and took the alien's shot. The sound of his voice when he said, "You're doing great, Miki."

Luka still hasn't answered my last text. I'm so frustrated and anxious that I actually called again this morning, and this time, I left a message. Then another. And another. Stalker much?

"Real pancakes?" Dad asks suspiciously.

Whole grains are real; they just aren't what he's hoping for. "With real maple syrup and sliced bananas," I say, knowing that once they're made and in front of him, he'll polish off the plate, whole grain or not.

I set out the ingredients, pausing for a second to stare at the empty bottles lined up on the counter yet again. Only five of them this time. I want to ignore them almost as much as I want to turn around and ask Dad why he leaves them out like that. Because he wants me to see them? Because he doesn't care if I see them? There's a world of difference between the two. Sort of like the difference between suicide and murder.

In the end, I keep my back to him as I put them in the box under the sink, then wipe the counter even though it isn't dirty.

We both ignore the elephant in the room and get on with breakfast.

"How was fishing?" I ask.

Dad lights up like a kid. "Caught a ten-pound steelhead. Look!" He pulls out his phone and shows me the picture—he's a catch-and-release kind of guy so I never actually get to see his catch, just pictures of them. It's at an awkward angle and I can only see about two-thirds of the fish, but Dad's thrilled. He launches into the details of the catch. I chew and listen, not that I'm really into fishing but because I like seeing him like this: happy. He hasn't been fishing much in the past few months, and I'm glad he decided to go yesterday. It seems like the more often he drinks, the less interested he is in doing all the stuff he used to like to do.

Or maybe it's because he's less interested in life that he drinks so much.

He flips to the next fish picture—a blurry shot of a swishing tail—and launches into more details of his day.

It isn't until later when we're standing side by side at the sink—me washing pans, Dad drying—that he asks, "You okay?"

No. I can't sleep. I'm having nightmares. And I spend every waking second wondering if—when—I'm going to get pulled again. "Of course I'm okay."

Mostly honest, but sometimes not.

He nods. "Thought I heard you walking around last night."

"Upset stomach," I lie. "Probably the garbage plate I had at Mark's."

"You? A garbage plate? Burger, hash browns, grilled cheese, gravy? If that's true, then you really aren't okay." He lays the back of his hand against my forehead as though to check my temperature.

I smile and slap his hand away. "I shared one and a big salad with Carly and Kelley."

"Meaning you ate the salad and they ate the rest."

Pretty much, but I don't bother to admit it. "The salad had grilled chicken. And cheese."

"Dressing?"

"Actually, yes." Low-fat raspberry vinaigrette.

He stares at me, saying nothing, his expression solemn. "I love you. You know that." Not a question.

My breath catches. I know he loves me; it just isn't something he actually says all that often. "I know, Dad."

You just don't love yourself, at least not enough to stop drinking before something terrible happens. But there's no point in saying that because if I do, he'll just turn around and walk away. No deep convos for Dad, at least not if the deep end is on his side. I smile a little sadly. "I love you more."

At my reference to our childhood game, he smiles back and I have to look away before I throw my arms around him and babble out all my fears like I used to do when I was five, worried about the monster under the bed.

With a shudder, I remember the way the Drau was sucked in by my weapon: legs, then torso, and finally head. It knew what was happening the whole time it was dying. Its end wasn't fast and easy.

So who's the monster now?

A couple of hours later, I give up on homework. I can't concentrate. My mind keeps going back to the aliens, the lobby, the weapons. Tyrone. Richelle.

Jackson.

I'm so mad at Luka for being stubborn. He doesn't have to betray any secrets. I could stick to general questions and he could stick to one-word answers. I grab my phone, ready to tell him exactly that, when it hits me.

I don't need Luka.

He won't talk to me? Fine.

Richelle Kirkman from Philadelphia just might.

I log on and enter her name in the search engine. Richelle will talk to me. I know she will. Even if there's some sort of edict against talking to anyone outside what Luka refers to as the game, Richelle isn't an outsider. She's as much part of it as I am. And if even the insiders aren't supposed to discuss it, I'll keep my questions generic. There must be something she'll be willing to divulge.

My connection is slow, the little circle spinning and spinning. Come on. *Come on.*

Nothing. Three minutes' worth of nothing.

"Dad," I yell. "Dad, can you reset the modem? The connection's slow."

No answer. I run downstairs to Dad's home office. He's not there. I can hear him outside, running the mower over our too-long grass. Good, the neighbors were starting to give me pointed looks every time I left the house. I reset the modem. The row of lights flickers back on one by one.

Success. I do a little victory dance and pump my fist in the air.

I tear back up the stairs. I have a plan. A solution. I'll get the answers I need. I am in control.

In that second it dawns on me that this is the most excited I've been about anything in ages. Gingerly, I feel around for the gray fog, sort of like a tongue poking at a sore tooth. It's there, at the edge of my thoughts, but it's hazy and weak rather than thick as pea soup.

A search for Richelle's name pops up a bunch of results. A real estate agent. A funeral home. The third is a link to the census bureau. Strike one. Strike two. Strike three. But

I'm not out because the fourth is a social network site. I click it and grin when her picture pops up. I did it. I found her. I'm back in control. I jump up and do another victory dance as I study the page—

I stop mid-dance and sink into the chair.

The page that popped up is wrong. My breath rushes out and I can't get it back. I'm gasping, dizzy, my hand flying up, my fingers splaying over the screen.

I shake my head, but it doesn't change anything.

On the left, there's a picture of Richelle looking pretty much the way I saw her on Friday, wearing her cheer uniform, a smile on her face. Her hair's different, tied back in a ponytail. But the sparkle in her eyes is the same.

Across the top of the page is a series of smaller pictures: one of Richelle with the squad, one in street clothes with friends, one with a couple that I assume are her parents, one with a small white dog. There's no doubt I found the right person, but the words above the pictures are wrong: *Richelle Kirkman's Memorial Page.*

I scan down, frantic.

In celebration of Richelle's life . . .

Miss you, Rich. xox

Thinking about Richelle while I study for finals . . .

There's post after post from her friends and family and even people who say they never met her but knew someone who knew someone who knew her.

And there's a post with a brief article from the local paper, outlining the circumstances of her death. I scan it, then go back and read it in more detail. She fell to her death trying to save a little boy who'd climbed out on her neighbor's roof. She managed to save him but not herself. I stare at it. Read it again. Two things jump out at me: the fact that Richelle was on a roof when she was scared of heights and the date of her death.

"No." I don't understand. According to this page, Richelle died more than seven months ago. "No," I say again, louder. It's not possible that she's been dead all that time. It's not possible that she's dead at all. We were healed. Luka and I . . . we came back healed. That's what's supposed to happen when we get pulled back from the mission. Luka and Richelle said so.

But Richelle's dead. Has been for seven months.

This can't be right.

I open a new tab and search the word *respawn*. *To generate or give rise to an entity or player after its death or destruction in the game.*

Luka and I regenerated; we came back with nothing more than a couple of scrapes. And Luka said he's been part of the game for over a year, getting pulled again and again. He'd been hurt and healed again and again. *I* was hurt and healed. We got hit by the truck; we respawned in the lobby. We were shot by the Drau; we respawned in real life. But every gash and break and scrape disappeared when we came back.

It isn't a game. It's a nightmare.

I close that tab and return to Richelle's page. It makes

no sense. Richelle can't have been dead for— I look at the page and check the dates again.

How can she have been dead for seven months when I just saw her Friday? I talked to her. Laughed with her.

My recollections writhe and twist. *The bracelet's your con. The color's your health. Don't let it turn red.*

Red.

Images flash through my thoughts like a strobe light: The truck's bumper, stained with cherry-juice smears. Blood on the ground. Blood on Luka's broken arm. Blood staining my jeans dark crimson.

I wrap my arms around myself, trying to hold it together as I remember Luka's look of horror when my con turned orange. And right before we got pulled back, Richelle's screen was red. I saw it. We all saw it. They knew what it meant, but I didn't. Oh God, I didn't know.

Richelle is dead. She's not coming back.

With a moan, I lower my head and press the sides of my balled fists against my forehead. My eyes sting. My throat feels thick.

I thought it was a game. Luka called it that. I know he did. Tyrone treated it like one. Richelle said he wants to sell the rights. . . .

But Jackson said it was no game. He said it was real, and that what we did determined our survival. I thought he was crazy. I *wanted* to think he was crazy.

I'm shaking as I grab my phone. No more texts. No more evasions. I call Luka's number and when it goes to voice mail, I start to babble, "She's gone. Oh my God, she's gone. She's dead. For real dead. As in *dead*. I need to talk to you. Please, Luka. I need to talk to you."

I hang up and pace the length of my room as I dial his number again, my hands shaking. My stomach churns and rolls.

Voice mail again. My babbling is even less coherent the second time. And by the third, I'm not even talking, just breathing hard, willing Luka to answer.

Panting, I stare at my phone. I want to call Carly. I need to call Carly. But I don't dare drag her into this. I can't put her in danger. The thought of Carly dead like Richelle is more than I can bear. What if one phone call seals her fate?

I hear the slam of a car door. I look out to see Dad pulling away. I stare blankly for a second before I recall that at breakfast he told me he planned to do the grocery shopping. I'm alone, all alone, which is both a bad and a good thing. I don't trust myself at the moment. If Dad hadn't left, if he'd walked into my room right now, I might have told all.

At which point he probably would have done a room search for drugs and then hauled me to the ER at Rochester General for a mental health assessment.

Hugging myself, I rub my palms up and down my upper arms. I feel like the walls are closing in on me, like my skin is too tight, my blood too thin. I turn and stare at my computer and see Richelle looking back at me.

I dial Luka again. "Luka, please. I'm begging you, pick up. I need to talk. I need—"

Anger surges and I disconnect the call. I'm alone, and the only person who can help me deal with this is me. Have I learned nothing? Everyone leaves. Gram. Sofu. Mom—

In the end, you can only rely on you.

I drag on running gear, lace my shoes, fill a small water bottle and tuck it into the holster at my waist. I'm moving on autopilot, not thinking, just doing.

I don't usually—*ever*—run in the afternoons. I don't run on Sundays. But this isn't just any Sunday afternoon.

Richelle is dead. Richelle is dead. Richelle is dead.

The thought feels both immediate and distant at the same time. I stare at her picture on the screen and somewhere buried underneath my pain is the calm, cold voice of reason. I need to hide my tracks. The game can't bleed into real life; Luka made that very clear.

At least this small thing I can control.

I stand up and walk over to my computer, double-check that I was set to private browsing, then close the window. I hit Reset. And then I say a silent word of thanks to Carly, who's always trying to make certain that her multitude of brothers can't find out what sites she's been to. She's the one who told me that my operating system could cache entries, even when I'm set to private browsing. And she's the one who taught me the command to clear it. Not that I've ever needed it before, but she was insistent that one never knew when something like this would come in handy.

I type the command: Terminal: dscacheutil—flushcache.

All evidence wiped clean.

"Good-bye, Richelle," I whisper.

I feel like a robot as I lock the front door, then run down the driveway. My music. I forgot it. I spin toward the house but can't face going back inside. I spin back toward the road and slam into something hard. Hands close on my upper arms, steadying me. My head jerks back, I look up a good six inches, and my breath locks in my chest.

"Hey," Jackson says.

CHAPTER**NINE**

I RUN. JACKSON RUNS BESIDE ME. WE DON'T TALK. WE DON'T even look at each other. No, that's not quite true. I sneak sidelong glances, not trusting myself to speak yet.

He's not wearing the aviator shades anymore. He's switched them out for a pair of wraparound Oakleys, black on black, the lenses so dark that I wonder how he can see through them even in the sunlight.

We've done a mile before I ask, "What are you doing here?"

"Running."

"Just once, can you be something other than an asshole?" I don't think I've ever wanted to hurt anyone as much as I want to hurt Jackson Tate in that moment. I imagine punching him in the head.

"You want to punch me in the head," he says, and when I stop dead and turn to stare at him, he shakes his head. "No, I can't read your—"

"Mind," I finish for him. "So you've said. More than once, I think. I'm not sure I believe you. After all, I could hear you in my mind. What's to say you can't hear me in yours?"

"Me. I'm saying it. And I'm telling you the truth."

"The truth? Would you recognize it if it bit you on the ass?"

He smiles a little but says nothing.

I sigh. "Why are you here, Jackson?"

"I'm here for you, Miki. To try and help you figure things out."

My breath catches, then rushes in to fill my lungs. "Only if I ask the right questions."

He gives a short nod. "True enough."

I start running again, afraid that if I don't, I really might hit him. Or dissolve in tears. Neither option will lead to anything good. I'm out of control and I don't like it. My feet pound the sidewalk, the rhythm familiar. I cling to that familiarity, letting it ground me. I think that if I don't hold on to something, my sanity will slip away.

Richelle's dead. I want to know how and why. I want to know how it's even possible. Those are the questions I need to ask, along with dozens of others. I need to do it in a way that doesn't break the rules Luka alluded to. And since Jackson's so fond of nonanswers, I need to do it in a way that'll get me what I want. I center my thoughts, using every trick Dr. Andrews, my grief counselor, taught me. Breathing. Visualization. Distraction.

"Plotting my demise?" Jackson asks, turning his head toward me for a second as we run.

"Something like that."

"I'm not good at this, Miki."

"At what?"

"Explaining."

My laugh is short and hard and dark. "No shit." I feel a little bad as soon as I say it. He's trying. Sort of. I should meet him halfway.

"Does it break the rules if I say her name?"

"It breaks the rules for me to be here at all. But there are breaks"—he pauses—"and there are *breaks*."

We run side by side, keeping a steady pace. After a few minutes, I ask, "Who makes the rules?"

"Let's just say . . . they're decided by committee."

He said something like that before, when I asked him who decided on the name for the con.

"Are you on that committee?"

He makes a sound somewhere between a grunt and a laugh. "No."

He slows to a walk, and I slow with him.

"What happens if we break the rules?" I ask.

He doesn't answer, either because he doesn't know or because he doesn't want me to know. Whatever the consequences are, they worry Luka enough that he won't even talk to me. Or not. Maybe there are no consequences; maybe it's just an amorphous threat that's holding Luka hostage. I'm not brave enough—or maybe it's that I'm not foolish enough—to take the risk. So I come at things from a different angle. I keep my comment generic and say, "She's dead."

Jackson nods. I take that as a sign that I can safely continue.

"For seven months." Every syllable is laced with my pain and confusion.

Jackson nods again.

"So I fought beside—"

"*Tsss,*" Jackson hisses through his teeth. A warning. So apparently there *are* lines I have to be careful not to cross. No talk of fighting. Probably avoiding the mention of weapons or aliens is a plan.

"So I *met* . . . what? Her ghost?" I ask.

"No," he says. He stops. I stop. We're at the park, which is surprisingly empty for a sunny Sunday afternoon. He walks over to the swings and leans back against a wooden post, watching me. He's long and lean, his black running gear outlining the muscles of his limbs.

Angry with myself for noticing, I look away. The last thing I need to do is to think of Jackson Tate as anything other than a source of information.

"You catch on quick," Jackson says.

"What does that mean?" My gaze shoots to his, except it doesn't because his eyes are hidden. I wish I could see them. I wish I could tell if he's looking straight at me or avoiding my eyes. My mom always used to say, if wishes were pennies . . .

"It means what I said. That you catch on quick. I notice that you aren't mentioning specifics."

"Does it matter?" I glance around at the empty park. "Who's listening?"

His smile is tight and dangerous. "Who knows? That's the point. That's the danger. They could be anywhere."

He's talking about the Drau. Dread knots in my belly as I realize what his words mean: the Drau aren't confined to the game. They could be here, in my world, my real world. I glance around the empty park. "Are you trying to scare me?"

"No. I'm trying to answer your questions."

I give him the thumbs-up. "And doing a great job, too." I slump down onto a swing, dragging my feet on the ground as I surge forward and back. "Why are you here, really?"

"You called Luka."

"Yeah, I called *Luka*. To talk to *him*. What exactly does that have to do with you?" I pause, considering, and then feel the heat of mortification in my cheeks. "He called you? He asked you to come see me because I'm this crazy girl who won't stop calling him?"

Jackson laughs. The sound is low and a little rusty, like he doesn't laugh often. I feel that laugh somewhere inside me, like butterflies. "Not because you're the crazy girl. He called to tell me he was going to break the rules and meet you."

That's a big deal. Even though I ended up here with Jackson, the fact that Luka was willing to break the rules for me feels like he was offering me a gift. "Why would he call to tell you that?"

Jackson's shoulder lifts in an easy shrug. "Either he wanted my blessing or he wanted me to talk him out of it."

"Which route did you decide to go with?"

"Neither. I headed him off at the pass. Got to you before he could."

"Why?"

He doesn't answer right away, and when he finally speaks, I feel like he's holding a lot back. "I trust myself not to screw this up."

Which tells me everything and nothing. Because he already told me that he's not good at explaining, so he must mean that he trusts himself more than he trusts Luka to give answers that don't break the *rules*. Or maybe—

"So do the rules apply to everyone equally, or are you exempt?"

"Depends on the rule."

"That's not an answer."

"Ask a different question."

The first one that jumps into my head is: Why does Luka have Jackson's number if we're not supposed to have contact? I almost ask, but I can't think of a way to do it that won't make me sound like maybe *I* want Jackson's number, too, so I let it pass.

But thinking about that makes me wonder how Jackson got to me so quickly. Richelle said that people don't get pulled from the same geographic regions, so how could Jackson be close enough to get to me before Luka?

I remember the weird feeling I had yesterday when I was standing at my window, and a chill crawls up my spine. "Oh, no, no, no. Please tell me you are not some creeper guy."

"I am not some creeper guy."

I huff a sharp exhalation and narrow my question. "Were you watching my house yesterday?"

"Yes."

"Spying on me?"

"One of my responsibilities is ensuring the acclimation of new recruits."

"'Ensuring the acclimation,'" I repeat. "You're supposed to do that without making contact or offering any explanations?"

"Pretty much."

"That's the most asinine thing I've ever heard."

"I doubt it's the *most* asinine."

I don't want to play word games or argue about semantics. "Are you in charge of the game, Jackson?"

He scrubs his fingers along his jaw. "When we're on assignment, there are things I know that others don't. In charge of the game?" He gives a dark laugh. "No."

"You're in charge on assignment? So isn't it your responsibility to keep your team alive?"

I don't even see him move, but he's suddenly right in front of me. His hands fist around the chains of the swing as he bends close, his face inches from mine. He smells faintly of citrus shaving cream, and I have a crazy urge to lean a little closer and breathe him in.

"No team," he whispers. "Every man for himself, remember?"

I do. And I ought to hate him for throwing it in my face again. But there's . . . something . . . his tone, or maybe the hard line of his mouth . . . Something makes me think he doesn't like saying it, that he doesn't believe his own words. That Richelle's loss is his torment and his responsibility.

"Tell me what happened to her." I hold up my hand, palm forward. "Don't tell me she died." There's a knot in my throat that makes it hard to speak. "What I need to know is how and when."

"First tell me how you figured it out. You didn't realize it before we got pulled back. I saw it in your face. And Luka wouldn't have told you."

I almost refuse. After all, he's not exactly being forthcoming. A little tit-for-tat might be a worthwhile lesson for him to learn. But I just don't have it in me. Not right now. So I tell him about the memorial page. Then I tell him how I cleared my cache and erased any possible trail.

"Did you now?" he asks, and smiles, white teeth and that dimple carving deep in his cheek. Jackson Tate's full smile is something to behold.

I swallow and look away. "Your turn," I say. "Explain the missing seven months."

"She went back to the place where she originally exited."

I digest that for a second. "Richelle went back to the moment she was first pulled." A moment that in some alternate reality ended in her death rather than her inclusion in the game. Even in my thoughts, I stumble over that word. It isn't a game. We're not playing there. Some of us are dying there. "As if she had never been pulled at all, never . . ." I hesitate, wondering if I'm breaking all the rules now, if he'll stop me. He doesn't, so I keep going. "As if I had never met her, never almost had the chance to be her friend. But I did meet her. I remember the time I spent with her. What about all her family and friends? From the comments I read, they don't remember her as alive for the past seven months."

"No."

"My outcome would be the truck," I say.

I would save Janice's sister. I'd get hit by the truck. It would kill me.

No aliens. No battles.

No coffee with Carly. No pancake breakfast with my dad.

No moment here in the park with Jackson.

"And everything after that would just . . . disappear? Like it had never been? People wouldn't remember anything about me after that?"

"Pretty much. Except for those of us who met you else-where."

By *elsewhere,* he means in the game that isn't a game at all. "How is that possible?" I force the words out through tight lips. "What is it? Some sort of time paradox?"

Tangled, impossible threads of time that merge and diverge.

Thinking about it makes my brain hurt.

Jackson takes his time answering, and when he does, there's definitely a thread of humor in his tone. "Time dila-tion. Time passes more slowly the closer you are to the speed of light."

The words sound familiar, and suddenly I'm certain he's amused. He's playing me. "Laughing at my expense, Jackson? I saw the same show last Thursday night. That theoretical physicist was interviewed, right? I watched it with my dad. But according to the expert, time dilation only accounts for movement forward in time, not back. Nice try. Don't bullshit a bullshitter." I play sleight of hand every day of my life, pretending to be like everyone else. I can recognize when I'm being played.

His lips curl in that barely there smile, dark and sar-donic and sexy. Why does it make me want to reach over and touch him? I curl my fist to keep from doing exactly that.

"You're right. I watched the same show, but it could only cover what *people* know." The way he says *people* makes me think he means humans, but he's being careful like I'm being careful.

"It couldn't cover what people don't *yet* know." Or what *aliens* already know.

"It's a combination of time dilation, mass, gravity, and a positional wormhole."

I narrow my eyes. "Do you even know the answers? Everything you're saying could be bullshit."

"But I make it sound so good you can't be sure it's not the truth."

"Is it?"

He goes quiet, and then shocks me when he reaches out and strokes a strand of my hair back off my cheek. My skin tingles where he's touched. I want to jerk away. I want to lean closer and ask him to do it again. The rush of confusing emotions takes me by surprise.

"Do answers help?" he asks, and the moment is gone.

I don't even need to think about it. "No. Especially not when they're coming from you."

"Because?"

"Because you aren't really saying much of anything, and I don't know if I should believe what you do say."

"Trust me, the how and why don't take away the pain." His tone is cool and even, the words flat. Yet, for some reason, I think he knows a bit about pain.

CHAPTER**TEN**

JACKSON AND I ARE SIDE BY SIDE, FACING OPPOSITE DIRECTIONS as we swing. We're quiet. We've been quiet for a while. Twenty minutes. Maybe thirty. Oddly, the silence is a comfortable one. I pull out the little water bottle at my waist, take a drink, then hesitate. Cutting him a sidelong glance, I think about his lips on my water bottle, then mine, then his. I look down at my lap and take a slow breath. Then I turn my head and hold the bottle out toward him.

He smiles a little, like he knows what I'm thinking. I feel that smile shimmer through me all the way to my toes. His fingers brush mine as he takes the bottle from my hand. He tips his head back and takes a drink, and I watch the muscles of his throat move as he swallows.

"Thanks," he says, and hands the bottle back, our

fingers brushing once more.

I'm breathing faster than I should be. I'm glad for the excuse to look away as I settle the bottle back in its holder at my waist. Maybe he senses my discomfort and confusion, or maybe he just decides to move. Either way, Jackson gets up from the swing, takes a few steps, and looks around, not nervously or shiftily, more of a casual scan of the area, just like he did back in the lobby. I realize that he did that while we were running, too. He's always on alert.

"So, can I ask some more questions?"

He turns to face me. "We shouldn't talk about this here."

"We already did, so it shouldn't matter if we do again. Besides, there's no one else anywhere near us. Who's listening? The grass?" Frustration punches through my carefully manufactured facade of calm. "And we'd see *them* coming from a mile away. They're not exactly easy to miss." I can't help but notice how he grows unnaturally still. I rewind what I just said, and a chill crawls across my skin. "We *would* see them, wouldn't we?"

"Not necessarily."

Oh, I did not want to know that. Does he mean that the Drau could be here, right now? I swallow.

"Where can we talk? Is there anywhere safe?"

He paces a few feet, then turns and paces back. It hits me then that cool, icy Jackson Tate isn't so cool at this moment. "Depends on your definition of *safe*." He tips his head back, his face toward the cloudless sky. "Satellites can see you anywhere."

"Now you're just trying to freak me out." Isn't he? I'm getting nowhere on this topic, so I do a quick switch. "Who were the other people in the clearing?"

"Richelle. Tyrone. Luka."

"I thought we weren't supposed to say their names."

"Did I say that?"

I frown and think back. "No, I don't think you did. I think you just sort of avoided answering. Was that a test?" When he doesn't answer, I sigh. "Tell me about the people in the other clearings."

"You see them." He sounds both pleased and wary. "Not everyone can."

"Yeah, I figured that out. Luka can't, but you can, and I can. So who are they?"

"You'd call them other teams."

"You can use a different word if it makes you feel better. What would you call them?"

"Let's just say they're others just like us."

"Do Luka and Tyrone know there are other teams?"

"In the abstract, yeah. But they've never seen them."

"Why can I see them and they can't?"

Jackson shrugs.

"I could hit you. I really could." I'm so angry in that moment, so sick of his nonanswers, that I almost do hit him. I'm appalled by that. How does he do this to me? How does he break through my control so easily?

"You could try," he says, and his smile is all white teeth and amusement. For a second, all I can do is stare. He's enjoying this, and if I'm honest with myself, so am I. I'm angry at Jackson, at everything and everyone. I'm resentful that he's here. And I'm so glad he's here, that he didn't leave me to struggle through alone. How's that for contradictory?

He pulls emotions out of me that I'm not used to feeling. For some reason, when I'm with him, the things that drag me down feel thin and weak, and I feel strong.

I'm enjoying matching wits with him, and that realization makes me feel horrible because the only reason we're together right now is because Richelle is dead.

Jackson reads the change in my expression. "She's gone," he says, his tone gentle. "You can't change that, and you shouldn't feel guilty because you're alive." There's something off in his tone. Something that makes me think he wants me to believe those words even though he doesn't quite believe them himself.

I look away, unsettled that he can read me so easily, that he gets it. I do feel guilty. About Richelle. About Mom. And Gram and Sofu. How am I supposed to go on living when they don't get that chance?

"We did the mission. We made it through," I say. "So we were all supposed to go back to our regularly scheduled lives. She was supposed to get to go back."

"Not all of us made it through. Only the ones who did can come back. Remember what I told you about . . ." He taps his wrist.

The bracelet's your con. The color's your health. Don't let it turn red.

"It's because her—" I stop myself before I say the word *con*. "Because of the color change." Because her con turned red.

Jackson takes a step closer. "Health points, damage . . . you know what they are?"

I nod. I play sometimes with Carly and her brothers. "They're gaming terms. They measure how much damage a character can withstand."

"So you know that when the life bar . . ." He pauses, to make sure I'm still following.

"*Health* bar," I interject, seeing the pattern.

"Health bar. Or just health," he agrees. "When the bar changes color fully, it's game over."

Game over. Death.

Horror sluices over me like a bucket of icy water.

So that really is the answer. I'd suspected, but a part of me thought it should be something else. Something bigger.

"She's gone because of that? Like this really is a game? It isn't. You're the one who said that. It isn't a game. And she's dead. Forever dead." Because if you die in the game, you die for real. Of course. I should have seen that right from the start. I should have seen all of it.

I surge off the swing and step closer, breathing hard, my face inches away from Jackson's.

"In a game, you get to respawn. You get to go back to

the spawn point." A designated reentry point. That's what Luka and I did. We went back to the moment it started, the instant before the truck hit us. "That's what we did, isn't it? We respawned. Why didn't she?"

"I just told you why."

Because her con turned red. I remember the battle in flashes and blurs. Richelle's scream. Jackson kicking the weapon out of the alien's hand. He protected me. Why didn't he do the same for her?

"Why didn't you help her? Keep her safe? Why did you let her die? Why?" I'm screaming, raising my fists without even realizing I'm doing it, pounding them against Jackson's chest.

And then I'm not. He catches my wrists and holds them, just tight enough that I can't hit him anymore, but not so tight it hurts. I freeze, heart slamming against my ribs, because I'm angry and afraid, and because he's touching me, his hands on my wrists, our faces inches apart.

My pulse races; my cheeks feel hot. Lots of people touch me, and it never feels like this.

"So now you know," he says. "Happy?"

I pull my wrists free. "No," I say. "Not at all."

"I know." He lifts his hands and closes them on my upper arms. I stand there, too numb to jerk away. Slowly, he pulls me closer. I let him. I let him wrap his arms around me. I let myself rest my cheek against his chest. And for a few moments, I just breathe and listen to the steady beat of his heart.

"I'm still an asshole," he whispers, his breath fanning my hair.

"I know," I whisper back.

"Good." Last word.

Luka is sitting on my front steps when I get home. He's hunched over, head down, forearms on his knees. At the sight of him, warmth kindles in my chest. Not like the butterflies I felt with Jackson. Something else. A feeling of the familiar, the known and safe.

He lifts his head at my approach, his dark eyes wary and assessing. "I waited for you."

I stop a few feet away. "So I see. Thanks."

"For waiting?"

I nod. "For waiting. For coming at all. I know you're breaking the rules."

"Yeah." He offers a lopsided grin, easy and open. "Seems like everywhere we turn, there are rules. I wonder if we'll ever just get to make our own."

I don't know what to say to that. I'm not sure I want to be a rule maker, or even a rule breaker.

"He found me," I say.

Luka lifts his brows. "Who?"

"J—" I press my lips together, not certain I'm supposed to say his name. Then I throw my hands in the air. "This is ridiculous." It is. I'm supposed to censor every word I say because some invisible entity might be watching? I understand the need for a certain amount of discretion, but second-guessing my words is making me paranoid. "Jackson," I say. "Jackson went running with me." Only as I say it do I remember that it must be okay because Jackson said names out loud, too.

It's confusing to try to play by rules when I don't even know what they are.

Luka's eyes widen. "Wow. Okay." He doesn't sound happy. "Wasn't expecting that."

"Neither was I." I hold out my hand. Luka takes it, and I pull him to his feet. Once he's standing, I have to tilt my head back and look up to meet his eyes. He definitely got taller during the year he was away. His shoulders are broader, his jaw leaner. "Why'd you call him?"

"Because I couldn't stand letting you—" He holds his hands to the sides, elbows bent, palms up, obviously looking for the right word.

"Freak out," I supply.

"I was going to say lose your shit, but that works. So where is he?"

"Jackson? I left him at the park."

"Couldn't stand another minute in his company?"

I press my lips together, remembering the way I felt with Jackson's arms wrapped around me, the way I rested my cheek against his chest and listened to his heart beating slow and steady. I don't know how long we stood like that. I think that given the choice, I might have stayed there forever, but at some point Jackson dropped his arms and stepped away from me, leaving me feeling awkward and weird.

While he was holding me, it felt right. But once it was over . . . well, that was another story. Suddenly, I'd wanted—*needed*—to be away from him, because standing so close, breathing in the scent of his skin and feeling his arms warm and strong around me, had pushed me into water far out of my depth.

Luka laughs, mistaking my silence. "He has that effect on people."

"Actually, I couldn't imagine running back here with him and having my dad pull in as we arrive," I say. "That'd be great, trying to explain who he is and where I know him from." Dad had been the perfect excuse, and Jackson hadn't offered any argument. So either he'd been as anxious to ditch me as I was to ditch him or he'd sensed my discomfort and decided to be kind. If I were a betting sort of girl, I'd lay money on the former.

As if my mention of Dad summons him, the Explorer pulls into the drive.

"Perfect," I say at the same time that Luka says, "Perfect."

We look at each other and laugh. Which actually *is* perfect because Dad climbs out of the SUV to see two classmates laughing together instead of a boy and a girl standing tense and awkward and uncertain.

Dad walks over and I make the introductions. It's easy. Painless. "Dad, this is Luka. He goes to school with me. He's on the track team." Dad grabs hold of that last bit of information and decides Luka's trying to convince me to join. He grins and pumps Luka's hand because he thinks an organized sport would be good for me. I don't bother to correct him.

He glances at me and, taking in my running gear, frowns. "It's Sunday," he says. He thinks I run too much and eat too little, which is actually funny because I'm not the one who skips lunch half the time.

"Yup." I offer no explanation. What am I supposed to say? That I changed my ironclad schedule because of aliens and a girl who died seven months before I met her? "Hey, it's pretty hot out," I say. "I'd better get the groceries in before the ice cream melts." I unbuckle the belt that holds my now-empty water bottle and hand it to Dad. "Take this in for me?"

Dad heads inside, and Luka follows me to the car.

"I tried to talk to you," he says. "Before my dad got transferred. After you lost your mom."

Lost my mom. Stupidest euphemism ever. I didn't misplace her; she died. I swallow a quick retort that I know I'll regret. "I know. I remember. I wasn't up for advice."

"I get that."

He does. Luka's mom died when we were still at Oakview. Grade four. He got really quiet and withdrawn for a couple of years after that, and I'm not proud of the fact that I was just like most of the other kids and went on and lived my life and didn't really make a huge effort to stay friends with him. By the time he wasn't quiet anymore, we were at an age where, for the most part, the boys hung with the boys and the girls hung with the girls, and when the two mixed, there was a lot of giggling and punching in the shoulder. If I'd known then what I know now about the grinding pain of losing someone you love, I would have tried harder.

My expression must give away my thoughts because Luka says, "Hey, we were kids. What do kids know about dealing with death?" He juts his chin toward the Explorer. "Ice cream's melting."

We reach for the groceries at the same time. My hand's already on the bag's handle, and his hand closes on mine. I pull back. He leans forward. We end up with arms tangled, his chest against my back. He bends. I straighten. His chin bumps my cheek. We both laugh. An easy laugh. One I don't have to force.

"Cozy." I turn my head at the sound of Carly's voice. She's in the passenger seat of Sarah's mom's silver van, which is currently stopped at the end of my driveway with Sarah behind the wheel. Carly's eyes skate over me to Luka and back.

"Wanna help?" I heft the bag at her as Luka straightens and steps away. I expect Carly and Sarah to hop out and grab a bag each.

Instead, Carly turns her head and says something to Sarah, then turns back to the open window. "Not today," she says. "Have fun." But she doesn't sound like she means it. There's an odd tightness to her voice that I recognize.

Carly's pissed.

Sarah waves. Carly doesn't. The van pulls away, and I watch it move down the street.

"You're the one who said the ice cream's gonna melt," Dad calls through the open front door. He's right. Whatever's up with Carly, I'll have to text her once the groceries are put away.

I can't help feeling angry with her. There's a lot more at stake here, a lot more going on, than whatever wasp stung her on the ass. A girl's dead. My world's upside down. Maybe everybody's world is upside down if Jackson's right and we're really fighting to save mankind. But Carly doesn't know any of that, and I can't tell her. So do I have a right to be angry when she's completely in the dark?

With a frustrated hiss, I grab a bag and hand it off to Luka, then grab another as he heads for the door.

"Just put the bags inside the door," I say, following at his heels. "Once we've got them all out of the car, we can get them to the kitchen." Mom had this thing about shoes. We always take them off at the door and switch to slippers; we never tramp through the house in shoes. It was important to her, so it's important to me. One small way I can keep her here with me rather than letting her go completely.

Luka sets down his bag and I'm just behind him when he freezes, then spins, his eyes wide and . . . blue.

That's all the warning I get.

Color and sound explode, too bright, too loud. Even the air on my skin feels like it's too much. My fingers go lax. The bag's handle slides down my palm, then along my fingers to the tips, impossibly slow. The world tips and tilts and I flail for balance.

Luka grabs my hand and holds tight.

I blink. My house, my open front door, my dad, they're all gone. My breath comes in short gasps and every muscle in my body feels like it's knotted up tight.

I'm standing in a grassy clearing bounded by trees.

The lobby.

We've been pulled.

CHAPTER**ELEVEN**

"IT'S TOO SOON," LUKA SNARLS, HIS FINGERS TIGHTENING ON mine as I bend forward to rest my free hand on my thigh. I take a couple of deep breaths to steady myself. I feel a bit woozy, but no headache. I guess I'm getting better at this. Practice makes perfect and all that. Soon I'll be a pro. The thought isn't exactly comforting.

As I straighten up, I see Jackson striding toward us, still dressed in his running gear and wraparound shades. Of course, I can't see his eyes, but I sense him looking at me. At my hand. Clasped in Luka's. His mouth tightens.

I take my time letting go of Luka's hand, pretending Jackson's expression has nothing to do with my actions. I notice that my con is back; the feel of it on my wrist makes terror gnaw at me with sharp little rat teeth. I want to tear it off and fling it into the trees. I force myself to do the breathing thing and get my heart rate under control. The screen's green. I intend to do everything possible to keep it that way.

I look around for Tyrone. He's there, by the boulders, his jaw clenched tight. I want to go to him, to comfort him, to say—

What? Anything I offer will be empty and shallow, and won't bring Richelle back.

"Gear up," Jackson says.

"There are only four of us," Luka points out.

He's wrong. There are hundreds of us. I can see them in clearings that mirror our own, some of them small teams like ours, some of them teams of more than a dozen. If I try and look at them, they disappear and all I see are the trees bordering our own clearing. If I don't look at them, I see flashes of movement and the never-ending reflections of team after team, just like Gram's powder-room mirrors.

"Four's all there are going to be this time," Jackson says.

How does he know these things? He knows when we'll get pulled. He knows things about the mission—I remember that from the last time we were in the lobby.

"Miki."

I turn just in time to catch the harness Jackson tosses in my direction. I slide it on the way he taught me and then jog over to the open metal box on the ground where there are four weapon cylinders nestled in dense black foam.

I glance up and ask, "Does it matter which one I take?"

"Hold your hand over the box, fingers straight, palm down," Jackson says. "The weapon you used last time will come to you."

I do as he said, and a cylinder shoots up and slams against my palm, making me gasp. I slide it into my holster and look at Jackson. He has the knife strapped to his thigh again.

"What about one of those?" I ask.

"A weapon's no good unless it's more of a threat to your opponent than it is to you."

"But everyone knows you run faster with a knife," Luka says.

Jackson's brows rise above the frame of his shades. I whirl to face Luka, uncertain what he means.

"It's an in-joke," he says, spreading his hands palms up in a gesture of conciliation. "Gaming term. First-person shooters carry a ton of weapons. They pull out a big one, like . . . a bazooka? They run slower. They pull out something small . . . say . . . a knife? They run faster."

I nod. "Even though they should be running at the same speed, because either way, they're carrying the same amount of weapons, right?"

"Right. First game that concept appeared in was Counter-Strike," Jackson says.

Luka glances at him. There's some sort of guy exchange between them that involves nods and knowing smirks, as if that bit of trivia is super important. Whatever.

Jackson turns to me. "You still don't get a knife, no matter how fast it'll make you run. If your enemy grabs it, he can use it to gut you."

"Thanks for the graphics." He's right. Even though I know quite a bit about kendo swords, I know nothing about knives. But I can learn. I mentally move "knife research" to the top of my to-do list for when I get back. If I get back. I close my fist tight and dig my nails into my palm. *When* I get back. "So how come *you* know how to use a knife?"

Jackson tips his head, and for a second I think he isn't going to answer—answering questions isn't exactly his forte. Then he says, "Combat application technique training."

"Seriously?" Luka asks, looking impressed. "Like, you took a class? They actually have a class?"

"Yeah. Eleven months of training in Fort Worth."

"I've known you for a year, and you're only telling me this now?" Luka asks.

But that's just it. Jackson wasn't telling Luka, he was telling *me*. A small distinction, but one that matters, though I don't exactly know why. I'll figure it out. I just need to come at it from a different direction.

In typical Jackson fashion he closes the topic right when it's getting interesting. "Discussion time's over. Let's move."

I cast a look over my shoulder at Tyrone. He hasn't said a word. He's just standing there, jaw clenched, hands shoved in the pockets of his jeans.

Luka collects his weapon, then turns back to Jackson.

"Four isn't enough. We've never gone with less than five."

"Four's what we have."

Never gone with less than five. I freeze. *I* was the fifth last time. I was the new addition because someone didn't make it back, didn't respawn. Who? A boy? A girl? What did he look like? What were his dreams? And how could Jackson and Luka and Tyrone bear to lose Richelle so soon after losing someone else?

Snippets of a forgotten conversation come at me— Richelle's and Tyrone's voices from the first time I respawned in the lobby.

"*. . . selfish jerk . . . Put all of us at risk so many times. Hanging back and stealing the hit points . . . all he cared about was himself and getting out . . .*"

"*Doesn't mean he deserved to . . .*"

"*He put* you *at risk. As far as I'm concerned, that means he deserved . . .*"

Their words meant nothing to me at the time, but now I get it. They were talking about the boy who didn't come back, the boy I replaced.

Horrified, I whisper, "You're expecting a replacement for Richelle to show up."

Luka cuts me a glance and nods, lips set in a tight line, all traces of his grin gone.

"But no one's coming." I look at Jackson, who has his arms crossed over his chest and his head turned away from me.

"How do you know no one's coming?" Tyrone asks,

speaking for the first time.

"Isn't that the question," Luka mutters. "But you don't answer questions, do you, Jack? You just bark orders. And step in and take over. You're good at that, too, aren't you?"

Jackson turns his head, saying nothing. I don't need to see his eyes to know he's glaring at Luka.

For about three seconds, I'm completely confused. What happened to the easy camaraderie of a minute ago? Luka's gaze flicks to me, then away. Suspicion blooms. Their little macho display isn't just about the number of people in the clearing. It's about me and Jackson running together. It's about Jackson getting to me before Luka did. At least, I think it is. I'm about to tell them to knock it off when I'm hit by doubts, unsure why I'd imagine this new tension has anything to do with me. It's just a feeling, one without substance.

This is one of those moments that I wish Carly were here because she'd be able to call it for what it is.

The second I think that, I feel sick. I don't want Carly anywhere near here. I don't want her involved in this nightmare. I want her safe and happy and normal. I want everyone I care about to be safe and happy and normal.

But as I look at Luka and Jackson and Tyrone, I realize that I'm not going to get what I want because somewhere in the past few crazy days, they've been added to the list of people I care about.

"Four weapon cylinders in the box," I say. "That's how he knew." I turn away and head over to Tyrone, who's standing by the same boulder that he was sitting on the first time I came to the lobby. But this time, Richelle isn't there beside him. He looks pale, sick, exhausted. I remember the way he knelt beside Richelle's body. I remember his sobs.

"This is too soon." He repeats what Luka said earlier, but there's no emotion behind the words. His tone's flat, his expression even flatter.

"Too soon?" I repeat, thinking he's talking about it being too soon after Richelle's death. I try to think of something comforting to offer and come up blank. I know how worthless even the most well-meaning words can be in the face of such loss. Nothing can make it better.

"Too soon after the last time we were pulled." His voice is hoarse, like he's spent days shouting. Or crying. I'm guessing he's been doing some of both. "We need recovery time." He shoots a look at Jackson and raises his voice. "They know that. They trying to kill us all?"

The question is all the more terrifying because Tyrone doesn't actually sound like he cares.

"Who?" I ask. "Who are *they*?"

Jackson picks up a holster and strides toward Tyrone. "What they know or don't know has no relevance," he says. "What matters is that we've been pulled. We have a job to do. And we'll do it." *Or we'll die,* he doesn't say. He doesn't have to. We all know it.

"Who are *they*?" I ask again.

"Don't bother asking," Tyrone grumbles. "He'll just say it's decision by committee."

Jackson tosses the holster at Tyrone's feet. Tyrone stares straight ahead, his expression blank. I know that look. I've seen it in the mirror. I stared at it every morning for months after Mom died. Some mornings, I still do.

Tyrone's broken, like I was—am—broken, the gray fog weighing so heavily on his soul, he's barely even aware it's there.

I'm better now than I was two years ago. At least now I can use the tricks Dr. Andrews taught me. I recognize the bricks sitting on my chest and the endless need to sigh for what they are. I feel them pressing down on me right now.

Tyrone might start to heal, in time. But time is one thing we don't have. This is only my second mission, but I already know that it's going to go forward whether we're ready for it or not.

"Tyrone," I say, moving to stand directly in front of him. I rest my palms on his cheeks and stare straight into his eyes. "I'm sorry. I'm hurting and I barely knew her. I can't imagine what you're feeling." But I can. I know what it is to mourn.

He swallows. Rage and anguish flicker in his expression. "I can't talk about her back at home."

"Because of the rules."

He nods. "I can't talk about her to anyone. They'll want to know who she was, how I knew her. And I can't tell. That makes it worse. I want to remember her laugh. Her eyes. Her smile." He pauses. "She never had a boyfriend. Now she'll never get the chance." He looks away and whispers,

"I was waiting for her to grow up. Now, she never will. I shouldn't have waited."

"How old are you?"

"Nineteen."

"How old was . . ."

"Seventeen."

No, he shouldn't have waited. Two years isn't such a big gap.

Sorrow claws at my chest, making it hard to breathe. Richelle won't get the chance for a lot of things. Prom. Graduation. College.

"It hurts to think about it," I say.

"It hurts not to."

I know exactly what he means.

"Nothing's the same," he says. Then he laughs, the sound twisted and ugly. "I used to play all the time. Every night. I'd play and I'd think about the game, *this* game, and I'd jot notes about scores and points and badges. I had plans. Big plans. Sell my game for millions, you know?" He snarls and spins away, breathing heavily, his back toward me. "Every time we got pulled, I'd see her numbers climb. She was almost out!" He slams his fist against his palm with such force that I jump and gasp. Then he repeats, very softly, "She was almost out. Almost free."

Almost out. Almost free.

. . . all he cared about was himself and getting out . . .

I feel like someone just turned on a spotlight, making the whole world shine bright. I cut a glance at Luka.

"There's a way out? Other than dying?"

Before he can answer, Tyrone rounds on him. "How can you still play?" he asks, his voice a low rasp. "How can you laugh and joke and talk about running faster with a knife, like this isn't life or death? Like the score isn't the most important thing for us now? Our ticket out?"

Luka looks abashed, and for some reason I feel angry on his behalf.

"He didn't choose to be here any more than you did," Jackson says, his voice low and smooth.

I rest my hand on Tyrone's arm. "He's just doing the best he can. He's stuck in this, same as you. If he's laughing, it's because that's better than crying, isn't it?" Better than feeling nothing at all. If you force yourself to laugh, to pretend you feel okay, eventually you *will* feel okay. At least, that's the theory.

Tyrone stares at me, then scrubs his palm over his face. "I don't know. I don't know."

"Tyrone, you need to gear up," Jackson says. Maybe I'm imagining things, but I swear I hear a hint of sadness in his voice. Or maybe I just want to hear it. For a second, no one moves. Then Jackson grabs the harness off the ground and nudges Tyrone, who does absolutely nothing to aid the process.

"That's gonna cost me," Tyrone mutters.

"Cost you?" I ask.

"Points deducted for the cost of weapons," Tyrone says. "Primary weapon costs fifty. Harness is twenty-five.

He"—he juts his chin toward Jackson—"has a secondary, the knife. That's another fifty off his score."

Score. Points.

Every time we got pulled, I'd see her numbers climb.

All the pieces click into place. We earn points, as if this really is a game. When he talked about that in Vegas, he wasn't just talking about the imaginary game in his head. Earn enough of them and—

"They're pretty generous in the charges they levy. Not so generous with the points they pay out for hits," Tyrone snarls.

"Save it," Jackson says, low and fierce. "Save that anger for the Drau, Tyrone."

Tyrone stares at him, jaw set, eyes flashing, and then he snatches the harness and gears up.

When Jackson points to the weapons box, Tyrone holds his hand out to draw his cylinder. Jackson's shoulders tense, then he turns his face a little and I can't tell if he's looking at Tyrone or me.

"You live through this, Tyrone," he says, so low I barely hear him. "Don't you die."

I swallow, not sure exactly what's going on here, because even though he says Tyrone's name, I feel like he's speaking to me, too.

"Strong language for someone who claims it's every man for himself," I say.

Seconds tick past. "I just don't want to have to train someone new."

"Asshole," Tyrone mutters without heat, sounding almost like himself. Jackson smiles a little.

"Scores," Luka says from behind me.

Tyrone turns. I follow his gaze to the center of the clearing. The air dances like heat shimmers off a hot sidewalk. Something glossy black and rectangular begins to take shape. It looks like a massive, flat-screen TV, but when I walk over and reach out to touch it, my fingers pass through. As I draw them back, that corner of the image wavers and warps, then settles back into the shape of the screen's corner.

Luka walks over to stand beside me, followed by Tyrone. A picture of Jackson bounded by a black border appears on the screen. He's dressed in the clothes he was wearing the first time I met him, complete with the old-school aviator shades. In the picture, there's blood on his clothes and a scratch on his cheek. The picture is odd and more than a little eerie because it isn't a photo. It looks like a truly awesome 3-D rendering of a person. 3-D Jackson turns end over end, then zooms to the top left.

A new picture appears: Luka. He's leaning against the wall, holding his arm, and I can see the white shards of his broken bones. I gasp. These pictures are from the end of the last battle. I take a step back, feeling uneasy as 3-D Luka turns end over end, and then lines up in the top left. Jackson's image moves down a notch.

Tyrone's next. The picture rotates up and over. He ends up above Jackson but below Luka.

I want to look away. The next picture will be Richelle's. Or mine. Either way, I don't want to see. But something pins me in place and I can't tear my eyes from the screen.

The black frame forms. The picture shimmers into place. My heart clutches. It's Richelle. Her last battle. Her last moment. Her skin is gray, her hair tangled, matted with blood. Her eyes are open, but she isn't there. Beside me, Tyrone exhales in a rush, the sound like a deflating balloon. My gaze still locked on the screen, I reach for him blindly and loop my arm around his waist. He shudders beneath my touch but doesn't pull away. I shudder right along with him, remembering the way Richelle touched me in the dark warehouse before the aliens came at us, offering silent support. Tears prick the backs of my lids.

We could have been friends. We *would* have been friends. I didn't help her, didn't do anything to help her stay safe. I barely managed to keep myself safe. And Jackson? He was busy keeping me from getting my brain sucked out through my eyes—at least, that's what it felt like. Would he have been able to save Richelle if I hadn't been there? Would he have even tried?

I cut him a sidelong look. He's standing rigid and still, not even breathing. *Every man for himself.* He keeps insisting on that. And at the park, he told me not to feel guilty for being alive when others aren't. But if he stands by his own philosophy, why does he look like the world is sitting heavy on his shoulders, his muscles tense, his lips pressed to a thin line?

Richelle's picture dances to the left, nudging Luka's down. She's at the top.

Then comes my picture. I feel like I'm looking at someone I've never met. The girl looks pale and pained and wild. There's fear in her eyes, but the tilt of her chin and the set of her mouth say she's not quite out of the game, yet. She is me, but not me. Topsy-turvy I go, and then I'm in rank above Jackson and below the others.

Two columns of numbers pop up beside our images. The numbers beside Richelle's name are red while everyone else's are white. Red, like her con. Red, like her blood.

"What are they?" I ask.

"Scores," Luka says. "The first column is our score from the last mission. The second column is cumulative for all the missions. The rank is according to the cumulative total."

I stare at the numbers. Richelle had the lowest score for the last mission, but the highest cumulative total. That's why her name is first. "Richelle was kick-ass," I whisper.

"Yeah," Tyrone says, his voice catching. "She was. And she almost made it out."

My pulse kicks up a notch because I think I understand, but I barely dare hope. "Her cumulative score was nine twenty-five. How much did she need to make it out?"

"If she'd hit a thousand, she'd have been done."

"Done . . . you mean finished? Finished with the . . . game?"

Jackson makes a sound of denial, but not because I'm

way off base. It's because, for some reason, this is something he wasn't ready for me to know. I whirl toward him. "If she hit a thousand, she could have . . . what? Left? Retired? Escaped?"

"All of the above," Luka says.

"It's a rumor. You don't know for certain," Jackson says.

"So just to be clear, the rumor is that a thousand points buys your freedom?" I wait for Jackson's nod. "And we get points for killing"—I glance at Luka—"Sorry. I mean *terminating* aliens?" Again, Jackson nods.

"How many?" I ask, and when no one answers, I ask louder, "How many points?"

"Five for a sentinel. Ten for a specialist," Luka says. "A leader's fifteen. A commander is twenty."

So few points. It would take a very long time to get to a thousand. Maybe that's the plan. Maybe whoever is running this bloody game wants to dangle the dream of freedom without ever delivering.

I turn to Tyrone. "You told me this. In Vegas." I struggle to recall what he said. "You talked about multi-hit points and bonus points for . . . stealth hits. And . . . penalty points." I pause. "When I first woke up here, I heard you say something about the boy who was here before me. . . ."

Tyrone's expression darkens. "He was all about getting out. He didn't care about the rest of us."

"He was a griefer," Luka says.

"Another gaming term?"

He nods. "We use it for someone who causes grief. He

stole hits. He'd let me or Tyrone or Richelle wear down the target, then dive in and steal the hit. Steal the points. He couldn't care less if we got killed. He just wanted the points for himself. He wanted out."

"Doesn't everyone want out?"

"Yeah, but we won't sacrifice our teammates to get there."

I cut a glance at Jackson. *Every man for himself.* The more I find out, the more I think he's full of crap when he says that. From what I saw on the last mission, he's no griefer. None of us are.

I turn back to the scores. Richelle's from the last mission is only twenty-five. But I remember the way she fought, and I'm certain it should have been higher than that.

"Her score is so low last time because she died. She lost points." I stare at Tyrone. "You said we have to pay for weapons. How else do we lose points?"

"Twenty-five per injury."

I stare at Richelle's score, wondering how many injuries—and how much pain—she suffered on that last mission to bring it so low. I feel sick.

"If your con goes beyond yellow-orange, you lose even more," Jackson says.

"So I lost points last mission?"

"Yes."

I look back at his weirdly low score. It's doubly confusing because even though his score is the lowest, he's the only one of us who has some sort of rank insignia or prestige badge next to his name. It's bronze colored, in the shape of a star, and at the center is another, smaller star. "And you?" I ask. "Did you lose points?" He must have because I remember him killing Drau, but his score doesn't really reflect that.

"I seem to lose points every mission." There's a thread of dark humor behind the words.

"He leaves the hits for us," Luka says.

I don't know what he means. And then I do. I remember how Jackson kicked the weapon out of the Drau's hand rather than shooting it. He only used his weapon when he had to, when it was absolutely clear that I wasn't going to figure things out without a little help. And I remember the way he leaped in front of me and used his body to shield me from the Drau's weapon, twisting to take the shot in his back.

It's almost like he doesn't want to gain points. Or like he wants the rest of us to gain points instead of him.

I flick a glance at his oddly low score. "Don't you want to be free?"

"The thousand points is a rumor," Jackson repeats.

"You don't believe it?"

"I don't know anyone who made it to a thousand."

I inhale, ready to fire my next question. Instead, I pause. Jackson's careful with his words. He doesn't waste them. *You* don't know for certain, he said to Luka, not *we* don't know. That implies that Luka doesn't know, but does Jackson? And saying that he doesn't know anyone who made it to a thousand points isn't the same as confirming or denying the truth of the rumor.

I glance at the scores and frown. "Why didn't I see these last time?"

"They came and went before you woke up," Luka says. "You didn't need to see them. You didn't have a score yet."

"Who's been in the game the longest?" My gaze slides from Jackson to Luka to Tyrone.

"Jackson was already here when I got recruited," Tyrone says.

I nod and look at Luka, who says, "They were both here by the time I came on board."

So Jackson's been here the longest, but his cumulative score is the lowest. Then mine. Then Tyrone's. But he's been here longer than Luka. . . .

"Why is your score so low?" I ask, rounding on Tyrone.

"It's higher than yours," he points out.

"I just got here. I haven't had time to build a score. You have."

Tyrone swallows, and then says, "I didn't try as hard as I could have. In the beginning, I thought it was fun. Exciting. I thought I was researching *my* game. Then . . . once Richelle showed up . . . I didn't try as hard as I might have. It was a chance to . . . to see her. To be with her."

We're all quiet for a moment. I turn to Jackson. "You've been here the longest. Why is your score so low?"

He gives that lazy shrug I'm coming to recognize. "Guess I'm not very good," he says, lying through his teeth.

He's good. Better than good. He's making a choice to keep his score low, and I want to know why. Suddenly, it feels like the most important question of all.

"Do you get points when you use your knife?"

"We jump in thirty," he says.

"That's not an answer."

"It's the only one you're getting."

I narrow my eyes at him. "I'll figure it out."

"Will you, now?" He offers a close-lipped smile. "Game on, Miki Jones."

CHAPTER **TWELVE**

WE'RE PULLED INTO COOL, DAMP DARKNESS SO COMPLETE that I can't make out even the hint of a shadow. Fear flicks its forked tongue. Palms damp, breath coming too fast, I stand perfectly still, waiting for my eyes to adjust, but as the seconds tick past, I realize they aren't going to. We are entombed in utter darkness, and the only thing that tells me I'm not alone is the rasp of someone else's breathing.

There's a snapping sound, like a twig being broken in two, and then a greenish light illuminates a ring about five feet in diameter. I'm inside the ring, along with Jackson, who's holding a phosphorescent wand that looks like a pregnant version of the glow sticks you get at concerts. I can just make out the shapes of Luka and Tyrone a few feet away, at the far edges of the ring. It's Luka who's breathing

139

rough and hard, and after a second I realize that I'm there right along with him. I need to slow it down before anxiety turns to full-on panic. Deliberately, I do my thing: breathe in, hold, breathe out.

On the next inhale, I notice that wherever we are, it smells like sulfur and damp rock and something slightly unpleasant and halfway familiar: Kelley's hamster cage.

A quick glance around reveals little. My field of view is restricted by the light of Jackson's glow stick. I can make out walls and a floor of stone. I'm guessing the ceiling is more of the same, but I can't see it. The light fades away into claustrophobic darkness before it hits the top of the cave. Cavern. Tunnel. Whatever. The hamster cage smell takes on new meaning. Is that bat guano?

In a distant recess of my brain I hear a whisper, just as I did in the alley in Las Vegas: *enemy.* Something's out there, hiding beyond the ring of light. Instinct tells me far beyond it. The threat isn't imminent, the feeling of horror just a whimper rather than a roar.

I make a hand motion at my lips, asking if it's safe to speak. Jackson leans close and I whisper against his ear, "Where are we?"

He turns his head and whispers back, "In a cave." He's smiling. I can hear it. Pushing my buttons has become one of his favorite pastimes.

I take a deep breath and clench my fists by my sides, but at the same time, the knot of tension inside me eases a little. He wouldn't be teasing if we were about to be attacked. "And where is this cave?" I whisper, syrup sweet.

"Puerto Rico. It's one of the largest cave systems in the world. We're in an isolated part of the system that hasn't been mapped."

Getting that answer was easier than expected. I gesture at the glow stick. "Won't the light give us away?"

"Our arrival gave us away." He's not whispering anymore. "We might as well be able to see."

Well, that's comforting.

"Our arrival gave us away, like it did in Vegas?" I ask, remembering what Tyrone told me that first night.

"Yeah," Tyrone says. "But there aren't a lot of people here to mask us, so we've been dropped farther. Less chance the Drau'll be able to pinpoint us. And once we're here, the con scrambles our signal. Makes it tough for them to get a lock. But we're in for a bit of a hike."

I look over at Jackson. "Why not just drop us right on top of them? The advantage of surprise, you know?"

"They don't publicize their exact location," he says. "We know the general vicinity. Our cons don't get a lock on them until we're dropped in."

"So we're dropped in blind? Sort of knowing where we're going, but not really?"

He shrugs. "Once we're here, the con figures out the rest of it."

Yet more comforting information.

"In Vegas, if the Drau knew we were there even before we went inside, why didn't they attack?" I ask. "Why didn't they come out into the alley to get us?"

"They don't want to risk being seen. Not yet. They aren't ready for humanity to know they're here. They'd rather face us in confined spaces and"—he sweeps one hand before him, indicating our surroundings—"underground caverns where there are no human eyes to see them and alert the world."

I frown. "Why?"

"Humanity will be easier to kill if they don't know what's coming."

I shudder, horrified by that. "Why don't we tell someone then?"

"Like who?"

"The police. The government. I don't know." I glance at Luka and Tyrone for help.

"Who'd believe us without proof?" Luka asks. "And, trust me, the game won't let us bring out proof."

"How do you know?"

"Been there, tried that. Brought my weapon back once. Shoved it in my pocket to make sure it came with me. Only, it disappeared at some point during the respawn. Took pics with my phone. When I got back, there were no pics."

"You mean they didn't turn out?"

"I mean there was nothing there. Like I'd never taken any. And before you ask, I tried more than once. So trust me, trying to tell anyone isn't an option. If I came to you a week ago and told you I was part of a game that really was fighting off an alien invasion, would you have believed me?"

He has a point.

Jackson tosses a glow stick to Tyrone. Then he turns back to me, offers an easy shrug, and says, "We're it, Miki. We're the defenders. Don't you get that?"

I'm starting to, and I can't say I like it.

"We and the other teams," I say, and glance at Luka to see if he's surprised to hear that. He isn't. So he does know there are others even if he can't see them.

Jackson tosses another glow stick to Luka. They snap the sticks, then attach them to their harnesses so their hands are free. I wait, but Jackson doesn't offer a light to me. "Forget someone?" I hiss.

"You ever been caving?"

I shake my head.

"It's disorienting. There's no horizon line, and we won't always be walking on the horizontal. The more lights there are, the more shadows are cast, and that can get confusing. Besides, I don't want you wandering off and getting lost. If you're relying on my light, you aren't going anywhere."

"That is pure condescending bullshit. Having my own light source would be less confusing, not more." I glance at Luka. He frowns and shakes his head. I'm guessing he doesn't like this any more than I do, but he's not the one in charge. I turn back to Jackson. "What happened to every man for himself?"

"I'm bending the rules," he says.

I roll my eyes. "What if I get separated from you?"

"Don't."

He moves forward and I stay close at his back, not wanting to fall outside the circle of light. I'm not afraid of the dark and I'm not claustrophobic, but this experience just might make me both. After a few minutes, Jackson reaches back and grabs hold of my hand. His fingers are warm; mine are like ice. I want to hold on tight and never let go, which is precisely why I pull my hand away.

"Why the glow sticks?" I ask. "Why not those helmet-mounted lights you see on TV?"

"We don't have helmets."

Good point. "But why the glow sticks?" It really doesn't matter, but I need to know. I need explanations. Control. Information means I rely less on others and more on myself. Because in the end, that's all anyone has.

"These don't need backup batteries. They last as long as we need them to last. If we relied on human technology, we'd eventually run out of juice and end up in the dark." He snaps his glow stick and we're plunged into pitch black. I gasp and freeze, then Luka comes up behind me and his light catches me in the edge of its circle.

Jackson snaps his light back on. To my surprise, he takes it off his holster and attaches it to mine. "Better?"

"Yes." It *is* better. "Why didn't you just give me a light in the first place?" I'm both angry that he didn't and grateful that he's given me one now.

He says softly so only I can hear, "It seemed like a good excuse to keep you close."

My breath locks in my throat. He can't mean that the

way it sounds. I tell myself he wants me close because I'm still new and he doesn't want me to mess up. And I try not to look too closely at the reason I don't want that to be true. Ambivalence—he brings that out in me.

"Why'd you change your mind?"

"It was obviously stressing you out. That isn't the outcome I was going for."

I stare at him, completely confused now. I don't know what to think about him, how to feel. "Are you admitting you made a mistake?"

"Never." He laughs and just like it did in the park, the sound reaches inside me and flutters around. "Can't decide if you love me or hate me?" he asks.

"You make it sound like it has to be one of the two. Love. Hate. Those are strong emotions. What makes you think you're worth either one?" My tone is flippant and I purposely don't look at him, but I can feel him watching me.

Behind me, Luka snorts, telling me he's heard every word.

Jackson leans close so only I can hear. "If you're smart, Miki Jones, you'll choose hate."

I roll my eyes. "Why? What's so terrible about you? I mean, other than the fact that you're an annoying asshole who's insanely fond of mixed messages?"

Luka steps between us and asks, "We stopping here for a reason?"

"Call it a whim." Jackson cracks another glow stick and attaches it to his harness.

I poke at the glow stick on my harness. "So . . . these aren't human technology?"

"No."

"Why not just bring one of these out of the game? Show it to someone? That'd be proof."

"Tried it. Twice," Tyrone says from behind me. "They disappeared, just like Luka's pics and his weapon."

"And if you did succeed?" Jackson asks, his tone soft. "Have you forgotten the rules? The fact that we can't tell anyone about the game? What makes you think you'd survive long enough to divulge a thing?"

The way he says that makes me shiver.

As he moves off, I see what he meant earlier. The shadows *are* weird and disorienting, dancing and weaving, then ending abruptly as they're swallowed by the dark.

In Vegas, Jackson said that the Drau were sluggish in the dark. I wonder why they chose these eternal-night caverns to set up camp. I wonder how our arrival gave us away. I wonder where we are and exactly what our mission is. I hope I live long enough to find out.

The longer we walk, the more I think. The more I think, the more out of control I feel. There's no Richelle this time to chat with me and keep my mind from going along a dangerous path, one that has any number of not-so-pleasant outcomes.

The air is cool, but we're moving fast and I'm too amped to feel really cold. Still, I worry about what we'll do if the temperature drops. "I don't think we're dressed for this." The words run together in a rush. "And the caving environment . . ." I'm babbling now. "I saw this show about how spelunkers have to be careful because the environments are fragile. Even a touch can destroy—"

Jackson stops and turns to face me, the light on my harness reflecting off his ever present über-dark lenses. Which he's wearing even in a cave. I start humming: *I wear my sunglasses at night.* . . . Then I start laughing, a little too loud. The sound bounces back at me.

He steps closer, close enough that I'm staring straight ahead at his chest, remembering how it felt to rest my cheek against it in the park. "Miki, you can't control this," he says.

"I—"

"We're here. It is what it is. We don't get a choice about that."

"You make it sound like we get a choice about anything."

His fingertips skim the back of my hand, just like they did that night in Vegas. "We could sit down here and refuse to move. That's a choice. But I don't recommend it."

"Then what *do* you recommend?"

He's so close that I feel his breath against my cheek. "That you hang on and enjoy the ride."

Jackson leads us through a maze of tunnels. Everything is disorienting: the darkness, the restricted field of vision, the ever-changing shadows that have nothing to do with sun or moon. I can barely tell which way is up. There's no real color here, only shades of gray cast in a greenish glow by the lights we carry. The textures blur and fade. Passages branch and change directions. I have a hard time knowing for certain if we're moving on the horizontal, and I have an even harder time knowing how long we've been at this. Sometimes we can walk. Sometimes the tunnels narrow and dip so much we have to crawl, the rocks scraping my sides and back. Each time the passage branches, Jackson doesn't hesitate. He goes right. He goes left. And we follow.

Every so often, he stops and turns and studies what's behind us. "What are you doing?" I ask.

"The path is going to look different on the way out than it does on the way in. I'm doing a look-back. Memorizing the landmarks."

"But we won't have to find our way back. We'll be pulled when we're done."

He stoops and takes some loose stones in his hand, then arranges them in a neat pyramid. This is the third or fourth time he's done that.

"Just in case. Better safe than sorry," Luka says, stepping up, positioning himself between Jackson and me. He studies my face. "You okay?"

"Yeah." I nod, then turn and take a good, long look at the tunnel behind us, memorizing the outcrop high on the wall that looks like a bird's beak.

Jackson saunters over. He makes a big show of looking at me, then Luka, and back again. His lips twitch as he shoulders his way between us.

Luka narrows his eyes at Jackson. Jackson holds his ground till Luka steps back. I'm starting to feel like a raw steak between two pit bulls. The thing is, it's pit bull nature to fight, even when the steak isn't there.

Then Luka juts his chin toward a group of large boulders ahead of us in the tunnel positioned perfectly at a fork in the route. "Good place to camp," he says.

"Camp?" I ask.

"Hunker down and pick off the enemy as they run past," Tyrone says from behind me. I glance at him over my shoulder. "In a game, it's a good way to get a lot of points very fast."

"Right." I nod. "I've done that."

Luka's brows go up.

"Mostly Carly and I camp in paintball."

"Makes sense." Luka grins. "*Carly* and *running* are words that do not belong in the same sentence, even when you're talking about paintball."

"She doesn't believe in achieving sweat unless the activity involves dancing." And/or a guy. "So we usually just end up lying in wait."

"But if the enemy figures out where you are," Tyrone says, "you're screwed."

"Pretty much. Which is why we never win."

"I'm a little surprised that Carly does the paintball thing," Luka says. "They hurt when they hit."

"And leave bruises. But Carly has a bunch of brothers.

If she didn't paintball, she'd have to miss their birthday parties."

"My sister wouldn't much care about that. She wouldn't go paintballing if I paid her," Luka says.

"Well, your sister only has one brother, so maybe she doesn't feel as much pressure to paintball. Carly, on the other hand . . ."

"How many brothers?"

"Two older. Two younger."

Luka looks away for a second, then back. "Maybe we should all go sometime."

"Um . . . yeah . . . I guess." I glance at Jackson. He's been unnaturally quiet. I would have thought he'd break up social time before it got started. He's watching us with his head tipped slightly to one side, his expression indecipherable. If I were forced to put a name to it, I'd say he looked wistful. Sad. But I can't think why that should be the case.

"So what do you think, Jack?" Luka asks. "Good place to camp?"

"Would be, *Luka*, if the Drau were going to come looking for us," Jackson says. "But they aren't."

"Why not?" I ask. "You said they know we're here. Why haven't they sent any security patrols to stop us? It isn't like Vegas, where they don't want to risk people seeing them. There's no one else down here. Only us."

Neither boy looks at me. They're too busy glaring at each other. At least, Luka's glaring, and I assume Jackson's glaring even though I can't see his eyes. I step back, leaving them a clearer sight line. Who am I to get in the way of macho posturing?

"For one thing, why expend the energy to hunt us down when they know we're coming straight to them?" Jackson asks.

Comforting thought.

"They're waiting for us to come to them so they can pick us off like a trash mob," Tyrone says, sounding disgusted.

I glance at him. "Trash mob?"

"MMO term—"

"Massively multiplayer online," Luka interjects. "Virtual game world. Gajillions of players."

"Thanks. Actually knew that one already," I say. "But still waiting for the explanation of *trash mob*."

"Enemies that are just annoying because they travel in bunches and are too easy to kill." Tyrone jumps in. "Not much of a challenge."

"Like shooting fish in a barrel," I say with a grimace.

"Just like."

"And nothing like us." Jackson's tone is soft but laced with steel. "The Drau aren't going to pick any of us off. We're not so easy to kill."

Maybe not easy, but still killable. The thought is sobering. I turn toward Tyrone. He's leaning back against the wall watching us, one knee bent, the sole of his boot pressed to the stone. His gaze slides to Luka, then Jackson, his expression deadpan. "You done with the chatty-chat?" He lifts his brows. "We moving, or what?"

"If by *moving* you mean walking, I'm up for it," I say. "Crawling through more of those tunnels? Not so much." I put my hands on my lower back and arch, easing the strain. "It feels like we've been down here for days."

Tyrone pushes off the wall. "How long *have* we been down here?" he asks Jackson.

"Six, maybe seven hours."

"What?" I gasp, stunned that we've been moving that long and I didn't notice the passage of time.

"When we're on a mission, we can run longer and harder. We're faster. We don't have the same physical requirements that we usually do," Luka says.

I remember him telling me that in Vegas. He said it had something to do with our cons. "Physical requirements like eating or drinking."

"Or taking a leak," Tyrone chimes in, with a ghost of a smile.

"Thanks for that." I roll my eyes at him, trying not to make a big deal of how pleased I am that he's offered up a joke, however lame. I know how hard it is to do that when your heart is broken in a million pieces and every word uttered takes a billion pounds of effort.

Then I remember something else Luka said, the first time I was in the lobby. Something about how we're not really alive during the game. My good mood sours because some of us might not be alive at the end, either.

I swallow and look away, not wanting any of them to read my expression.

"Rest time's over. We split up here," Jackson says.

"Split up?" The thought sends a bolt of panic through my heart. "That sounds like a crappy plan. We should stay together."

"No." He doesn't sound negotiable. "Luka, you're with Tyrone. Miki, you're with me."

"I don't think we should split up."

"Not open for discussion."

"This is a dictatorship, not a democracy?" I ask.

The muscles in Jackson's jaw tense. He doesn't usually bother to explain himself, so I'm surprised when he says, "There are two main entry points to our target. One at the north, one at the south. We need to clear both. It'll take half the time to send a separate team to each rather than hitting one together, then moving on to the next. So what do you suggest?"

The way he asks that . . . it's as if he actually wants my opinion. As if he wants me to make the call. I feel like my answer's important, but I can't imagine why. I'm not the one in charge here.

"We split up," I say after a minute of figuring all the options. "Tactically, it's the only good choice. But I still don't like it."

"Fair enough." He turns to Tyrone. "You and Luka take north."

Luka crosses his arms over his chest. "Miki stays with me. I'll watch her back. I'll keep her safe."

Whoa, where did that come from? Before I can come

up with an appropriate comment, Jackson answers, his tone harsh. "And that's why she's staying with me. Watching her back? Keeping her safe? That's a good way to get yourself killed, Luka. Miki can take care of herself."

He sounds so certain of that.

"He's right," Tyrone says, sounding bleak. "You know it, Luka. If you're trying to keep an eye on her, you'll split your focus. It might get you killed. And you might end up getting her killed, too." There's so much pain in his tone that I wonder if that's what happened to Richelle. If she was trying to keep an eye on Tyrone and that's part of how she ended up dead. I remember hearing her scream his name right before she screamed in pain.

Luka's eyes narrow. But he doesn't answer Tyrone directly; he's saving all his venom for Jackson. "And you're not gonna watch anyone's back but your own, right, Jack?" He hits the *k* hard. "You don't care what happens to Miki."

But he does. For some reason, Jackson cares. I know that, and I don't trust it. From what I know of him, Jackson isn't the type to offer things up at face value. There are layers and layers of motivations behind everything he does. I don't know why I feel certain of that, but I do.

And I don't think Luka's being fair. Jackson took more than one hit for me in Vegas.

"Look at your con," Jackson says with a little shake of his head. He's always so calm, so controlled. What would it take to push him across the line?

Luka lifts his wrist and grimaces.

"What?" I ask.

"The con decides how we split up," Luka says, his voice vibrating with anger as he glares at Jackson. "Mine's not doing anything. Look at Tyrone's." Tyrone lifts his hand. His con has a green border, but the majority of the screen is showing a live stream of our surroundings, and in the left corner is a small map with green triangles clumped together. Four of them. *Us.* "It's a map. His con's like a GPS." Luka lifts his wrist and shows me that his con is still green. "Mine won't tell us where to go. Neither will yours. Looks like either you're with Jackson or I am, Miki."

The look on Luka's face is frightening. For a second, I think he actually might haul back and punch Jackson in the face.

"Hey," I say, "it isn't like this is Jackson's choice. He doesn't decide who does what."

"Doesn't he?" Luka shoots a dark look at Jackson.

I'm not sure I understand what's going on here. I swear that back in the clearing there was some sort of guy-bonding thing going on. And I don't recall this much animosity between them on the last mission. Maybe separating them for a while is the best option.

"I'll go with Jackson."

Luka takes a deep breath, then steps close and stares down at me. "Stay safe. We have groceries to unpack when we get back."

Then he and Tyrone are gone, and it's just Jackson and me, all alone.

We move on, not talking, just walking, falling into a numb routine of one foot in front of the other. We must have been down here forever . . . or at least for days. My mind wanders and then settles in to think of nothing at all. Right foot. Left foot. Right. Left.

And then I'm jerked from my lethargy as our glow sticks snap out and we're plunged into darkness so thick and heavy it chokes the breath from my lungs. Something grabs me, arms like bands of steel, a hand pressed tight to my mouth, stifling my cries. I struggle and push, but the grip on my body only tightens until I can't breathe at all. Light-headed, I take the only option I can see. Hoping to catch my captor off guard, I let my legs drop out from under me.

CHAPTER **THIRTEEN**

MY PLOY DOESN'T WORK. THE HAND THAT'S PRESSED TIGHT against my mouth and the arm across my waist only tighten all the more, taking my weight as I try to drop, holding me immobile. My struggles are worthless. Whatever has me is stronger than I can ever hope to be. Panic chokes me. I fight it down. I need to think. I'm not stronger, so I need to be smarter.

I need to—

"*Tsss.*" There's the faintest hiss in my ear. It's enough. That hiss is familiar, and I realize who's holding me and why. I stop struggling and nod, hoping my message is clear. I won't fight. I won't make a sound. Jackson drops his hand from my mouth and changes his hold on me so he doesn't have me pinned against him anymore and he's leading rather than dragging.

The darkness is smothering, thick and black. The second he became aware of the threat, Jackson must have snapped off our lights without me realizing he'd done it.

I try to compensate for my loss of sight by straining my ears, listening for the slightest sound. Jackson thrusts me behind him, and I'm trapped between cold rock at my back and his lean, hard body in front of me. His hand closes on mine, and he guides it to my cylinder. I get the message and pull my weapon free. It molds to my palm, hugging my fingers, and I feel the same connection to it that I felt last time.

My chest feels tight. My limbs buzz with hypersensitivity. I press my lips together and think about breathing as quietly as I can. I don't want to give us away. I lift my weapon cylinder but have no idea in which direction to point it. Jackson closes his fingers on mine, stilling my movements. Whatever we're hiding from he doesn't want to engage. He wants to let it pass, at least for now.

The darkness is suffocating. I can't breathe. I can't think.

I can feel the movement of Jackson's chest as he breathes, not fast and rough like mine, slow and steady. It's enough to steady my own rapid inhalations. I can do this. I can hide in the dark and, failing that, I can fight.

I don't hear footsteps or conversation. I don't hear anything at all. But I sense them passing close by us. The horrific fear that I felt in the alley in Vegas unfurls in my limbs, my gut, my chest. I need to scream, to fight, to flee.

Can they sense me as I sense them? Will they find us? Will they kill us?

Run. I need to run.

They're close. Close enough that I could stretch out my hand and touch them. I know they're here, even though it's only my instinct telling me so.

My nerves are twisted so tight, I think they'll rupture like an overwound guitar string. Then Jackson snaps his light. The greenish glow forms a neat circle with two terrifying figures at the center—almost human but not quite. The second Jackson's light hits them, their bodies flare with a blinding white light, like the magnesium strip in chem class.

The instant the flare roars, something inside me demands I close my eyes. I obey, but the flash is bright enough to pierce my lids and make me see stars.

Temporarily blinded, I don't think, I just act. My hand comes up, and then I see them, moving so fast they're visible only because of the light trail they leave behind.

So I aim just ahead of the light.

I thought I remembered what it was like in Vegas, but as the cylinder hums its high-pitched song and the darkness punches from the muzzle, I'm struck again by the horror of it. The force of the recoil jerks my arm back. The dark pulse surrounds the Drau, engulfing it, sucking it in. I think of an amoeba digesting its dinner.

And then the Drau is gone, snuffed like a match.

The other one comes at us. Jackson slashes at it with his knife. The Drau bares its jagged teeth as Jackson hits the mark, and I smell something sharp and astringent. Then the Drau fires its own weapon and a thousand sparks of light rain down on Jackson's chest. He gasps and dodges. I know the shards of pain he's feeling, the bite of agony that tunnels through skin and muscle and bone. I've felt it myself.

With a cry, I put myself between Jackson and the Drau. Defend. Protect. I take out the second threat. The sound it makes as it's swallowed by the black surge is bone-chilling: a high, keening wail that makes my skin prickle. I feel sick with horror even though I had little choice—it was the Drau or me.

My whole body shakes. Gasping for breath, I press my palm flat to the rock and struggle for control. I did it. I took them out almost before they realized we were there. After a few seconds, I straighten and realize that Jackson snapped my glow-stick light back on. My pulse slows, and as it does calm returns.

I lift my head to find Jackson watching me with his hip cocked so his weight rests on one leg and his arms are crossed over his chest. His expression is unreadable, but something intangible gives him away. He's anything but pleased.

"You got a problem?" I ask, eyes narrowed, breath still coming too fast.

"I was hoping to question the second one," he says. "Next time, maybe wait till I get information before you shoot."

Oh. That must be why he was using his knife instead of his weapon cylinder.

"Question it? The Drau can speak?" I haven't heard them. Not during a battle, and even now, just before we fought them, they weren't holding a conversation. "Can they speak English?"

"No."

I close my eyes and strive for patience. "Which of my three questions does that *no* apply to?"

The corner of his mouth kicks up in the barest hint of a smile. "They don't speak English."

Well, at least he answered something.

"So glad I amuse you," I grouse.

He leans close and whispers against my ear, "Me too. There hasn't been much that makes me smile in a very long time. But you do. So thank you for that."

"You're welcome," I whisper back, feeling off balance. He never says or does what I expect.

So I cross my arms over my chest and shift my weight to my right leg, mirroring his stance. "And next time, if you want to question one of them, tell me your plans before I shoot."

"Point taken, well made," he says.

"And while we're on the topic of next time, maybe just tap my arm to give me a heads-up rather than grabbing me right before we're attacked."

"Did I scare you?"

Not ready to acknowledge that, I say, "You threw off

my game. It could have cost us."

He's quiet for a few seconds, then he says, "And I scared you. I'm sorry."

Jackson apologizing. I'm left speechless.

"By the way," he says, "I was expecting you to ask whether or not I speak Drau."

"Call me unpredictable."

"Don't you want to know?"

Of course I want to know. That isn't even something I need to acknowledge aloud.

"No, I don't," he says. Just that, nothing more. But something inside me loosens a little because Jackson just offered up information voluntarily.

We stand like that, facing off.

"You did good." That incredible, dark, sexy smile carves the dimple in his cheek and bares his white, white teeth. "I think I like you, Miki Jones."

I find myself smiling back. I think I like him, too, and that is not smart. Not smart at all.

Fatigue tugs at me. The adrenaline rush of our encounter with the Drau faded a few thousand steps ago. I don't know how long we've been walking—hours? days?—but my feet are starting to drag. Jackson's in front of me, leading the way. We're moving at a good clip, and the exhaustion slithering through my muscles doesn't seem to be hitting him. Some time ago, he reached back, took my hand, and drew my fingers to the loop of the harness that angles across his hips. I was already tired enough that when he told me to hang on, I didn't argue. I'm still hanging on, and that's helping me keep pace.

"You okay?" The sound of his voice jars me. It's the first thing either one of us has said in quite a while.

"Exactly why are you asking me that?" I can't help the suspicion that curls through the words. I'm not sure why, but I don't want to admit my exhaustion. Stubborn, I guess. If he can keep going, so can I. Or maybe I want to prove I'm as strong as he. A holdover from my kendo days when I was the only girl in the class, driven to be faster, better, hit harder than any of the boys. But the most likely reason is because I don't trust solicitous Jackson. It isn't a persona he wears easily.

"You think I have an ulterior motive in asking if you're okay?"

I stare at his back. Broad shoulders. Lean hips. Honey-gold hair falling in ragged layers almost to his shoulders. Even in the weird, greenish light, he really is beautiful from any angle. "Actually, I think you have an ulterior motive for pretty much everything you do."

"You don't think much of me, do you?" He sounds amused rather than offended.

"I figure you think highly enough of yourself." But the truth is, I sort of admire the complicated layers of his personality. The way he's always thinking and planning.

The way he's in control.

He gives a short laugh. I feel it inside my chest, a soft flutter.

"And since you asked, I'm fine," I say as I sidestep a deep dip in the stone floor, my fingers tightening on the harness. Other than the fatigue, I *am* fine. I now have my own light. I know what our goal is, thanks to Jackson's earlier explanation. I feel a measure of control. Well, as much control as is possible when I'm who-knows-how-many miles underground, getting towed along like a stalled car, on my way to face the next attack by a deadly enemy.

"Can I ask you something, Jackson?"

"Ask away. I might even answer."

Funny guy. "What did you mean earlier when you told me to hang on and enjoy the ride?"

"How do you feel?"

I frown, annoyed that as usual he's evading my question. Doubly annoyed that he's asking me that again. He must be sensing how tired I am, and he's going to make me admit it. Well, I'm an old hand at avoidance, so good luck to him. "I told you already, I'm fine."

I let go of the harness and push myself to keep up, just to prove the point.

He reaches over, catches my wrist, and settles my fingers back on the harness. "No, I mean how do you feel when you're here, underground, walking into the unknown? How did you feel in Vegas? How did you feel a little while ago facing down the Drau? How do you feel when you get pulled?"

I open my mouth, then close it. How *do* I feel? "Scared. Out of control. Freaked out."

"And?" That one word pushes me, challenges me. It's like he wants to climb inside my mind. But he's already there. From the second he started talking inside my head, calling my name, Jackson Tate's been front and center in my thoughts.

"How do you feel?" he asks again, forceful, insistent.

For some reason, I think of Tyrone and the way he seemed better down here, more focused, more— "Alive," I whisper. It hits me then. When I'm on a mission, I don't feel the gray fog weighing down every thought, every action. "I feel alive and it's a rush."

"*That's* what I mean. You have no choice about whether to be part of this or not. You'll be pulled no matter what. But you can choose to make the best of it."

I recoil, appalled. "The best of it? We kill things and run the risk that they'll kill us. Whoever I replaced is dead. Richelle is dead. We had no choice about that, no say. How do you make the best of that?"

"By grabbing hold with both hands and steering the nightmare instead of just huddling in the corner and watching it unfold." The words are low and intense. He knows what he's talking about. He knows what I'm feeling.

Does he know that just being with him is a rush, too? Does he know what he does to me?

"You call what happened on our last mission steering the nightmare?" I ask.

"What I could control, I controlled."

I have a flash of memory: Jackson kicking the weapon out of the Drau's hand. Richelle's scream. Is that what he means about controlling what he could? Did he choose between us because he couldn't save both? A terrible possibility.

"Your definition of control was watching my back, keeping me alive."

"Yes."

"How long have you been steering your nightmares, Jackson?"

There's a long pause. I hear the faint scuff of our footsteps as we keep moving, and I think he isn't going to answer. Then he says, "Too long. Forever."

"Then why don't you get your score to a thousand and get out?"

Another long pause. "There's only one way out for me, Miki." Every syllable is nuanced and laced with meaning, but what that meaning might be, I can't say. I almost ask, but at the last second, I hold back. If he wanted to tell me, he would have. Instead, I ask, "Do you ever think of giving up? Just saying 'No more' and giving up?"

He stops and turns to face me, his expression fierce. "No, and you won't, either."

"How do you know that?"

"Because you haven't given up, no matter how much shit's been dumped on you. You're a fighter. You fought to be the best at kendo. You fought for your mom. You fought your grief. You fought to be normal."

I stare at him, stunned. "How do you know all that? How do you know things about me?"

He steps closer. Then slowly, so slowly, he lifts his hands and curls his fingers around the back of my neck so they meet at my spine. He cups my face, his palms resting against my cheeks. I freeze, heart pounding, my mouth going dry. My skin tingles everywhere he touches.

"I know you," he whispers. He sounds so certain that I almost believe him. I almost believe that I know him, too, that there's something in each of us that clicks with the other, like two pieces of a puzzle.

I shake my head. "You don't. You can't."

I don't know how long we stand like that, so close I can feel his holster pressed against my hip, feel his breath touch my lips.

He lowers his head a fraction of an inch.

I'm breathing too fast, heart slamming against my ribs, blood rushing, leaving me light-headed.

My lips part. My gaze drops to his mouth. He's going to kiss me, here in this underground labyrinth, far from the world, far from reality. And I'm going to let him. Electricity dances along my nerves, lighting me up.

But the kiss never comes.

His mouth tightens into a hard line, and he lifts his head and turns his face away. I almost grab him and drag him back. His whole body is rigid. Controlled. I suspect he's purposely looking somewhere over my shoulder, somewhere other than at me. His jaw is set, his expression harsh.

The moment is lost. Or, more likely, he gave it up on purpose.

I'm both disappointed and relieved. He does that to me, twists me up in crazy knots and leaves me to pick at them until they untangle. I hope I do the same to him. It's only fair. But miles underground on a mission to kill Drau really isn't the best place to lose myself in a kiss, and I have no doubt that once his lips touch mine, I will be lost.

"Okay," he says, dropping his hands and stepping back. "You win. I don't know you. And you don't know me." He pauses. His voice lowers. "Don't get to know me, Miki. You won't like what you find."

I'm confused for a second, and then I remember what we were talking about: he was claiming to know me and I was telling him he didn't. Now he's agreeing with me, but his words leave me completely off balance, and I don't like it.

I stare at him, and then I lose my patience. It's gone in a snap. "Enough cryptic warnings. What's so wrong with you? Webbed fingers?" I grab his hand and spread his fingers. "An extra toe?"

"Tainted motives."

I throw my hands in the air. "What am I supposed to say to that? What am I supposed to think? Talk about mixed messages. You are the most confusing, arrogant, self-absorbed, obnoxious—"

"You can call me an asshole later. Right now, you're fighting exhaustion." He hunkers down and then settles himself with his back against the wall and legs stretched out straight. "So we rest."

I almost argue, but I'm smart enough to recognize that this is a concession. He's doing this for me. He's not the one who's tired. So I bite my tongue and gingerly get myself settled on the ground, stunned by how grateful I am to be off my feet.

"You can lean on me," Jackson says.

"I—"

"Lean on me." Not an offer this time, an order.

I scoot over and lean my weight against his arm.

"Not like that." He shifts both of us around until my back's against one side of his chest, my head lolling sideways onto his shoulder, our legs stretched out in front of us, side by side. Not perfect on the comfort score, but better than it was a minute ago. He rests his chin lightly on the top of my head and tells me, "Sleep."

"What about you?"

"I'll keep watch. I've been doing this long enough that I don't need rest while we're on a mission."

"What about Luka and Tyrone?"

"They won't need to rest, either. You're still getting used to the jumps. By the next mission or the one after that, you'll be like us. A robo-soldier." And there it is again, that thread of humor, like he's laughing at himself.

"Is that supposed to reassure me? 'Cause I gotta tell ya,

thinking about upcoming missions doesn't exactly thrill me."

I jump when his hands settle on my shoulders. Then I sigh as he kneads my muscles. Long fingers. Strong hands. Some of my tension slips away, and I relax more fully against him. "How long have we been here now?"

"A little over seventeen hours."

Wow. "But when we go back, it will be the exact second we left?"

"Yes."

My eyes drift shut. After a minute, I say, "You're answering all my questions. What happened to the rules?"

"We've been pulled. We're in"—he pauses, and when he continues, I can hear that he's smiling—"what Luka calls the game. So the rules don't apply. We can speak freely."

"So you're conceding on the name? Now it's okay to refer to this as a game?"

"For lack of a better option."

"Are there really rules, or you're just making that up as a way to control everyone?"

The easy rhythm of his breathing shifts ever so slightly.

"Think you know me so well, do you?"

"Well enough to know you're a control freak. Answer the question . . . please," I add as incentive.

"There are rules." He pauses. "And some of them are ones I put in place."

"With the others."

"The others?"

"The ones in charge of the teams in the other clearings, the ones only you and I can see. Are they on that committee you mentioned?"

"No teams. Every man for himself."

"So you keep reminding me, but you're just talking the talk because here you are, watching out for me. Again. Who are the people in the other lobbies?"

"There are no other lobbies. They're all parts of the same lobby."

"Can they see us?"

"Some of them can."

"Why can I see them when Luka and Tyrone can't?"

Again, the easy rhythm of Jackson's breathing shifts, telling me that whatever answer he offers, it won't be the whole truth and nothing but the truth.

"Because we're alike, you and I."

"Aaaand you're back to being cryptic." I change direction and ask, "So while we're here, in the game, you can tell me things that you can't talk about back in the real world."

"Yes."

"Which means the issue isn't about me having the knowledge. It's about something else. It's about people—humans—overhearing, or about the Drau listening in."

"Yes."

"The Drau can't listen in here?"

"No."

I think about that, and then offer a theory. "Because

171

they're piggybacking on human technology to do their spying. Like the satellites you mentioned in the park. And human technology doesn't extend to the game."

"Yes." He sounds pleased as he says it. I get the feeling he wanted me to figure that out. I wonder why, if that's the case, he didn't just tell me in the first place.

I sigh. It's like pulling teeth. He's giving me only what I ask for and not a single word more. Maybe an open-ended question . . . "So tell me about them, the Drau."

"Information is power?"

"Too cliché?"

"Maybe. But still true. They come from a planet that's . . . harsh. Harsh terrain. Harsh climate. Limited resources. Vicious predators."

"But it's mostly sunny. That binary star thing, right?"

"So you do listen to what I say."

"Every word."

His hands leave my shoulders and he wraps both arms around me, settling me more fully against him and holding me close. I blow out a shaky breath. I'm lying on the ground, in a cave, in the dark, wrapped in a boy's embrace. Not just any boy. Jackson Tate. Infuriating, arrogant, gorgeous, competent, deliciously warm Jackson Tate. "They fought each other on their own world for thousands of years, and eventually they destroyed it."

"Destroyed? Completely? Like they blew up the planet?"

"Close. They turned it into a wasteland. Their weapons

weren't nuclear based, but it's a good comparison. Think about what we'd do if we unleashed a nuclear holocaust." I cringe at the images that conjures. "They lived in that wasteland for centuries, and all the while, they worked and planned and plotted how to get off their broken hunk of rock. You'd think they'd have learned from their mistakes. You'd think that when their technology finally reached a level allowing them to go elsewhere, they'd be different."

"But they weren't."

"No. They wiped out entire populations. They raped planets for their resources. They left a trail of broken worlds behind them. They are predators, and they don't care what destruction they leave in their wake. In fact, they enjoy it. The worlds that fight the hardest give them the most pleasure."

As if the entire explanation weren't bad enough, that last bit shoves a blade in my gut and twists. "What you said in Vegas, about how our ancestors fled to Earth and lived among humans . . ."

"They chose Earth because they knew they could survive here, not just for one lifetime, but by having offspring. The DNA was compatible. Their appearance was compatible. Their needs for oxygen and sustenance similar."

"How do you know all this?"

I feel him shrug. "It wasn't just physical similarity," he says, continuing as if I hadn't even asked a question. "Our ancestors believed humans were tenacious and brave and honorable, that they would fight for what mattered."

"You're talking in generalities here. Not all humans are like that."

"Agreed. But the good ones outnumber the bad."

I shake my head. "Wow. You're an optimist. Wouldn't have expected that."

"I'm all about the unexpected."

I fall silent, trying to figure everything out. There are things here that don't add up. I don't know why Jackson's telling me all this. He's not exactly a forthcoming kind of guy, and I have a feeling that if I ask Luka about any of this, he won't have a clue because Jackson won't have told him any of it. So why is he telling *me*?

"You know this is a lot to get my head around." Even to my own ears, my words sound slurred. The fact that I'm so tired isn't helping my confusion. I'm already half asleep, despite the mind-boggling information he's dumping on me.

I swear I feel his lips against my cheek. Then I tell myself I must have imagined it.

"Go to sleep, Miki," he whispers, and his lips touch my cheek again. "I'll watch over you."

CHAPTER**FOURTEEN**

I DON'T KNOW HOW LONG I SLEPT CRADLED IN JACKSON'S arms. I only know that when I wake up, I feel much better than when I fell asleep, and Jackson is back to his usual self. He walks. I follow. I try to ask him more questions about the Drau and our ancestors, about the game. But I guess he's used up all his words for the day.

I remember the way he cupped my cheeks and leaned close, his mouth a breath from mine. I can't believe that for a second I actually wanted to kiss him. I'm back to wanting to punch him. Hard.

Eventually we see Luka and Tyrone coming toward us.

"We hit three of them in the tunnels, and then Tyrone's con led us back to you," Luka says after I tell them about our Drau encounter.

"Huh. Seems like there should have been more of them."

"I don't trust the lack of defense," Tyrone mutters.

Neither do I.

"Maybe they figure they don't need much security because they can't imagine anyone being able to find this place," Luka offers, but he doesn't sound convinced.

I shake my head. "Even if that's so, it was still too easy. Plus, I thought that they can sense us when we're dropped in, even if they can't precisely pinpoint our location."

I glance at Jackson for confirmation and he says, "True enough."

"Back to being all chatty-chat," I mutter, stealing Tyrone's description.

Tyrone snorts. Jackson says nothing.

"The Drau . . . ," Luka prods.

"The ones we encountered didn't even seem like they were trained properly," I muse as I think back on the two Jackson and I came up against. "They almost seemed like new recruits." I glance at Jackson again, waiting for him to throw his opinion out there, but he seems content just to listen. No . . . more than content; I have the feeling he wants me to reason this out on my own. But . . . why?

"Does it matter?" Jackson asks, and for a second, I think he's answering my silent questions. Then I realize he's referring to the Drau level of training. He glances at his con. "Move out," he says, and heads off down the tunnel, Tyrone behind him.

The tunnel's just wide enough for two, and Luka falls into step beside me.

"They were like new recruits?" he asks, picking up where I left off. "What makes you think that?"

"Well, remember in Vegas . . . I thought the Drau were so fast, and I asked about that because you guys said they're slower at night?"

"Yeah . . ."

"You said that *was* slow for them. But the Drau we went up against here were really slow in comparison. It just seems . . . off."

"Maybe because we're in these caves and it's way dark down here. Maybe that slowed them down."

"Maybe. But then why would they set up a facility here if it slows them down and makes it hard to defend?" I'm not convinced. "I feel like it's more than that. There's too few of them, and they don't seem well trained. It's like the place is almost deserted and all that's been left behind to guard it is a disposable group."

I take a few quick steps and catch up to Jackson. "If you know something, now would be a good time to share."

"Know something?" He doesn't even glance at me, just keeps walking.

"Why did they set up here?"

"Can't say for certain, but my guess is that it's isolated, no chance for humans to stumble on them since these caves aren't on the spelunker radar, and because the space is large enough for what they have in mind."

"So why's the security so light?"

He shrugs.

I grab his arm and stop walking, which in turn makes him stop walking. Actually, no. I can't *make* him do anything. He let me drag him to a stop, so maybe he's willing to offer up a few answers. With him, it's hard to know for sure.

"Are we walking into an ambush?"

"No," he says, then turns his head toward Luka and Tyrone. "It's like the situation in Arizona."

They both nod. I'm the only one in the dark.

"Situation in Arizona?" I look back and forth between them, and they look at Jackson.

His mouth tenses, and after a few seconds he says, "It's easier to believe if you see it." His tone is flat.

I figure he'll just stalk off like he usually does. Instead, he stands there for a long minute, and then he stalks off. Which makes me give a dark huff of laughter.

"Predictable," I call after him softly.

He doesn't give the slightest indication that he's heard. But after a few steps his voice carries back to me. "And proud of it."

Tyrone follows, with Luka and me taking the rear again.

"Tell me about Arizona."

"It was a poorly guarded facility. The Drau left only a skeleton staff because they clearly weren't expecting us to hit. They thought they were too well concealed. We were in and out pretty quick."

His explanation makes me nervous, not because of what he said, but what he didn't say. There's something in his tone that tells me Arizona wasn't quite as easy as he's making it sound. His expression is closed, his fists clenched. Whatever happened in Arizona, Luka didn't like it.

"And you don't think they'll have learned from that? You don't think this might be a trap?" I ask.

"No," Tyrone says, surprising me with how certain he sounds. "One weird thing about the Drau . . . they don't seem to learn from their mistakes. It's as if one group doesn't communicate with the others very well."

"They don't," Jackson says, stopping and turning to face us. "The Drau are violent. Predatory. Think of a pride of lions with rage issues. They have a degree of community within the pride, but they fight with rivals. It's a predator thing. The Drau are like that, and it's one of the few things working in our favor. Whatever organization they have in regard to attack, there's infighting and aggression within their ranks. Groups are only loosely affiliated, and half the time they'll as soon kill each other as work together. They're poor communicators, and the right hand doesn't always know what the left hand is doing."

I consider—and decide against—pointing out that he's not exactly the king of communication either. Instead, I ask, "If they're so bad at communication and organization, how have they managed to conquer so many worlds?"

"Tenacity, brutality, viciousness, and sheer numbers," Jackson says, his tone hard and ugly.

Last word, as usual.

We walk on, and after a bit Luka says, "I think their predatory nature must make them competitive to an astronomical degree."

"Makes sense." Tyrone glances back. "And that would just drive them to conquer more and more worlds, even if they aren't exactly working together."

"Like the space race," I say. They all look at me. Even Jackson stops and waits to hear what else I have to say. I'm more than surprised. It isn't like I've offered up anything brilliant. Maybe they don't know what I'm talking about. "The space race in the 1950s. You know . . . the Soviets launched Sputnik, and that drove the race to the moon. . . ."

"Are you saying the Drau are like humans?" Jackson asks, and there's something in his voice that makes me think my answer is enormously important.

"I don't know. I don't know much about the Drau." I give him a look that says, *And whose fault is that?* "I think some people are predatory. Some people are competitive." I pause. "And some people are just secretive, uninformative, reticent—"

"—assholes," Jackson finishes for me with a tight smile. "Got it. Let's go." He heads off down the tunnel.

Tyrone's brows shoot up. Luka looks back and forth between Jackson and me, his jaw slack. I shrug and start walking. I can't explain Jackson's actions any better than they can, and trying to figure him out just makes my brain hurt. On the one hand, I feel like he's trying to let me get to know him a little. On the other, I feel like he's put up this solid metal wall between us that even a tank couldn't break through.

Tyrone moves ahead, with Luka and me bringing up the rear.

"Luka, what happens to the Drau after we fire our weapons? I mean, they're there and then they're gone, and I have this horrible thought that it's like the amoebas we learned about in bio. That the Drau get engulfed and digested by the black stuff."

He glances at me, his expression somber. "I'm sorry, Miki. I don't know what happens to them. But I've had similar thoughts to yours." He pauses, looking faintly ill. "So I try not to think about it."

Before I can say anything else, Jackson holds up a hand to halt our progress. "Weapons."

I pull mine out, my adrenaline rush so forceful it actually makes my head spin. I would have thought it would start to get easier. But it doesn't; it isn't. I'm still terrified. Jackson grabs my arm and hauls me back so we're side by side against the tunnel's wall. Tyrone and Luka fall back on the opposite side. My entire body feels like it's a spring compressed until it's ready to explode. We wait in tense silence, each second an eternity.

I get this weird feeling in my gut, telling me to close my eyes a millisecond before Jackson orders, "Close your eyes."

The light that explodes in front of me is so bright it pierces my closed lids and feels like it's burning clear through my eyelids and pupils to my retinas.

My gut clenches and I'm already dropping to the ground when Jackson barks, "Down." His hand is on my shoulder, a light pressure silently telling me to stay down.

"Now," Jackson says.

Cracking my lids, I squint and see the shapes of two aliens coming at me from far down the now-bright tunnel. They're fast and fluid, bright white, their skin like glass, their features almost human. Jackson's already on his feet, in front of me and a little to my right. I come up on my knees and aim. Inhale. On the exhale, I force my will into the cylinder and feel gratified when it releases its greasy, powerful surge.

But life's not that easy. The two aliens veer apart, and my shot misses completely. They're faster than the last two. Not so easy to take down.

Luka said there were sentinels, specialists, leaders, commanders. What are these? What were the ones we encountered earlier? How can I tell?

I push to my feet, familiar kendo patterns taking hold. *Okuri-ashi:* basic stance. *Zenshin kotai:* forward backward. *Hiraki-ashi:* pivot. I need to make sure I'm not where I was a second ago, because if I am, their shots will get me. I'm quick and sure as I evade them because I've defended myself in practice and competition so many times I don't even need to think. Terror only makes me faster.

Two more come at us, and from an offshoot tunnel, at least three more. I lose count. All I know is pivot, aim, shoot. The metal of my weapon cylinder is icy cold in my hand. My arm jerks from each recoil, but I force it to hold steady. Kendo's trained me to bear up under the strain. There's no time to think, to plan. There's only me, or them.

I don't look in their eyes. But that doesn't keep me safe from their weapons. More than once, I feel the acid burn of thousands of needle points of light digging deep. I drop, roll, fire, evade, push to my feet and fire again. I don't allow myself to process my fear. I just move. But on some level, I sense something off. They're definitely faster than the two we encountered earlier, more organized in their attack, but still not as quick as the Drau we encountered in Vegas.

Tyrone gets one. I think Luka gets another. I spin, and there's one directly in front of me. My instincts scream for me to retreat. I force myself to go on the attack, and all the while, I keep telling myself not to look at its eyes. I shoot. I score. The thing makes a sound, high and eerie. My head jerks up, and for a split second, I *do* look in its eyes, mercury gray, swirling like storm clouds around long, slitted pupils. Terrifying. Deadly. Beautiful.

A predator's eyes.

Do I see fear mirrored there? Pain?

Doubts wing at me like a colony of bats. What if this is all wrong? How do I know these aliens are evil? How do I know I'm justified in taking their lives? Yes, they've attacked us every time, but we were the ones who invaded their turf. What if they're like the dudes in that old show *Star Trek* who just want to observe life on other planets?

But if that's the case, why attack us? Why not just try to communicate somehow?

I have no chance to know because the alien's gone, sucked into the black oblivion that spews from my weapon.

Panting, shaking, I look around. Jackson's watching me, his expression unreadable, his weapon pointing at the spot where the alien was standing only a moment ago.

"Watching my back?" I ask.

"I need you safe," he says.

Unexpected words spoken in an indecipherable tone. He needs me safe because I'm part of his team, or he needs me safe because I mean something to him? Given the way he's always insisting there is no team, it's every man for himself, I have a hard time picking option one. But going with option two means asking myself why I want to mean something to him, and thinking about things that I just can't face right now.

"Don't feel pity for it. Don't feel anything," he says, his tone rough, angry. "Trust me, it wouldn't feel pity or empathy for you."

"How do you know that? How do you know what I'm thinking?"

"Because I thought the same things when I was fresh and naive. Give them the chance, and they will kill you. If they happen to be hungry, they'll eat you alive. They like their prey fresh and bloody." He yanks up the left sleeve of his running shirt, all the way to the shoulder. The scars there are horrible. It looks like chunks of Jackson's flesh were torn clean off the upper part of his arm, then tossed back in place by a careless hand.

I gasp and rear back, remembering the Drau in Vegas and how it bared its jagged teeth.

"But we heal. When we go back, we heal."

"Do we now?" Jackson asks, whisper soft. "This didn't happen in the game."

I think that might be the most horrific thing I've ever heard, the fact that the Drau aren't confined to this alternate reality, the fact that somehow one got at Jackson in the real world and savaged him. At the park, he told me they could be listening. But I thought he just meant through satellites, not that they really might be there, close enough to touch. Close enough to hurt us.

I reach out toward his arm, but he takes a step back and yanks down his sleeve.

Luka and Tyrone jog over, panting. I wonder if Jackson yanked down his sleeve because he doesn't want them to see his scars or because he doesn't want me to touch them.

"Are there more?" Luka asks.

The four of us move to stand in a tight circle, backs toward each other, weapons ready.

My gaze darts back and forth, but nothing comes at us.

"Why don't we make the jump?" I ask. "We seem to have"—I can't make myself say the word *killed*—"*gotten* all of them."

Jackson steps away and turns a slow circle. "They weren't the mission. They were incidental. This way." He strides off to the right—the direction most of the aliens came from—and we follow.

I glance at Luka. "What happened in Arizona?" It feels like the answer to that question is incredibly important.

His expression closes down, and he shrugs.

As far as answers go, that one's pretty shitty.

"Luka, if you know something, tell me. It might save my life."

He looks at me then, desperation etched in his face. "If it isn't like Arizona, then there's no reason for you to know. It's too horrible for anyone to know. I wish I could scrub it out of my mind."

"And if it *is* like Arizona?"

"Then you'll know soon enough."

I've never heard Luka sound so bleak.

We're not using the glow sticks to light our way anymore. The aliens' appearance brought bright white light, and it seems to have hung around even though they're gone. We keep moving down the tunnel, the sides of which have been polished to a smooth, shiny finish. No one appears to stop us, and that only makes the uncertainties plaguing me grow stronger.

The hairs at my nape prickle and rise. My steps slow, and I fall back behind the others. It's pure instinct that makes me turn, makes me lift my weapon and fire, but not before white-hot needles of pain burst in my chest. I cry out as the Drau's shots hit me, piercing deep.

CHAPTER FIFTEEN

THE PAIN MAKES ME STUMBLE BACK UNTIL I HIT THE CAVE'S cold rock wall.

"Miki!" Tyrone yells from somewhere to my right.

I don't take my eyes off the Drau. There's only one. No backup. I notice things that I didn't notice before when we were fighting so many of them that all I saw was light; all I knew was fear. The glowing, glassy surface of the Drau's body . . . I think it isn't naked skin as I get a good look. I think it's some sort of suit that covers everything, with openings for its eyes and mouth. There are no nostrils, and I don't see any ears.

My first shot went wide. I shift my angle and fire again. The Drau is silent as the blackness surges from my weapon; it appears frozen in place by terror. My shot is true, the darkness engulfing my enemy from its feet up. At the last second, the Drau's eyes catch mine and pain tears at me from the inside out. Then it's gone, swallowed whole, and the agony wrenches away, leaving my whole body prickling with painful reawakening, like the blood rushing to a limb after it's fallen asleep.

"Miki!" Luka's beside me as I drop to one knee, Tyrone right behind him.

I look up and see Jackson a few feet away, his weapon in his hand, pointing to the spot where the Drau stood seconds ago. I terminated it, but if I hadn't, Jackson had my back, again.

"I'm okay," I rasp as Luka hunkers down beside me, worry and uncertainty etched in his features.

He studies my face, then offers a faint smile. "Nice shot, but whatever points you gained were more than eaten up by penalty. Sucks to be you."

I drag in a breath, the pain sharp and bright. By the third breath, it's easing to a dull ache, more like a bruise than a stab. I turn my wrist and check my con. It's still mostly green with just a hint of yellow. Not so bad, then.

Jackson strides over and pauses by my side. Then he holds out his hand, and when I take it, he pulls me to my feet. His fingers are warm against mine for a brief second, then he lets go and steps away. Not a word of comfort, just that all-too-brief touch.

"I'll live, thanks for asking," I mutter.

"How did you know it was there?" he asks, and even

though the question is simple, asked in a low, casual tone, I feel as though there's a lot riding on my answer.

"I just knew. Instinct, I guess. And back when we got hit by the whole group, I knew to close my eyes before the bright light flashed and I knew to drop to the ground before the first shot was fired."

"I told you to do those things."

"You did, but I was already doing them before you said. The longer I'm in the game, the more my instincts seem to be taking over."

He doesn't say anything to that, just offers a spare, sharp nod. Of course, I can't see his eyes. But I know that he's looking at me, and I know he likes what he sees, that he's . . . I don't know . . . I guess *proud* is the best word. Yeah, he watches my back, and he also trusts me to watch my own. But there's something else there, too. His expression is both pleased and angry. Ambivalent. I know better than to ask why. Jackson's not much one for sharing. But I'm patient. I can wait. I just need to figure out what angle to come at the question from, and I'll get my answer eventually.

"How did *you* know the Drau was there?" I ask, and only as the words slide free am I certain that he did know. He knew there was danger, and he was waiting to see if I caught it, too. Why?

"I just knew," he says. "Instinct, I guess."

I huff a short laugh and offer him the same nod he gave me.

Luka and Tyrone exchange a confused glance, and then we're moving again, Jackson in the lead, me behind him. I still feel the hit I took. Every breath reminds me, but the pain is dull, an ache, the same sort of pain I get the day after a good workout.

Holding up his hand, Jackson puts the brakes on and presses back against the stone wall. Then he leans forward very slowly and peers around the corner. Apparently satisfied by what he does—or doesn't—see, he signals us to move.

We round another corner. I'm hit by light so bright it's like sunshine on a July afternoon, the glare amplified by white walls, white floor, white ceiling, all polished to a perfect shine. I jerk to a stop, horror congealing like day-old bacon fat.

The room is full of people. Humans.

Dead humans.

Before me stretch rows and rows of girls, lying on their backs, eyes closed, limbs bare. Strips of white cloth drape their chests and hips, like tube tops and short skirts. At first glance, they look like they're floating, but when I look more carefully, I see that they're on white gurneys that blend with the walls and floor, white on white on white.

The sounds of beeps and hisses hum in the background. Their chests rise and fall in synchronized rhythm.

So I was wrong. They aren't dead.

They're all attached to machines and tubes. I don't know if the machines are human technology or alien knockoffs, but I recognize some and can figure out the rest. Three weeks into her chemo, Mom ended up in the ICU with pneumonia. One of the ways I coped with seeing her there was by finding out everything I could about the machines that were keeping her alive. A lot of the stuff here looks familiar. There are monitors that beep softly and respirators doing the breathing. There are tubes in the girls' legs or near their collarbones; one of the nurses in the ICU said those measure things like oxygen in the blood. The tubes in their chests drain fluid and keep their lungs from collapsing.

"Oh man," Luka says, and rakes his fingers back through his hair. "Oh man, this is not good. There are so many of them."

"What is this place?" I ask. "Who are these people?"

"This is bigger than the facility in Arizona." Luka shakes his head. "This is bad, Miki."

"Bad in more ways than one," Tyrone says. "Security was too light for a place like this, even if they were so sure of themselves that they thought we wouldn't find them. A handful of guards for a place this size?" He looks at Jackson. "You think it's a trap?"

"Lousy trap if that's what it is," Jackson says. "More likely, we got lucky. Could be a change in shift, or security was sent off-site to attend to something else." Something in his voice catches my attention, like he doesn't really believe what he's saying. And I silently curse those stupid shades because I suspect he's watching me, but I can't be sure. He shrugs. "Doesn't matter. Stop talking and start working. Tyrone, get the supplies. Smash everything that's breakable. Luka, Miki, help me with the machines."

"Who are they?" I ask again. "What's wrong with them?"

"There's nothing wrong with them." Jackson's tone is dark and rough. "And nothing right, either."

The sound of glass shattering makes me turn. Tyrone's standing near the far wall. I thought it was just a wall, but now I see that it's a series of smooth-fronted cabinets. Tyrone has one open and he's sweeping his outstretched arm along the shelves. Whatever doesn't break as it hits the ground, he shatters with the heel of his boot.

"Nothing wrong with them?" I turn back to Jackson. "They're unconscious. They're hooked up to machines."

I wrinkle my nose. The smell in here is off. Medicinal mixed with something sort of earthy, like Dad's compost bin. Not pleasant, that's for sure.

Jackson's finished offering explanations. I should probably count myself lucky that he gave me as much as he did. "Get moving," he says.

Luka crosses to the row of gurneys nearest Tyrone. With a grimace, he reaches out and turns off the respirator. The girl's chest deflates and doesn't rise again.

The sight of that dredges up horrific memories of Mom breathing her last, the sound of her exhalation and then just . . . nothing. Suddenly, I'm not here. I'm back there, with her.

"Wait! No!" I lunge forward but get nowhere because Jackson grabs my arm.

"They aren't people." He hits a button on the respirator closest to us, turning it off.

"What are you doing? You're killing them." I shove his hands away and reach for the switch. On some level, I realize that I'm not reacting in a way that makes sense, but all I can think about is Mom lying on the bed, gray and small and dead. "Help me stop him," I yell at Luka before I remember that he turned off a respirator, too.

Jackson catches my wrist again and says, "We don't have time for this," his words calm and low. "There could be an alarm. We could be seconds away from a fresh wave of Drau. This time *skilled* Drau rather than green recruits."

"You just killed an innocent girl." I feel sick. He's a monster. I remember the way he wrapped his arms around me in the park, the way I rested my cheek high on his chest, the way he made me feel, just for a few moments, that the world hadn't gone crazy. I let him hold me then. I let him hold me in the tunnels while I slept. I almost let him kiss me. I trusted him. *Liked* him. And now he's killing people and Luka's killing people, and they look like they expect me to do the same. Not aliens in a kill-or-be-killed standoff this time. *People.*

Once more, I reach for the respirator he turned off, tears blurring my vision.

He makes a sound of impatience. "Miki, pull it together. These are not people."

I whirl to face him, breathing hard, angry and afraid and sickened. I remember the rows of patients at the hospital, sitting in these recliner chairs, getting chemo. Men, women . . . kids. Mom. "Just because they're unconscious? Because they're in comas? They're still people."

"They're not. They never were. Look." He points at the feeding tube that's running into the woman's abdomen. I glance down, trying to see whatever it is he wants me to see—

The tube runs in above the belly button, except . . . No belly button. Just a feeding tube right above where her belly button should be. I shake my head.

He yanks a bunch of electrical wires out of the woman's neck. Then he looks around, fails to find whatever it is that he wants, and drags his knife with its deadly black blade free of its sheath. I cry out and lunge forward as he slashes at the top of the girl's head, twisting his hand in a rapid circle. The skin of her scalp peels back and I see to my horror that Jackson's knife has gone clear through bone. I think I'm going to be sick.

Jackson taps the hilt of his knife against the top of her skull and the dome of bone falls back, like flipping open the lid on a shampoo bottle.

An empty shampoo bottle.

There's nothing inside.

There's no brain, no blood. There's nothing. Her skull is empty, a clean box formed of smooth bone. The only blood is from her scalp.

"No brain. No belly button," I whisper.

"Because they weren't born, so there was no umbilical cord to cut," Jackson says. "This is an experimental facility. They were grown here to serve as vehicles for alien consciousness. They're like suits the aliens plan to wear. And we're here to stop them."

"In the park," I whisper, "when I asked who was listening, I said we'd see the Drau, but you said not necessarily. I figured it's because they can piggyback human technology, like satellites. Listen in to what we say. But"—I can't bear to look at the girl on the gurney. I can't bear not to—"it's not just that. It's because they could be right there and we'd never know it. Because they can hide. Inside human shells." The horror of that is immeasurable.

"Yes . . ." He hesitates, and I gasp. His scars. Those weren't made by a shell. They were made by a Drau in the real world. My hands are shaking. He grabs one and squeezes, then lets go. "It's our job right now to make sure they don't get the chance to hide in these shells. So move, Miki. Get the next row." I stand frozen, staring at him, thinking about how he once told me that I wouldn't believe stuff he said, that I'd have to see it myself. I could have done without seeing this. "*Now,*" he orders, snapping me out of my trance.

I jog over to the next row of gurneys. From the corner of my eye, I see him pull the breathing tube from the girl's throat. I don't think. I just work. I turn off the next respirator, drag out the tube, and that's when I notice the girl's face.

It's exactly the same as the face of the girl on the gurney I just left. Light brown hair. Long lashes. High cheekbones. She's lovely. There's something vaguely familiar about her features. I move faster, pulling out tubes, disconnecting machines, and then I'm at the next gurney and the next, and each and every face is the same as the last.

A horrid thought hits me. I turn my head and look at Jackson. "Does it hurt them?" My question echoes through the room. His hands freeze on the tube he's holding, but he doesn't look up at me.

"No brain," he says. "Nowhere to process the sensation of pain. You aren't hurting them and you can't kill something that isn't alive in the first place."

He's right, but I feel sick anyway. I shove my emotions into a box and work my way down the line, aware of Tyrone creating a symphony of shattering glass behind me. I kill the next respirator and the next, telling myself these girls were never alive. They're some sort of clones without brains, with machines breathing for them and feeding them. They're shells destined to be used in a war against mankind, the ultimate spies, or maybe the ultimate stealth weapons.

I keep my breathing slow and steady, forcing myself to be calm. The smell is stronger now, antiseptic overlying something that smells sweet and foul, sort of like burning rubber mixed with raw bacon mixed with the smell of the mushroom farm Dad and I once drove past on the highway. I glance at the others and notice that Luka has the back of one hand pressed up against his nose as he moves between gurneys.

"Done," he says a couple of minutes later. He's reached the end of his row.

"Done," Jackson says.

"What the hell is that smell?" Tyrone asks.

I hit the button on the last respirator and pull out the tubes and wires. "Done," I choke out, the word catching in my throat. I force a deep breath and almost gag. I look at the body in front of me, really look, and then I see things I missed up till now because I was so focused on just getting the job done.

The skin of her feet doesn't look right; it's pale and shiny and there are blisters all over her toes. I move up to her calves and see more of the same. Turning, I check the next body. Her limbs are worse. There are actually chunks of skin sloughing off her feet and the blisters extend up above her knees. The next body has huge sections of skin sloughed off her hands and her arms are discolored.

The smell . . . it's the smell of decay. The bodies are rotting, the ones at this end in worse shape than the ones at the far end of the row. I swallow against the bile that crawls up my throat.

"I think I know why security is so light," I say. The others turn to stare at me. "There's something wrong with them. Whatever the Drau have planned, this"—I wave my hands, searching for the right word—"*batch* failed. They're rotting. Decaying. That's the smell. The Drau didn't care about them because they didn't turn out right." I point at the girl's feet. "Why bother to guard something that's broken?"

Jackson walks over and looks down at her, his expression blank.

"Good call," he says. He doesn't sound surprised. A crazy thought hits me: Jackson knew all along why there was light security here. He was waiting to see if I'd figure it out. I shake my head and discount that thought. Why would he do that? Why wouldn't he just tell me?

"Is this a test?" I ask so only he can hear.

He turns his face to me. "A test of what?"

"I don't know."

"If it were a test, you'd pass with flying colors, Miki." So why does he sound angry about that? "Wait here," he says, then strides across the room and pulls on a door I hadn't even noticed before now. The handle turns, but the door doesn't move. Jackson pulls out his weapon cylinder, touches the side, and when he fires it, the black surge isn't greasy and oily, it's a thin, powerful stream.

"I saw this show once about how a company in Texas uses machines that shoot water at such high pressure that it actually cuts through steel," I say.

Jackson doesn't answer. There really isn't much for him to say. He turns his weapon on the row of respirators closest to him and destroys each in turn. Luka and Tyrone get to work on the other rows. But I stand frozen, watching Jackson. He puts his weapon away, taps the door handle, and it falls free. He steps into the room and makes a point of dragging the door shut behind him.

I look at Luka and Tyrone. "Does he always do this?"

"Do what?" Luka asks warily.

"Take a little personal time?" There's a touch of venom in my tone, and I don't really care. On the last mission he disappeared for a few moments there at the end while we were all waiting to make the jump. Now he's done it again.

Luka hedges. "Not always."

"Why keep any of them alive if the batch was tainted?" Tyrone asks, frowning at the nearest gurney. "Why not just destroy them all and start over?"

"Maybe they were hoping some would turn out okay," I reply absently, still staring at the door Jackson disappeared through. "Like when you burn a tray of cookies but you let them cool and hope that maybe one or two are still"—I hesitate as I realize how inappropriate the analogy is—"edible."

"That's disgusting," Luka says.

"Yeah." I glance back at the closed door. Maybe I should do what Jackson said and wait here, but the way I see it, I'm in this nightmare through no choice of my own. I can curl up and let it happen to me, or I can do as Jackson suggested when we were alone in the tunnels: I can grab hold and steer it. If information is power, I need to find out everything I can, which includes what's behind that door.

I take a step forward but find my way blocked by Luka's arm. "Miki," he warns. There's a boatload of worry in the way he says my name, and that only makes me all the more certain that I need to see what Jackson's hiding in there.

"Do you know what he's doing?"

Luka and Tyrone exchange a look, which could mean either that they know or that they don't want to know.

But I do. I duck under Luka's arm and sprint to the door, pull it open, and freeze. The room's the size of a large closet. It's a lot colder than the bigger room behind me. My breath puffs little white clouds. There's a single gurney in here, and a lone girl. She doesn't look like the ones outside. She's dark where they were fair, and she looks smaller, shorter, though I can't be certain since she's flat on her back. Hard to tell with her skin so pale and her eyes closed, but she looks older than the girls in the other room.

Jackson lifts his head. His fingers are clamped around the wires leading to her neck. His expression gives nothing away, but I don't think he's surprised to see me.

"You ever listen?"

I shake my head. "I'm more of a see-for-myself, think-for-myself kind of girl."

My thoughts spin, tumbling one over the next. Why did he need to shut the door? Why is this girl isolated from the others? What doesn't he want me to see?

And then the questions don't matter because I see it. Her belly button. "She's not a shell. She's a person," I whisper.

"She's an original donor," Jackson says, his tone flat.

"What does that mean? That they'll use her to make an

army like that?" I gesture toward the door behind me and the rows of shells beyond.

"Yes."

"But the clones out there are from a different donor. . . ."

"They harvest genetic material and distribute it to growth labs all over the world." He looks down at the body in front of him. "They're still harvesting this one. They'll keep her body alive until they've taken what they need, then ship out samples and terminate her."

"So you're just going to do the job for them and kill her? You can't. Jackson, she's not like the others. She wasn't—" I make a futile gesture, at a loss for words. "She wasn't grown like them. She's *human*."

"I'm not killing her. She's already dead," Jackson says.

I stare at the machines, the tubes and wires. "How do you know? She could still have a chance! She could—"

He pulls out his deadly black knife.

"No!" I lurch forward and clamp both hands around his wrist.

Tendons tighten beneath my fingers. He pulls away. His knife slashes down . . . around . . .

The top of her skull falls away. There are bloodstains inside her skull, but no brain. There's no brain. They took her brain. I shiver and wrap my arms around myself.

"Why would they do that? Why would they take her brain?"

I think he isn't going to answer me, and when he does, I wish he hadn't.

"It's a delicacy." His tone is flat.

I stare at him openmouthed.

"They need her body, but they don't need her brain for their purposes. So they took it."

I press the back of my hand against my mouth, trying to hold back a howl of fear and revulsion and horror.

"She's already dead," Jackson says again, softer this time. He lifts his head. I desperately want to see his eyes, to know what emotions are mirrored there, to connect with him in our common humanity. But all I see is myself, pale and shaken, reflected in the lenses of his sunglasses. And suddenly it's all too much.

Without a word, I reach up and rip the shades off. My gaze locks on his.

He stares back at me, his inhuman gray eyes beautiful and deadly and mercury bright.

CHAPTER**SIXTEEN**

I RESPAWN WITH AS MUCH GRACE AND ELEGANCE AS A PLANE crash. I'm on my driveway, facing my open front door, grocery bag in my hand, as though only two seconds, not almost two days, have passed.

The grocery bag's handle slides down my palm, then along my fingers, impossibly slowly, just as it did before I got pulled. The world tips and tilts, and I flail for balance.

My head jerks up. My gaze collides with Luka's. His eyes are wide and . . . brown.

I think of Jackson. His eyes. His beautiful, terrifying eyes. Confusion and panic swarm through my thoughts, spawning questions like maggots. But Jackson's not here, and Luka isn't the right person to ask.

The bag takes an eternity to fall to the ground, sending

cans rolling in all directions. But they're slow, too slow. I look up and see my dad coming out of the house, moving like he's walking chest deep through a swimming pool, his expression taking forever to shift into surprise. The only things moving at regular speed are Luka and me.

There's a throbbing behind my eyes and pressure in the joints of my jaw, then my ears pop and—as Luka said last time we respawned in real life—*bam,* we're back. The world snaps into gear and Dad's beside me, brow furrowed, hand extended.

Dropping to my knees, I reach for the rolling cans, glad for the excuse to avoid my father's eyes. I don't want to talk to him. Not right now. I can barely keep it together. The shells. The dead human girl. The machines.

Jackson's eyes. A chill slithers along my spine. Jackson's inhuman, mercury-bright eyes.

"Miki?" Dad says, and his feet are right there, beside me where I kneel by the fallen cans. I force myself to keep my head down. My hand is shaking. I grab a can and focus on that, only that, willing my dad not to notice my anxiety.

"Must be my day for clumsy," I mutter, relieved when the words come out fairly steady.

From the corner of my eye, I see Luka set his bag down inside the front door and turn to watch me, his expression neutral. He's better at the reacclimation thing than I am. No surprise. He's had more practice. Even so, he leans one hip against the porch rail like he could use the support.

Does he know about Jackson? *Has* he seen his eyes?

204

I suspect the answer to both questions is no. I can't believe Jackson let *me* see them, and I have no doubt that he did let me. He could have stopped me from pulling his glasses off. He could have caught my wrists or turned his head, and the fact that he didn't means he wanted me to see. Why? *Why?* I didn't get a chance to ask. He ripped out the wires and tubes, and we made the jump while I was still gasping in shock, and I think that he planned that, too. Maybe I'm giving him too much credit, but I really believe what he said about steering his nightmare. I think he's a master at it.

And even if I had managed to get my questions out before we got pulled, I'm skeptical he would have offered answers. He's the king of evasion, telling me only the tidbits he wants me to know.

At least now I know why he's always wearing shades, and the bizarre thing is, I'm shocked but not shocked. As I think about it, it's like somewhere deep down, I knew exactly what I'd see. Didn't he keep warning me that he isn't a good guy?

A can rolls away, toward the grass, and I crawl after it. To my horror, Dad gets there first and squats down. His eyes meet mine as he lifts the can. "It's okay," he whispers. "He's just a boy. Just be yourself. It'll be fine."

I stare at him, my brain struggling to catch up to his words. Then I get it. He thinks my weird, clumsy behavior is because Luka's standing on my porch. Carly was so excited because she thought I was crushing on Luka. Now

Dad has that same hopeful/pleased expression. Like he thinks that being interested in a boy will make me normal again. I bite my cheek to keep from laughing because I have a feeling that if I start, I won't be able to stop, and it won't be pretty.

When I nod, Dad offers a reassuring smile, then hands me the can, straightens, and says, "I'll let you two finish the groceries. I have some work to do." And off he goes.

As soon as the groceries are put away, I manage to get Luka out of the house without another Dad moment.

"You okay?" Luka asks.

I try to hold it back. I fail. I tip my head back and laugh. It's the sort of laugh that makes other people cringe and look away. I know I'm at the very edge, but I can't seem to pull myself back.

"Look at me, Miki." Luka takes my hand in his and weaves our fingers together, and that's enough—just barely enough—to steady me and keep me sane. With a last few weepy giggles, I get myself under control.

"Well, that was embarrassing," I mutter, purposely ignoring his directive and looking anywhere but at him.

Wiping the tears from my eyes with the back of my free hand, I walk down the driveway to the end. Luka circles me so we end up facing each other, my back to the house, his to the street. He's still holding my hand and I slowly pull free, wanting to keep it together all on my own. I can't start depending on anyone else. It's me and only me. I need to remember that.

"The first few times I got pulled—" Luka's eyes slide from mine, and he turns his head and looks off down the street, his jaw clenched tight. "The first few times I got pulled, I was a mess when I came back. I stood under a hot shower for hours, shaking and"—he pauses—"crying. There was no one to talk to, no one to help me understand. I'm sorry. I shouldn't have done that to you, shouldn't have made you go through it alone."

I don't remind him that I wasn't completely alone, that when I was freaking out over Richelle, Jackson was there for me. At the moment, I'm not even sure how I feel about that, about him. One minute I think we have some sort of connection, that he cares about me. The next, I see that his eyes are Drau gray, and I'm left thinking he's my enemy. I open my mouth. I almost blurt out what I saw. Instead, I say, "It's okay. You were just following the rules."

He offers me a lopsided Luka smile. "Rules are made to be broken, right? Anyway, I want you to know, I'm here. You can talk to me. I'll answer as best I can."

"Will you?"

"I just said so."

"Okay. Then I do have a few questions." More than a few, but only one is digging at me like a dentist doing a root canal. "Have you ever seen Jackson without his glasses?"

His brows shoot up. "Wow. Okay. Wasn't expecting that as your first question. Is there a particular reason you want to know?"

I cross my arms and hug myself. Is Jackson one of

them? Is he some sort of spy? Worse . . . is he a shell? Is he an alien inside a human form? I should come right out and tell Luka what I saw, but that feels like a betrayal. I don't want to stab Jackson in the back; I just want to make sure that he isn't going to stab me first. "You said you'd give me answers, not offer questions for my questions."

Luka scrapes his fingers back through his dark hair and frowns. "Okay. I did say that. No, I've never seen him without the shades."

More questions leap to the tip of my tongue. *Didn't you ever wonder about them? Didn't you ever ask him why he wears them?* But asking Luka will only make him suspicious, and I'm not ready to divulge Jackson's secret, not until I have the chance to stand face-to-face and demand answers from *him*. So I head in a different direction. "You've seen a room like that with all those . . . people . . . before. In Arizona."

"It was smaller. Not as many—" He looks around as though deciding if it's safe to talk. "Not as many rows of . . . people. But pretty much the same."

"Those—" I break off and consider my words. "Those girls—can we call them shells?"

"I guess." He looks around again. "Yeah, I guess we can."

"Did you know them? Did they look familiar?"

He frowns again and shakes his head. "No, why?"

"I don't know. Something about them nagged at me." He just stares at me, waiting for more. I'm frustrated because I don't have anything more, just a weird feeling that I'm missing something important. "Did you notice that they all looked the same?"

Luka nods. "Same original donor."

That's what Jackson called the dead girl in the cold room. "But the shells in Arizona came from a different donor?"

"Yeah." He sounds upset. I don't blame him. The Drau stole girls, killed them by taking their brains, kept their bodies alive with machines, and used their DNA to grow an army of mindless clones, also kept alive by machines. Clones who weren't quite right and ended up rotting from the inside out. I'd say that's reason to be upset.

"Do they use male original donors? Do they create male shells?" The questions come out in a rush.

Luka thinks about that. "I don't know. I've only ever seen females. But I've only ever seen two places like this, so that isn't much to go on."

The relief I'd like to feel doesn't come. Just because Luka hasn't seen a male shell doesn't mean they don't exist. I'm quiet for a second.

"Luka, have you ever heard them speak?"

He knows I'm asking about the Drau. His brows draw together in a frown. "I don't think so. I've heard them"— he cuts me a glance through his lashes—"I've, um, heard them scream. At the end, if you know what I mean. But not speak. I think they have this telepathy thing. . . ."

Unease crawls through me. "Do *we*? I mean, do you have a telepathy thing? Have you ever heard someone in your head?"

He's still frowning. Slowly, he shakes his head. "No. Why?"

I shrug, trying to look casual. "Jackson said something about wanting to question one of the Drau. I was wondering how he would do that." Through some sort of telepathy? Because he's one of them? The thought is like liquid nitrogen in my soul. I don't want Jackson to be one of the bad guys.

I can see that Luka's about to ask me something. I don't give him the chance because I'm not sure I want to offer answers.

"I appreciate that you're answering my questions, Luka. The thing is, I'd like to know why."

He looks confused. "You asked me to."

"But I asked before, too, and you refused. What's changed?"

"I told you, I'm sorry I left you alone before. That I didn't tell you stuff."

"I know. And I'm okay with that." Sort of. I'm not so good at the forgiveness thing. "But why are you telling me stuff now?"

Now he looks embarrassed. He shrugs. "Jackson told you stuff, and he didn't die a slow and painful death. Or a quick and painless one. So I figure that it's okay to talk, so long as we're careful."

"Okay, that makes sense." I think about my next words and choose them with care. "But I agree that we still need to be careful. I think that there really is a danger if we talk about stuff here in the real world. Maybe there are shells living right next door to us." My gaze slides along the street, then back to Luka. "After what I saw today, I think the rules really are there for a reason."

"I never thought they weren't."

A cool breeze dances across my skin. Except, there's no breeze; it's a hot, sunny, sticky day. Again, I look up the street, then down. There's no one else around. Just to be sure, I recheck, letting my gaze slide along the porches of the houses closest to us.

"Have you ever seen one—not a shell . . . a real one— here in the real world?"

Luka looks as horrified by that possibility as I feel. "No." He shakes his head. "That would be . . ."

"Yeah, it would be. I feel like I'm in a horror movie," I blurt out.

"Or a nightmare," Luka says.

Grab hold and steer the nightmare. Maybe that's exactly what Jackson's doing. Maybe he's steering all of us precisely where he wants us, like pieces on a chessboard or players in a game.

"Do you know what Jackson was doing just before we made the jump back to reality?"

"When you two were alone in that room? I think I do. And if I'm right, he does it so the rest of us won't have to."

So we won't have to terminate a body that was once human. I shudder.

"She was already dead," I say, wanting Luka to know

that Jackson didn't kill a person. "She wasn't alive. They took—" I swallow, then huff out a sharp breath. "They took her brain. Because it's a delicacy for them."

Luka's appalled expression mirrors my feelings precisely.

"You can do this," he says softly. "I've been doing it for a year, and I'm okay. This time was a bit weird because we got pulled again so fast, but usually there's at least a couple of weeks between missions."

"Who sends us on those missions?" My voice is equally soft. "Who sends the weapons? Who keeps score?"

Luka just shakes his head, saying nothing, because there's nothing for him to say. He doesn't know. I suspected that before I ever asked. Then he shrugs. "Jackson says it's—"

"—decided by committee."

We stand facing each other on the driveway, separated by about three feet. Separated by a million miles. I want to ask him so many things. He won't have the answers, not all of them. There's only one person who has those, and I don't know when he'll show up again.

"Luka, I want Jackson's number."

He hesitates, his hands clenching at his sides. "Why?"

"You have it," I point out instead of answering his question.

"Because he gave it to me. If he didn't give it to you, I'm not sure it's okay if I do."

Now it's my turn to study him, and I get the impression

that Luka's worries have nothing to do with the game and everything to do with the kind of person he is. "You don't mean *okay* because of the game. You mean *okay* because you don't want to mess with his privacy."

"Well . . . yeah . . . Just like I wouldn't give him your number without checking with you first."

"What about my address?"

Luka's eyes widen. "No! Never. Not without asking."

"So you never gave him my address when you told him you were planning to break the rules and talk to me?"

"No."

"Then how come he showed up on my driveway just in time for my run?"

Luka opens his mouth, closes it, then says, "I don't know."

"It's okay, Luka. There's probably a simple explanation." Like Jackson followed me home after the first mission. Or he has secret methods of getting info. Or he's a hacker. Or a stalker—actually that one I'm sure of. He already admitted he was watching my house. Whatever. I'm sure now that I won't get answers from Luka, because he doesn't have them.

On impulse I reach over and hug him. It's sort of nice and sort of awkward, and it feels pretty much like hugging Carly except Luka's taller and broader and his chest is hard and leanly muscled. It feels safe and pleasant.

It doesn't feel anything like hugging Jackson.

Luka pats my back in awkward little spurts, and then

he clears his throat and steps back. "So, uh, see you tomorrow," he says, even though he obviously wants to say something else.

"Wait, just one more question. If none of us are supposed to have contact outside the game, why did Jackson give you his number?"

"I never said we couldn't have contact outside. Just that we couldn't talk about it outside."

"Right." I manage to drum up a smile. "Guess we're all breaking all the rules now."

"Guess so." He backs up a few feet, still watching me, and raises a hand in an easy wave. "Call me if you need me, okay?"

"Okay."

And that's that. I watch until he turns the corner and disappears. Even then, I don't go inside. I just stand on the driveway staring at nothing, letting the hot sun warm my back.

CHAPTER SEVENTEEN

IT TAKES EFFORT TO FOCUS ON THE FACT THAT BETWEEN THE long trek through the tunnels, the battles, and sleeping in Jackson's arms, I've been gone for nearly two days, but in my world, my real world, only moments have passed. My *real world*. Is this it? Or are the missions my reality now? Thinking about it makes my stomach roll.

Well, if this is my real world, I have stuff here to deal with, too: friends, Dad, homework, laundry. It's hard to get my head around that. My focus for two days has been on staying alive, but Carly's furious with me for some reason, and for her it's only been about twenty minutes since she and Sarah drove away. It feels weird worrying about her issues when there are things so much bigger weighing on my thoughts, but in this world, the one where my life isn't at risk every second, her issues *are* big.

I tiptoe into the house, trying not to alert Dad to my presence. The last thing I want right now is a father-daughter chat about boys. I head up to my room, retrieve my phone, and call Carly. It shoots to voice mail. I pull the phone from my ear and stare at it. Voice mail? Since when does Carly not pick up every single call?

I dial again. This time, she picks up. "Having a nice day?" she asks. Not a loaded question, so why does it feel like one?

"Peachy," I say, my patience paper thin. Whatever's eating her is nothing compared to what I'm trying to deal with. I swallow, trying to bury that thought. I feel selfish for thinking it. It isn't Carly's fault that I can't tell her what's going on with me, and if I don't tell her, then she has no way to know. I keep my tone light, and ask, "What's with you?"

"Oh, I don't know." She falls silent, and I'm left wondering if anything is going to be simple today. Even putting groceries away felt like I was walking through a minefield.

After a few seconds, she says, "Anything you want to tell me about your day, Miki?"

It hits me then. She must think I had plans with Luka and didn't tell her about it. Of course. If she had plans with a boy, she'd talk my ear off before, after, and possibly even during the event. She's hurt that I didn't share, and I feel lousy about that. But she has it all wrong.

"I didn't have plans with Luka. I would have told you if

I did," I say, aiming for casual. "He dropped by unexpectedly while I was out running. He waited for me till I got back."

"Uh-huh." There's still an off edge to her tone. "And?"

Okay. She must think I have more to tell her than I do.

"I introduced him to Dad, who wasn't too embarrassing. He made himself scarce while we carried in the groceries and put them away."

"And?" She keeps asking that like she's waiting for me to say something specific. Something monumental.

"There is no *and*. That's all, the whole story. Not very exciting, I know. We talked for a few minutes on the driveway. Then he took off."

"And that's it?"

"That's it."

"You're sure?"

"Yes."

"Positive?" She sounds angry now.

"What's with you?" I ask again, probably sounding a little angry myself.

"Luka deserves better than you sneaking around behind his back!"

"What? I'm not sneaking—I'm not— What?" If I didn't know better, I'd say that Carly sounds jealous. Or delusional.

"I saw you," she says, the words low and ugly and laced with accusation.

My first thought is that she saw me get pulled. Saw me

217

fighting. Saw me on the mission. But that's impossible. We weren't here, and there's no way she was there. So something else is giving her a wedgie. "Carly, what exactly do you think you saw?"

"I saw you holding hands with Luka. On the driveway, when Sarah and I drove up."

She's talking about the moments before we got pulled. I run through them in my thoughts, but don't see what her problem is.

"I wasn't holding hands with him. And I don't get why you're so pissed. Aren't you the one who's pushing me to call him? Now you're mad that we were carrying groceries together?" In a snap, I get it. I remember all the things Carly's said about Luka since the first day of school. She's the one who freaked and couldn't stop talking about how much he'd changed in the year he was away. How tall he is. How much he's filled out. She's always heading for our spot when he's on the track. But I never really thought about it because we've been hanging out under the giant oak since freshman year.

Carly crushing on Luka? No, that can't be right. She would have said. I close my eyes and pinch the bridge of my nose. I am so not in the frame of mind for this right now. "We weren't holding hands, Carly. We reached for the grocery bag at the same time. The story's a lot less interesting when you don't add anything that didn't actually happen."

"Yeah?" Carly snarls. "So let's talk about what definitely *did* happen. You were with Luka right after you finished making out with Aviator Guy. Since when are you such a skank?"

"Aviator Guy?" And did my best friend just call me a skank?

"The park?" Carly's practically yelling now. "Sarah lives at the corner? I saw you making out with him. I know it was him even though he was wearing different glasses. And I don't know what hurts more, the fact that you lied to me about it, or the fact that I called first dibs on him and you didn't even care." Carly's crying. I can hear it in her voice.

"Carly, no, you've got this wrong. I wasn't— I didn't—"

"What's his name?" Carly clips out. "How do you know him? You never said you knew him when we were talking about him after school on Friday. What else are you lying to me about?"

"I don't know him. I mean, I didn't know him, not when you were talking about him on Friday." I'm breathing too fast, and even though what I'm saying is the truth, I know it doesn't sound like it. "I went running. He happened to be running the same way. We ran together."

"You don't run on Sundays!"

"Well, I ran this Sunday." Today. A couple of hours ago. Was it really only a couple of hours ago? I feel like I've lived a lifetime since Jackson ran with me to the park.

"And ended up making out by the swings? With a guy you just met?"

"We weren't making out. He hugged me. I had a—" A

what? A *moment*, and I let a stranger hug me? No wonder Carly thinks I'm lying. "I had a rough minute where I was upset and he just hugged me. That's all."

Carly makes a strangled sound. "Save it for someone who wants to hear it," she says, and the line cuts off.

I stare at the phone. She hung up on me. Carly. The one person in my life who I could count on not to leave. She just left. Hung up and left. I feel sick.

Then I feel angry. She's my friend. My best friend. Carly's the peacemaker. She gives everyone the benefit of the doubt. Shouldn't she at least hear my side before putting me in front of the firing squad?

But that's just it. I can't tell her my side. I can't tell her anything. My secrets are driving a wedge between us.

All she knows is what she thinks she saw—an eyewitness account tainted by both insider knowledge and lack thereof. Anxiety sits like a lead bar on my chest, buzzing through my limbs and crushing me at the same time. I need to do something. I need to—

"Miki!" Dad yells up from downstairs. "I threw in a couple of loads. Can you fold the one in the dryer and transfer what's in the washer?"

Normally I'd groan, but right now I'm happy to do it. Anything to distract myself. Once I'm in the basement, I see that it's sheets and towels in the dryer. Folding them won't take long, and I need something that'll take forever. So I grab the first sheet and start ironing. Good busywork for my hands; I just wish it could keep my brain busy, too.

A while later, Dad comes down and stands there, watching me. "I was wondering what was taking you so long down here. What are you doing?"

"Ironing."

"The bedsheets? Who irons bedsheets?"

"Me."

"You've never ironed them before."

"I'm ironing them now," I say.

He stares at me for a long time, his expression bewildered, and then he leaves. I slam the iron down hard and rub it back and forth on the sheet, which is a soft, pearly gray, just a little lighter than Jackson's eyes.

That night, I do something I haven't done in years. I climb out my window and sit on the flat roof of the overhang that covers the front porch, my back against the bricks below my window. Mom and I used to do this when I was little, sit out here on warm, clear nights. Mom always kept a solid grip on the back of my shirt even though there really was no chance that I'd fall.

We'd stare out at the stars and she'd try and pick out the constellations. *I think that one's Ursa Major,* she'd say. Or, *I think that one's Cassiopeia.* Sometimes she'd be right. Sometimes she'd be wrong. It didn't really matter. I just liked looking at the stars with her.

There isn't much of a moon tonight, just a thin crescent hanging on a velvet night sky. Compared to the tunnels I spent the last two days in, I wouldn't call it dark. There's too much ambient light from the neighbors' houses and the streetlamps and the glow from downtown that bounces up and back down, leaving everything tinged a little bright.

I stare at the stars, but the truth is, I'm not really looking at them. I'm waiting for the prickle that will tell me he's there, standing on my street, watching me.

It doesn't come.

He doesn't come.

My disappointment is bitter and chalky, like I chewed an aspirin.

It's past midnight when I climb back inside and pull my window shut. The glass reflects my own face back at me.

I stare, something gnawing at the edges of my thoughts, and in my mind's eye, I see a different face. A face that repeats over and over again. Smooth expression. Light brown hair. High cheekbones. Familiar, but not.

I feel like someone's punched me in the gut.

The girls lying on the gurneys, the shells, I know why their faces seemed familiar.

They looked like feminine versions of Jackson Tate.

Monday morning my run is rough. My head's not in it and my body can't seem to find its rhythm. I aim for the rush, but it never comes. I had a lousy night's sleep, and it doesn't help that the last time I ran, it was with Jackson. As my feet hit the pavement, chasing the dawn, a million thoughts buzz around in my brain like wasps: Jackson's eyes; the shells who looked like him; the people in the other lobbies that only he and I can see. The fact that he's a telepath who spoke to me inside my head and, according to Luka, so are the Drau.

Lots of questions, no answers.

The day doesn't get better from there. In English, Carly doesn't speak to me, but sends me the most heartfelt accusatory looks. It's the first time that I'm actually glad we only have one class together because her you-have-mortally-injured-me glances are more than I could bear for an entire day. I didn't do anything wrong. So why do I feel like I did?

All my other friends shoot furtive looks my way, trying not to take sides and blatantly dying to ask what's going on.

"See you at lunch, Miki," Kelley says after the bell goes. Her expression is both hopeful and wary, like she thinks lunch in the caf will either cause a massive implosion or fix the mess.

I shake my head. "I promised Maylene that I'd tutor her at lunch for the Spanish quiz. I'm meeting her in the library."

"Oh, okay. See you later, then." I think she sounds relieved. Maybe she figured the implosion was the more likely of the two options.

Dee offers a wave, and Carly leaves with a last soulful glance.

After school, I wait at Luka's locker. He never shows, but it isn't until I've wasted almost half an hour that I remember he has track. I head for our spot under the giant oak, thinking maybe I'll corner Carly and just try to talk to her, but no one's there. I'm batting a big, fat zero.

Then I head to the bookstore. Usually Carly and I go together so I can pick up the latest manga and she can grab a few fashion and scrapbooking magazines. We used to scrapbook together, but ever since Mom died, I can't bear to put those memories on pages with pretty decorations. I walk in feeling melancholy. It's not like I've never been to a bookstore alone, but with the huge wall between Carly and me right now, I feel like I'm missing a piece of myself as I walk through the front door. Disappointment surges when I check the shelf and find only older editions of my favorite manga.

"Excuse me," I say to the girl at the counter. "Do you have the latest edition of *Bleach*?"

"Sold out," she says after she checks the computer. "I can order it for you."

"Thanks," I say, disappointment tugging at me. I was hoping the new book would be the highlight of my not-so-great day.

I get home to realize it was garbage day, my week to carry out the bag, and I forgot. Dad will not be pleased. I'm not pleased. I never forget things, and the fact that I did leaves me feeling morose and edgy. I try to tell myself it's only garbage, that it isn't the end of the world, that I didn't fail at something monumental.

I freeze, thinking about the way I feel at the moment. It's like the gray fog is hanging on my limbs, dragging them down, and at the edge of my thoughts is the worry that I'm failing, that I'm not good enough, that I'm not in control. This is the worst it's been in a long time, bad enough that I revert to some positive self-talk, a staple in the arsenal Dr. Andrews helped me build. This day just keeps getting better.

With a sigh, I trudge up the driveway. Mrs. Gertner steps out of the house next door. "Miki," she says, beaming at me.

"Hi, Mrs. Gertner. How are you?" Mistake. Big mistake. I know it the second the open-ended question leaves my mouth. But it's too late. It's out there now.

"Not so good," she says. "I haven't been able to sit properly for a week. That doctor said I'd be fine right away. But he's wrong. I did everything he said. I sat in an Epsom salts bath and I put my medicine on like he told me. But it's terrible. Just terrible."

I'm not sure what she's talking about, but I know I don't want to ask. Then my attention falters. There it is, that weird prickling sensation that tells me I'm being watched. I try to look sympathetic as I nod at Mrs. Gertner while surreptitiously scanning the street.

Mrs. Gertner asks me a question, but I don't hear the words. I just nod at her and make an agreeable noise and she's off and running again.

I'm dying to turn and check behind me, almost certain he's standing there watching me. But Mrs. Gertner just keeps on going. For the next half an hour, she gives me minute details of her hemorrhoid surgery, putting the rotting cherry on top of my rancid ice-cream sundae of a day.

I feel like I'm going to jump out of my skin. But I still remember when I was little and Mrs. Gertner used to come out with cookies for Carly and me when we were playing out front. Every time I lost a tooth, she gave me a dollar. Every birthday until I was twelve, she gave me a little present wrapped in pretty paper with a big bow. So I don't have the heart to make some excuse and duck away. Instead, I listen to every gory detail. The only thing that saves me is when her watch beeps, telling her it's time for her medication.

Grabbing my one shining chance, I mumble, "Hope you feel better soon," and bolt. On my front porch, I pull back in the shadows and take my time looking up and down the street. The certainty that I'm being watched sinks its tiny hooks into me, but no matter how hard I try, I can't see who's doing the watching.

What if it's not Jackson? What if it's a Drau? A shell?

For a second, I have this horrific thought that Mrs. Gertner's a shell. And the girl at the bookstore. Maylene. Any of the kids or even the teachers at school. Any of the neighbors on my street. The postman. The—

They're not. I'm being ridiculous. I need to keep a grip because if I don't, I won't survive this. And I mean to survive. It's as simple as that.

I ditch my shoes, drop my bag in my room, but I'm too edgy to sit. Instead, I run the vacuum through the house, taking my time, following my pattern, doing each room in small, rectangular sections.

"Making chicken casserole tonight," Dad says when he gets home. It's his night to cook. Maybe he reads the hesitation on my face, because he offers a sarcastic smile. "Low-fat cheese, lots of broccoli, diced tomatoes, and mushrooms."

"Sounds great." It's still not the healthiest thing ever, but he's trying.

After I finish vacuuming, I throw together a salad to go along with the casserole. Dinner's actually not half bad. We talk about a couple of movie trailers that interest us both, and I start to relax, the edge of my anxiety dulling. At least until Dad gets done talking about the trailers and starts on a new topic.

"So, that boy . . . Luka, right?" Dad says. "You want to talk about him?"

I fork in a mouthful of food to avoid saying anything. But Dad just keeps looking at me as I chew and swallow, and I finally say, "He's just a guy I know from school."

"Do you, um . . ." Dad carefully sets his fork down on his plate. Then he reaches for his water glass and moves it a quarter inch to the right. He clears his throat. He moves his water glass a quarter inch to the left.

I shovel in another forkful of casserole. If my mouth's full, I won't have to speak.

"I was about your age when I . . . Well, there was this girl. She was a couple of years older, and she had these—"

I hold up my hand, palm forward. "Don't do it, Dad.

Once you say it, you can never unsay it." No matter how much I might wish he could.

He purses his lips and nods. "Did you, um . . . Did Mom ever . . . I mean, do you have classes about, uh, health . . . in school? I think you're too young to . . ."

Oh no. No, no, no. My day has been bad, but this is worse.

I lift my hands and dip my head down. "Yep. School. Classes. Health classes. Got it covered."

"Well, there are things you need to watch out for. Diseases and—"

"Wow, I forgot to tell you I saw Mrs. Gertner today on the driveway. She told me all about her hemorrhoid surgery. Fascinating stuff."

Dad stares at me. His mouth twitches. "Preferable to what I'm trying to talk to you about?"

"Pretty much."

He lifts his head and stares straight into my eyes. I want to crawl under the table and stay there. He takes a deep breath. "I think you should wait before you . . ." He gives a decisive nod. "I think you should wait until you're fifty."

"Fifty." I sigh. "Dad, we do not need to talk about this. I know the basics."

His expression darkens.

"Not because I have any experience," I hasten to reassure him. I don't. Not really. When other girls were starting to date, I was mourning. Oh, I played spin the bottle in sixth grade. Didn't everyone? I still remember my first

French kiss. I spun. The bottle pointed to Roland Davis. I puckered up and put my lips to his and he unexpectedly put his fat tongue in my mouth. I squawked like a chicken and almost hurled. Carly laughed till she cried, and in the end, I laughed too. Thinking back on it, I feel sort of sorry for Roland. I don't think he laughed.

I got to the hand-holding stage and a few okay kisses with Sam Pitt when we went steady for a month in eighth grade. And that's the sum total of my personal experience.

Except for Jackson, who's never kissed me, but who's held me in his arms and made me wish he'd kiss me.

The second that thought surfaces, I squish it like a bug. Thinking like that will only win me trouble and heartbreak. Jackson Tate is as dangerous as they come, and I'm more of a careful sort of girl.

"Just the basic textbook concepts, okay?" I add when Dad keeps staring at me.

He nods and starts eating again.

"So, how about this warm weather?" I ask, and launch into a pretty one-sided discussion of the sun and blue sky. Every once in a while, Dad adds a word or two, but I can see he's still thinking about our last topic. After a few minutes, I jump up and clear the plates and have a genuine reason to turn my back to him as I stack the washer and scrub the pots. By the time I'm done, he's settled in front of the TV and I can escape to my room.

"Going up to do homework," I mumble.

I close the door behind me, sink back against it, and

breathe a sigh of relief. The day's almost done. Tomorrow has to be better. Tears sting my eyes at the thought. How many times have I told myself that? How many times have I forced myself out of bed in the morning, trying to believe that this is the day everything will be fine?

Hasn't happened yet. Well, except for moments in the game. If I'm honest, there are times that I do feel normal there. And how messed up is that? The only time I feel really okay is when I'm in an alternate reality fighting aliens. That's just wrong on any level.

Except, maybe it isn't. Maybe I feel like I'm okay in the game because I'm doing something bigger than me. My sadness, my loss, they seem small compared to an alien invasion. Jackson seems to think we're saving the world. Four teenagers, saving the world. I roll my eyes. Right.

I drag on an old T-shirt and flannels and haul out my math homework. I wish I could talk to Jackson. I wonder if he's doing it on purpose, avoiding me so he doesn't have to answer questions.

I laugh out loud. Of course he's doing it on purpose. He knows where I live. He knows when I run. All he'd have had to do was show up and run with me this morning. We could have talked. He could have explained. The fact that he hasn't done that tells me all I need to know.

Turning my attention to my math homework, I try to get it done. It takes forever because my concentration isn't the best. I'm tired. No surprise there. I didn't sleep well last night. I dreamed of Jackson's eyes and the shells and the dead girl that Jackson killed, even though she was already dead. Just trying to get my head around that makes me dizzy. I'm exhausted, and by ten o'clock, I'm fighting to keep my eyes open. I'm in the place between awake and asleep when I hear a weird tapping. A couple of minutes later, there it is again, a light tapping from . . . there. The window.

A shiver chases up my spine.

And the sound comes again.

Wary, I cross to the window and peer out. My heart slams hard against my ribs.

Dark clothes, dark shades, pale hair gleaming in the moonlight, Jackson Tate's outside my window, sitting cross-legged on the porch roof.

CHAPTER **EIGHTEEN**

I SHOVE THE WINDOW OPEN. "WHAT ARE YOU DOING?" I WHISPER the words too fast, stunned and alarmed and secretly thrilled that he's here.

"Visiting."

"Now?" I shake my head. "How did you get up here?"

"Climbed."

I stare at him, at a loss. Should I go out to him? Ask him to come in to me? I look frantically up and down the street to make certain no neighbors are out there watching. I don't see anyone, not right now, but that doesn't mean someone won't come out any second.

"Get in here," I order in a whisper as I step back from the window. "Take off your shoes. And be quiet."

The next thing I know, Jackson's inside my bedroom,

less than a foot away from me. I leave the window open just in case he needs to make a quick exit, but pull the curtain halfway to shield him from street view.

"My shoes?" He looks baffled.

"No shoes in the house. My mom had this thing about that."

"How about we pretend this is the front hall and I just stay in this spot and not move? Okay if I keep my shoes on then? I don't love the idea of having to dive out your window barefoot if your dad comes in."

The image of that makes me feel ill. I can just picture Jackson diving out the window, his shoes staying behind like beacons of my transgression. "Fine. Keep them on. But don't move."

"You sure? I'll take them off if it's a big deal." He sounds both amused and sincere.

I strain my ears, trying to hear if the TV's still on downstairs. If not, it means Dad's already gone to bed. I can't hear anything, but what if he's up here and not yet asleep?

"Keep them on," I whisper. "I'm sure."

True to his word, Jackson stays rooted to the spot as he looks around, taking his time. My bookshelf is right beside him, and he runs the tips of his fingers along the spines of the books on my keeper shelf. They're eclectic, I admit it. Alcott's *Little Women*, *Ender's Game* by Orson Scott Card, *Frankenstein*, *The Giver*, *The Catcher in the Rye*, everything ever written by Christopher Moore, the complete works of Jane Austen, a scarred and well-loved set of Harry Potter, my mom's old dog-eared Stephen King titles, *The Last Wish* and *Blood of Elves* by Andrzej Sapkowski.

He stops when he gets to those and murmurs, "I haven't read these. But the game rocks."

"The graphics kick ass," I agree, then ask, "But you've read the others?"

"Some of them."

I try to picture him engrossed in *Little Women*.

His fingers dip to the next shelf, where I keep my manga. "You read *Bleach*."

I nod. "It's one of my favorites."

"You don't have the latest issue."

"They were sold out."

He turns away from the books, back toward me, but he doesn't say anything. I can't figure out how I feel at the moment. Thrilled that he's here. Afraid that Dad will find him. Stunned that he came. And a little weirded out that our conversation so far has been too normal. But the thing I notice most is how bright and true those emotions are. It's like he's a fresh breeze that blew in and chased the fog away.

Our conversation started out in whispers, but it's increased in volume until we're speaking in a normal tone, and that's dangerous. I drop back to a whisper. "What are you doing here?"

"I'll answer five questions, then I need to go," he says, equally low.

"You came just to answer my questions?"

"Yes. And to see you."

Wow. Okay. I have no idea what to say to that. So I say the wrong thing. "Why didn't you come last night? Or this morning to run with me? I spent the whole day freaking about stuff."

"Couldn't last night. Or this morning. I was out of town until about twenty minutes ago." He smiles a little. "And that counts as the first question."

I roll my eyes. "No, it most certainly does not." I take a breath and just lay it out there. "What are you? Are you Drau? Are you a shell?" My heart's pounding so hard it feels like it's going to burst out of my chest.

"I'm a guy, last time I checked." His smile curls up on one side. "Wanna check for yourself?"

The question is so un-Jackson-like that it throws me for a loop. Then I feel my cheeks heat, which freaks me out because I'm not the blushing type.

He laughs softly and continues, "No, I am not Drau. No, I am not a shell."

"How do I know that's true? Why should I trust you?"

For a long minute, he just stands there. Then he grabs the hem of his T-shirt and drags it up. My jaw goes slack and all I can do is stare. His jeans hang low on his hips, baring about an inch of the waistband of his boxers, and above that, there's smooth skin and ridged muscle, accented by the light leaking through my window. He looks like an underwear ad in a magazine. One that's been Photoshopped to make it better.

"What are you doing?" I whisper frantically, and shoot a wild look at the door. I'd die if Dad walked in right now.

I grab his shirt and try to tug it down. My fingers brush his skin, making the muscles of his stomach jump beneath my touch. My fingertips tingle, and I feel like I've been hit with an electric shock. Dropping my hands, I practically leap away.

"Proving I'm not a shell," he answers.

"What—" Then I get it. In the middle of all that smooth gold skin and lightly ridged muscle is a belly button, and below that, a thin line of light brown hair. Not looking there. Definitely not looking there. "Great. Thanks. Proved your point. Drop the shirt."

"You sure?" He's smiling. I can hear it. But I don't see it because I have my teeth sunk into my lower lip and my head tipped back so I'm staring at the ceiling.

"I'm decent," he says. "Shirt safely in place."

I look at him to find that he's telling the truth, about the shirt at least. I have a feeling he's never decent.

"Okay, so you're not a shell, and you claim you're not Drau, but your eyes . . . they're not like anyone else's eyes that I've ever seen. Except . . . theirs."

"Yes, my eyes are like theirs. No, they're not like anyone else's. And neither are yours."

I freeze. "What? Luka—" I cut myself off. Luka's eyes are the same indigo blue as mine only in the game, not in the real world. In this world, they're rich, chocolate brown. And Richelle . . . I think of her picture on the net. What color were her eyes? I can't remember, but I feel certain that they weren't the blue that I saw in the game.

"What color are Tyrone's eyes outside the game?" I ask.

Jackson shrugs. "Don't know. Not blue. And not Drau gray."

"Tons of people have blue eyes." A weak protest, because I know what he's going to say next even before he says it.

"Not like yours."

It's the truth. My eyes always make people stare the first time they meet me.

"Explain," I say, then add, "Please."

From the corner of my eye, I see him look around. He's evaluating the possibility that anyone might be listening. He leans over and pushes my window shut. "Remember I told you about our ancestors. About how they became part of humanity, hiding in plain sight. They had children and grandchildren. . . ."

"Yes."

"My eyes, and yours, are because we're rare progeny, ones with a stronger-than-normal strain of a particular set of alleles."

"Alleles are genes, right?"

"Forms of a gene. In this case, you have a stronger strain of nonhuman DNA."

"So Tyrone and Luka have alien genes, and you and I have alien supergenes?"

He opens his mouth, closes it, shrugs. "I guess you

could put it that way. The genetics of it don't really matter. What matters is the result. You're stronger, faster, more resilient than most people."

"I thought that was because of kendo and my running."

"In part, but that's not the whole of it. And you see things the others don't."

"By "the others" you mean Luka and Tyrone."

He nods.

"And the things I see . . . you mean the other sections of the lobby and the other people in those sections. Other . . . teams," I finish, even though I know he's always telling me we're not a team. Every man for himself. But when it comes down to it, he's more of a team player than any one of us. He's watched out for me. I feel like he watches out for all of us. "And you see them, too. The others."

"Yes."

"So tell me about those teams. Do we ever work with them? Do they know about us? Do—"

Jackson reaches for me and cups my cheeks with his palms. My questions die an abrupt death. His hands are warm against my skin, his palms callused where they meet his fingers. "I have to go," he says. "And that was more than five questions."

He leans a little closer.

"Wait," I whisper, frozen in place, heart pounding, half hoping, half dreading that he'll close the distance between us and touch his lips to mine. "You can't go."

"Yeah"—he smiles a little—"I can." His thumb sweeps

across my lower lip. My breath locks in my throat. "I have to."

"Why did you come here tonight?" My voice sounds weird, tight and strangled.

"Because you needed some answers. Because it felt wrong to leave you hanging, thinking I was a Drau shell. Because despite the fact that it goes against everything I am and everything I need to be, I can't stand the thought of you here, alone, wondering and worrying."

"What do you mean? What do you need to be?"

"Now you're way past five questions," he says. "I'm sorry I couldn't come yesterday or earlier today, Miki. There really was somewhere I needed to be."

I want to see his eyes. I want to look at *him*, not his glasses when we speak. I reach up, but he catches my wrist and holds it.

"One more reason, probably the most important one," he murmurs. "I came because I wanted to see you." He lets go of my wrist and takes a step away. "I have to go."

"Wait, please, last question, I promise. Why did Richelle die?" I'm not asking the mechanics of it, and I know he knows that. I'm asking why he didn't save her, but I'm not cruel enough to phrase it that way.

"Richelle was the best at the game. She knew how to get in and get out. She knew that when her con started to go orange, she needed to drop back to defensive position and watch her own ass. She knew not to let it turn red." He pauses, and I wonder if he's remembering as I am the way he told me not to let my con turn red. "I can't be everywhere at once, Miki. I was watching your back and Tyrone's. Richelle made the choice to attack rather than defend, and I couldn't get to her fast enough. So she's dead."

His tone is completely flat, not a shred of emotion, and that makes what he's saying all the more heartbreaking. Whatever words he's used about Richelle's choices, he blames himself, and it's eating him alive.

Every man for himself. Except him. He thinks it's the best way to keep his team alive. I think he's wrong, but now's not the moment to tell him that.

"Jackson," I whisper, my heart breaking for him. Without thinking about it, I step close and flatten my palm on his chest, over his heart. I feel the steady drum of his heartbeat and the tension arcing through his body. I don't bother to tell him it isn't his fault. He won't believe me.

He grabs my wrist and turns my hand, then lowers his head and presses his lips to my palm. Electricity dances through me, making me gasp.

His lips move to the crease of my wrist.

I stand perfectly still, my blood hammering through my veins.

I want him to do that again. I want him to press his lips to my mouth. I want the rush of sensation to fill me. I want—

He lifts his head. He releases my wrist.

Then he pushes up my window and climbs out onto the roof of the porch, and before I can think of an argument to make him stay, he's over the side and gone. I try to pick him out of the shadows. No chance. He's disappeared as if he was never here.

And now I'm supposed to sleep. I'm doubtful as I climb back into bed, but as I drift off in a matter of minutes the last thought I'm aware of as my mind grows muzzy is that I have two less nightmares to worry about. Jackson's not a shell, and he's not Drau. I saw proof about the first, and for some reason, I believe him about the second.

So maybe I will sleep tonight after all.

I curl my hand under my head and turn my face so my lips rest at the crease of my wrist, the exact place Jackson kissed.

"You want one?" Lizzie asks.

She has the radio turned up loud, one wrist resting negligently on the wheel, the windows open so the wind whips through the car. We're going faster than fast. Lizzie likes it that way. She's been a little wild ever since she was fifteen and something happened. Something that seemed to change her overnight. She never talks about it. I don't think she even ever told Mom and Dad what it was. I just know that we were sitting there on the couch, watching some stupid show, and then she was all pale and sweaty, looking like she was going to barf.

She mumbled a lot of stuff about death and killing and dying and then she passed out. Mom rushed her to the hospital. For months after, there were all these tests. There was even a time where Lizzie stayed at a hospital for a while. She was never the same, but she got well enough to come home, to make it through high school, to head off to college.

She glances at me now and holds out the open box of candy, shaking it to entice me. She's home from college for two weeks—just got home today—and I'm happy to see her, happy to be with her, happy that despite the six-year difference, she still wants to hang with me.

I reach for the candy and take it from her hand. She laughs and looks back at the road. I'm watching her face. I see her expression change, her smile freeze, her body tense. Her back arches as she presses against the seat, her right leg slamming hard on the brake, both hands on the wheel now as she cranks it to one side. The car skids, tires screaming. Lizzie, screaming. I turn my head to look out the front window just in time to see two bright lights coming at us and the metal front grille of an enormous truck.

The hood crumples in what feels like slow motion, the grille coming closer and closer. The sound is like nothing I've heard before, metal tearing, the car crushed like a pop can, with us inside.

I blink, rolling to my side, except I don't move because I can't move. My whole body is a single shriek of agony. Cold. So cold. And tired. I want to close my eyes again and just rest.

She whispers my name.

I force my eyes open.

Lizzie's looking at me, her face all wrong. There's blood on the side of her head and along her cheek. And her eyes are gray. Swirling, pale, silvery gray.

But that's wrong. Lizzie has green eyes. The same eyes as Mom.

242

She says my name again, and I look down to see that I'm covered in blood and I can't move because I'm pinned in place, jagged chunks of metal running through me into the seat behind me. I feel like I'm looking at someone else.

"I need to hang on. Just till I get pulled," she says. "I'll make them pull you. Everything will be okay."

I swallow, my terror oddly numb, like this is all happening to someone else. I want to tell her she's right. They'll pull us out. But my mouth is filled with the taste of metal and rust and salt, and when I open my lips, something warm trickles out.

Blood?

My eyes close. Tired. So tired.

I hear Lizzie's voice, frantic and afraid, calling my name over and over. But she doesn't sound like herself. She sounds so weak. And the name she's calling . . . it isn't mine. . . . She's not calling Miki. She's calling Jackson. But that's not right, is it? I can't remember.

I try to force my eyes open.

"Look at me," she says, and I can tell she's in agony. "Open your eyes; look at me."

A command. So bossy. Always so bossy.

I open my eyes.

"Listen to me," she says. I can hear the strain in every word. "Listen to me. I need you to take something from me. They do it. I think I know how. I can show you how. You need to survive. Look at me. Look at me."

I blink, trying to focus. Her hand is on my wrist, her fingers at the base of my thumb.

"I can barely feel your pulse," she whispers. It sounds like she's crying. "You have to do it now. Look in my eyes. Think how badly you want to live. Then open yourself to instinct. It'll tell you what to do."

I stare at her, focusing hard on what she's saying, trying to understand. And something inside me does understand. I stare at her. My eyes feel strange—burning and aching. There's terrible pressure, like someone's pressing their thumbs into my eyeballs. My vision closes in until all I see is Lizzie's eyes, swirling gray, fading to grayish green, then just green. Lizzie green, like they've always been.

With a cry, I struggle to get free. Something has me. Something's holding me down. Something—

"Shh, Miki, everything's okay. It was a nightmare. Just a nightmare."

Dad. It's Dad who's holding me, dragging me to a sitting position so he can better get his arms around me, stroking his palm along the back of my head. I'm panting, drenched in sweat, my heart still racing. I had nightmares every night right after Mom died. I dreamed I was in the cold ground, and I could hear the dirt falling on me as each shovelful was tossed in the grave. But those nightmares stopped coming a while ago. Months and months. This is the first one I've had in a long time.

"Same dream?" Dad asks.

I shake my head. "No. It was different. It was . . . I think it was a car accident."

Dad reaches over and clicks on my bedside lamp. I blink against the comparatively bright light. His hair is standing up at odd angles, his jaw shadowed by overnight stubble.

"Who's Lizzie?" Dad asks. "You were screaming her name."

"Lizzie. That was her name. In the dream. I think she was my sister. She had green eyes. And I had different parents, not you and Mom. And there was a truck. And—"

She died.

The weight comes down on me like a concrete block. That wasn't part of the nightmare. When I woke up, Lizzie was still alive.

But I know for certain that Lizzie died. And I know for certain that I killed her.

CHAPTER**NINETEEN**

THE BUZZ OF MY ALARM IS ABOUT AS WELCOME AS THE SOUND of a dentist's drill. I want to roll over, snuggle under the covers, and go back to sleep. Instead, I go for my run. The nightmare's pretty much faded from my thoughts, but I can't stop thinking about Jackson. I don't know what to make of the fact that he came here last night to see me, to give me answers when he's not an answer kind of guy.

I remember the feel of his lips on my wrist.

I think about him all during my run, but when I get back to find that there are a ton of texts waiting for me, my focus shifts. I guess everyone's tired of waiting for me to offer info about my fight with Carly, so now they're digging for it. There are texts from Dee and Kelley and Sarah. There's even one from this girl we sometimes hang with,

Emily. All of them want to know about Luka. Sarah wants to know about Jackson; I guess Carly was at her house when they both saw me with him in the park on Sunday. Dee wants to know why Carly's mad at me. Every text is about Carly or Luka or Jackson, but none are actually *from* Carly or Luka or Jackson.

My, but Carly's been a chatty girl—chatty with everyone but me.

She's so angry with me. Part of me wants to say, *Who cares?* But this is *Carly.* I need to make things right. Besides, I didn't do any of the things she accused me of, and I have no intention of letting her punish me for stuff she just thinks I did. The taste of her temper I had for the past two days was quite enough. She should win the award for passive-aggressive.

So once I'm dressed and my hair is dry, I call her. When she doesn't pick up, I leave a message in between mouthfuls of yogurt and granola.

"Hey, Car. It's me. I'm mad at you, too. Hanging up on me was a shitty thing to do. Ever heard of *talking?* You want info? Here it is. His name's Jackson Tate. I did not have plans with him on Sunday. I was upset because I found out this girl I met through . . . kendo"—I planned that explanation in the shower. It's a lie, but a small one—"died, so I went running and he was running, so we ran together and he happened to be there when I had a mini meltdown. For about thirty seconds, he stopped being an asshole and gave me a hug till I got my shit together." But that's just it.

Jackson isn't an asshole. Well, not all the time. He's different than I thought he was at first.

I rush on with my explanation, "I left him at the park and ran home to find Luka waiting for me. Unexpectedly. We did not have plans that I failed to share with you. And since he was still there when you pulled up, there was no chance to call you and dissect details. End of story."

I pause, trying to climb inside Carly's head and offer something that will make her smile and forgive me. Remembering what she said to Kelley and Dee on Friday, I decide on, "But Jackson's hot." He is, but he's more than that. Much more than he originally let me see. "And his guns ought to be licensed." I close my eyes, remembering that it isn't just his guns that are beautifully sculpted. His abs, his chest, he's like a work of art. "And, um, I guess Luka's hot, too. See you in English."

I put my bowl in the dishwasher, then freeze as I stare at the beer bottle on the counter. Just one. That's good, right? I think that's good. After a second, I reach for it and drag it closer.

"Just one," Dad says from behind me, his voice too cheerful.

"So I see." I glance over my shoulder at him. His hair's wet from the shower. He's freshly shaved. And he's smiling at me. Still, something feels off, but I can't quite pin down what it is. I grab the empty bottle, stow it in the box under the sink, and wipe the counter clean.

"Counter wasn't dirty," Dad says.

I swallow and turn to face him. "I know. It's a habit."

"You can't always control everything, Miki." He reaches for me and takes my hand. He doesn't bring up last night's nightmare, but I figure that's part of what he's talking about.

"Lately, I feel like I can't control *anything*. Not even in my sleep." I regret the admission the second I make it. Tears sting my eyes. I'm not good at this, at talking to him, at letting my emotions out when I'm with him. With any-one. I feel like if I open even a tiny crack, they'll all come pouring out, and I'll be broken and out of control.

I remember the way I lost it with Jackson in the park and again with Luka on the driveway when we came back from the mission and I started laughing like a hyena. That scares me. I can't be that girl. I need my life to be like an abacus, all my beads in neat rows.

"No one can control what they see in their sleep," Dad says. "Is this about that boy?"

Depends on which boy he's asking about. I sigh. "No."

"Did you and Carly have a fight?" Dad's voice is gentle. It's his daddy voice, the one that reminds me of when I was small and he'd pick me up if I fell and stick a bandage on my scraped knee. He doesn't use that voice often anymore. Now he's Dad instead of Daddy. I guess that's what hap-pens when you grow up.

My gaze shoots to his. He's so clueless sometimes, and others, he sees way too much. "Yeah, we had a fight. How did you know?"

"Yogurt and granola for one. And two days in a row," he says with a nod toward the dishwasher. He must have seen me put my bowl away. "I can't remember the last time you ate breakfast alone on a school day."

It's true. Carly's usually here long before now. Half the time she's the one setting out breakfast while I finish up in the shower after my run.

Speaking of *one* . . .

"So you . . . um . . . you only had one beer? You're cutting down?" I stumble over the questions, but since Dad opened the door to a discussion about his drinking, something he's never done before, I want to try and get him to talk. I've done some reading on the internet and I even went to a couple of Alateen meetings a few months ago. If I can just get Dad to talk to me, maybe I can get him to go to a meeting. . . .

"Miki," he says, still holding my hand. "I don't have a problem. I just like to have a beer now and again. Lots of people have a drink after work to unwind. My job gets to me sometimes. It's stressful. Especially now, with the economy . . ."

I know that. Dad works in a bank, in mortgages. Not a happy, happy place.

He focuses his gaze on some unseen spot on the wall somewhere over my shoulder; he won't meet my eyes. "I don't have a problem. It's all under control. I'm not one of those after-school specials, passed out on the couch, with three empty bottles of gin on the floor."

That's when I'm certain that something's off. *Three empty bottles.* On instinct, I pull my hand from Dad's, yank open the fridge, and count the bottles on the door. He makes an impatient noise but I ignore him, grab the box of empties from under the sink, and count the bottles there.

Anger and pain crush me.

Dad and I, we're mostly honest but sometimes not. And this time, it's definitely not.

"One on the counter," I choke out. "And three more you put in the box, hoping I wouldn't notice. Why leave one out at all? Why lie to me? Or why not just leave them all out and ignore my worry like you have been for ages?"

"Four beers over an evening is not a lot for a grown man."

"A grown man shouldn't lie about it to his teenage daughter! Who's the adult here?" I take a deep breath, and then continue in a more even tone. *Catch more flies with honey.* "You say you won't drink, and then I come down and find the bottles on the counter. Instead of going to your fly tying group, you stay home alone—"

"I go," he interrupts me.

"You haven't been in months. You stay home and drink. Alone. Now you planned some bizarre trick to make me think you drank less than you actually did. Why would you even do that? That's just"—I hold my hands out to the sides, palms up, and shake my head—"weird. You know it's causing problems between us, and you drink anyway. When Mom was alive, you never had more than a couple of beers a week. Now you have at least a couple every night."

His eyes narrow. "You sound like you're running through a checklist." I am. I read it on a site about alcohol abuse, but I don't think this is the moment to tell him that. "A couple of beers over an evening is not a lot for a grown man," he repeats.

"You keep saying that! Are you trying to convince me, or yourself? It isn't about the exact number. It's about the fact that you have them *every* night, that even when you say you won't, you end up opening a bottle or three or six and draining them. You have a problem. Please, Dad, please—" I swallow and shake my head, trying desperately not to cry.

Dad. Carly. The game. The shells. Being forced to kill or be killed.

Jackson. For all the answers he gave me, I still have so many questions.

My whole world is falling into tiny little broken pieces and I don't know how to put it back together, how to fix it. How to control this out-of-control spin.

Dad's jaw is set, his nostrils pinched, his eyes narrow. "We are not talking about this. We were talking about you and Carly."

"No, we weren't. We weren't really *talking* at all, just exchanging words."

His head rears back like I've hit him.

He glares at me and finally says, "Teenagers," before he stalks out of the kitchen.

"I'm not the problem here," I call after him. The only

answer I get is the sound of the front door closing behind him. Not slamming. Closing. With a neat, precise click.

And he tells me I can't always be in control. I roll my eyes.

I'm glad he's gone.

I'm furious that he's gone.

I feel broken and afraid and responsible even though the fight wasn't one-sided.

As I throw together a lunch, my phone lights up with yet another text. I haven't answered any of the dozens from before, and I can't ignore them any longer, so I text them all back saying I'll see them in school and we'll talk then. I grab my lunch and I'm on my way out the door when Carly finally calls me back.

"So Jackson Tate is his name? Love it. And he's an asshole? Really? Maybe he's just misunderstood," Carly says, not even bothering to say *hi* first. "I'm sure he's incredibly nice. Aren't all guys who look like that incredibly nice?"

I huff out a short laugh, so glad to hear her voice even if she still sounds sort of pissed. "Stereotype much?"

Now it's Carly's turn to laugh, but there's a brittle edge to it. She hasn't forgiven me, but she's willing to pretend. That's a step in the right direction. I haven't forgiven her, either. "Well, Luka's nice, and he's smokin' hot."

"Luka's nice," I agree, making no comment about his heat level, just in case my suspicions are true and Carly actually wants him for herself.

"Think Mr. Shomper will show a movie today?" Carly leaps to the next topic. "I didn't read the chapter."

I groan. *Lord of the Flies*. With everything going on, I completely forgot. "Neither did I."

"What? Really?" She sounds appalled. Which doesn't surprise me. I'm the homework queen. I never forget an assignment. Usually, I have them completed days in advance. Her voice softens. "You must have been really upset about that girl."

"I was. I am. And I was upset about other stuff, too." I close my eyes, willing her to take the olive branch.

"What was her name?"

My lips part. I hesitate, then offer, "Richelle." No last name. What Carly doesn't know can't hurt her.

"How'd she die?"

She was murdered by aliens while she fought for humanity. "She saved her neighbor's son and then she fell off a roof." My voice catches.

"I'm sorry." She isn't just talking about Richelle's death. She's talking about our fight.

Part of me wants to hang on to my hurt, to tell her how deep the pain of her turning on me like that was, especially when she's the one always trying to appease and placate, always willing to hear the other side of the story, but when I needed it, she didn't offer that courtesy to me. But I don't want to keep fighting with her. "I'm sorry, too," I say.

"Okay." The tone of her voice makes my heart sink. She's talking the talk but not walking the walk. It's not okay. I could hear her hesitation. I press my fist against my forehead. I can't do this right now, so I pretend I don't hear the strain behind the word and tell her I'll see her soon.

A few minutes later, I'm at school. I jog up the stairs to the second floor and head to the last room at the end of the hall.

English is the only class I have with Carly, Kelley, and Dee. I walk in feeling wary. The problem is, our fight wasn't private. Their texts were a not-so-subtle hunt for deets, so I know Carly talked to Dee, Kelley, Sarah, Emily, and who knows who else. Despite our mutual apologies, I'm still hurt and a little pissed, but a part of me gets it. From Carly's point of view, the facts are the facts. She knows what she thinks she saw, and I can't exactly tell her the whole story to fill in the parts she's missing.

Still, her rejection is like a knife in my back. Just because she pulled the knife out doesn't mean the wound isn't aching.

I slide into my usual seat, back of the classroom, beside Carly, behind Dee. Kelley's in front of Carly. I'm more of a front-of-the-room kind of girl, but since this is the only class I have with all of them, I sit where they sit. Right now, I'm tempted to put in my earbuds, stay quiet, and ignore Dee's and Kelley's questioning looks. But that's the coward's way out.

Carly stares at me for what feels like an hour. Then she offers a small smile. "We're discussing costumes."

It takes me a second to catch up and realize she's talking

about the Halloween dance.

"Are you in or out?" she asks.

"Ummm . . ." I'm hesitant to commit until I hear what she has in mind.

"I'm going as mustard, Dee's gonna be ketchup, and Kelley's relish. We came up with it last night."

The fact that they decided without me and I'm the last to know sort of smarts.

"What are you planning to make the bottles out of?" I ask, surprised that they're going this route. All the other costumes they'd been considering involved very high heels and very short skirts.

Carly offers a cat-got-the-cream smile. "No bottles. Too bulky. We're thinking spandex. Mine'll be yellow. Dee's will be red."

"And Kelley's will be green." I get the picture. "I'm not sure people will know exactly what you're dressed as. Colored spandex doesn't exactly scream condiments, you know? Are you all going to wear pop-top lids on your heads?" The second I say it, I feel a wave of unease, the memory of how Jackson popped the shell's skull like the lid of a shampoo bottle freaking me out a little.

Carly laughs, and I force myself to let go of the memory. "Maybe," she says. "But I'm thinking colored wigs to match the spandex. And maybe little labels drawn on our tummies or something. So . . ." She lifts a brow. "You in or out?"

A minute ago I was upset that they hadn't invited me

to join in. Now, I'm trying to think of a graceful way to decline. Before I can come up with something, Carly says, "No . . . wait . . . there's three of us and, well, mustard, ketchup, and relish? That's kind of a trio thing. Guess you're on your own."

"Guess so." I duck my head and reach into my bag for my copy of *Lord of the Flies*, hiding my expression. By the time I lift my head again, I have my hurt hidden. I actually feel insulted and slighted and pissed that my friends made this plan without me. How's that for confusion? I don't know whether I'm upset that I'm upset, or glad that I'm upset because I'm feeling something more than the usual anger or pain. I can't help it. I laugh. My friends all look at me like I've grown a second head.

"It's all good," I say. The truth is, wearing skintight, reveal-all, red, yellow, or green spandex with a matching wig or a pop-top lid on my head isn't my idea of fun. Inspiration hits. "I might go as a ninja." If I go at all. Dress all in black—or if I wear my kendo outfit, navy blue—wear a mask, and strap my wooden kendo practice sword across my back. That could work. I catch Carly's eye and lower my voice. "Oh, and Carly? Don't do the bitch thing. Either we're okay or we're not."

I'm stunned by how calm I sound. Her eyes widen.

"A ninja," Carly says, ignoring my last comment completely, which tells me she'd rather be okay than not. "Black spandex. Nice. And you're hair's already dark, so you won't need a wig." She nods and turns back to Kelley and Dee, who are watching us with avid attention. They both look relieved to see that Carly and I are talking, and wary because they can sense something's still off.

At that second, Mr. Shomper walks in pushing an old TV set on a metal rolling cart. Relief is sweet as syrup. The cart gets stuck in the doorway and Mr. Shomper struggles a little, wheezing. He's seventy if he's a day, rumpled and stooped. He's organized and meticulous, always handing out a detailed description and rubric for every assignment. I like him even though pretty much no one else does. With a grinding rumble, the cart slides into the room. Mr. Shomper reaches back and closes the door behind him.

"Movie day. Nice," Kelley says. "I didn't read the chapter."

"Me neither." Dee rolls her eyes. "Actually, I haven't read a word of it yet. I was planning to just watch the movie. Guess Mr. Shomper has that covered."

"Good thing," I say. "Because I didn't read the chapter, either, and I was thinking it'd be just my luck if we had a pop quiz."

Dee and Kelley stare at me.

"You didn't read the chapter?"

"You always read the chapter."

"I had stuff on my mind."

They both look at Carly, who looks pensive, and it's easy to guess that they all think I'm talking about her and the fact that we had a fight. Which is true, to an extent. But as I lay in the dark last night listening to the house shift and settle before I fell asleep, I wasn't just thinking about how much I hate fighting with Carly. I was thinking about Luka and Tyrone. About Richelle. I was thinking about the aliens, the shells we shut down, the girl in the cold room.

But mostly, I was thinking about—

The door to the classroom opens. I look up and my chest locks down. I can't breathe. I can't think.

Jackson Tate just walked into my English class.

He's wearing jeans that have faded to the palest blue, holes at the knees, hems ragged. His dark gray T-shirt hugs his shoulders and chest and hangs loose at the waist, and the canvas backpack he has slung over one shoulder looks as well-worn as his jeans. His honey-blond hair is tousled and wild. And his eyes are hidden by a pair of bronze wraparound shades. On anyone else, sunglasses inside school would look ridiculous. On Jackson Tate they look . . . amazing.

His style is his own, and it works. And I'm not the only one who thinks so, because pretty much every girl in the room stares.

I'm not surprised to see him. Not exactly. There were enough warnings that on some level I knew he'd show up at Glenbrook eventually. My friends were talking about the hot new guy with the aviator shades right before I got pulled for the first time. Then Carly was all pissed at me because she saw me with the guy she'd called dibs on— with Jackson—when I was at the park. So it isn't as though I didn't know he was the new guy. But knowing it and actually seeing him standing here in my classroom, on my turf, are two totally different things.

I wonder why he wasn't in class yesterday, then I remember what he said last night about being away.

Dee gasps, then whirls and starts whispering to Carly. Kelley has her palms pressed together, her fingertips against her lips, her eyes wide. I can hear the murmurs from some of the other girls in the class. I don't turn my head. I don't look at anyone, don't talk to anyone. I just watch Jackson as he hands Mr. Shomper a couple of sheets of paper, then turns to survey the room.

Mr. Shomper says something to him. I don't hear it over the thudding of my pulse, but as he heads down the center aisle, I figure Mr. Shomper told him to find a desk.

My heart's pounding so hard, it's a wonder it doesn't jump right out of my chest. There's an empty desk beside me, and another on Carly's far side. I don't know if I want Jackson here, or there. Doesn't matter; I don't get a say. He cuts between desks and takes the one on Carly's far side, and as her smile widens into an all-out grin, I find myself glad he did. Carly's just started talking to me again. If he'd chosen to sit next to me, that wouldn't have been healthy for our reunion.

As Jackson drops into the seat, Mr. Shomper looks at the paper in his hand, looks at Jackson, looks back down, and says, "Mr. Tate, I don't know about the rules in your previous school, but at Glenbrook High there are no hats or sunglasses permitted in the classroom."

"Understood, sir. I'm not wearing a hat."

The room's dead silent, everyone waiting for the explosion.

Mr. Shomper blinks. "The sunglasses, Mr. Tate."

"Medical necessity, sir. It's there in the papers I brought you. There's a doctor's note and a memo from Guidance." Jackson's tone is calm and even, completely respectful, and completely inflexible.

"I'm not familiar with any medical condition that requires sunglasses, Mr. Tate. Please remove them. Immediately."

I shoot a glance at Jackson. What happens if he takes off those glasses? What happens if people look in his eyes? The same thing that happened to me when I looked in the Drau's eyes? I shiver. Then I tell myself that Jackson won't let it come to that. He'll just leave. He'll find another option. He won't risk exposure.

Jackson rubs his palm against his jaw, then says, "Are you familiar with scotoma, sir? Macular degeneration? Congenital amaurosis? Glaucoma? Any and all of the above require sunglasses."

The whole class gasps. No one challenges Mr. Shomper. But did Jackson really challenge him? There was nothing inflammatory in his tone. He sounded completely respectful.

Mr. Shomper stares at him, then does something I've never seen him do, not once, and this is my second year having him for English. He smiles. It's a little scary to look at. His teeth are yellow with a few brown spots and his pale, papery skin crinkles so much it looks like it might crack.

"Point well made, Mr. Tate," he says. "You appear to have some skill with argument. I look forward to reading your essay on *Lord of the Flies*." The smile disappears. "How many times have you presented your case to a dubious teacher?"

"This is my eighteenth school."

Eighteen schools? Even Mr. Shomper looks stunned.

"That includes elementary and middle schools," Jackson clarifies, as if that makes the number any less shocking.

That night, teeth brushed, ready for bed, I go to my window and look out. My skin isn't prickling, I don't feel that electric certainty that Jackson's out there, but I look for him anyway. Hoping. English was the only class we had together, and though I looked for him in the halls, I didn't see him for the rest of the day. I'm honest enough to admit that I'm disappointed.

I'm about to turn away when I see it: a white package on the porch roof. I open the window and lean out far enough to grab it. It's a book, wrapped in a white plastic bag that's taped down like weatherproof gift wrap. I smile. I can't help it. Whatever book it is, it's from Jackson.

I run my finger under the tape, open the bag, and peer in, feeling like I'm about six years old and it's Christmas morning.

The latest edition of *Bleach* looks back at me. I sink my teeth into my lower lip, smiling and trying not to.

There's a sheet of white paper, folded in half, sticking out from inside the front cover. I pull it out.

> Almost had to give you my copy. Sold out in two stores, but finally found this in the third. So it's yours.

No signature. None needed. I know who it's from, and my heart does a crazy little dance. I give up on trying not to smile and let my grin stretch.

With a laugh, I put the book on my bedside table, grab my copy of *The Last Wish*, tuck it in the bag, and tape it down. No note. None needed. I put the package on the roof, in a different spot than where he left the one for me, hoping that will be enough to tell him it isn't his package just sitting there unnoticed.

Then I close the window, sit down on the floor, and settle in to wait. At some point, I nod off, and when I wake up, my hip sore from lying on the floor, my neck cricked at an odd angle, the book's gone.

CHAPTER **TWENTY**

IT'S FRIDAY. AGAIN. I SURVIVED ANOTHER WEEK, AND I DIDN'T get pulled. But that doesn't mean I didn't spend the week worrying about getting pulled even though I remember what Luka said about usually having some time in between missions. I'm glad he turned out to be right.

wht is green & leafy?

I roll my eyes as I read his text, careful not to let Ms. Devon see my phone. She'll freak if she catches me using it in class.

We've started doing this a couple of times a day, sending each other the most ridiculous jokes. I text back:

Salad?

a green leaf

It takes a lot of self-control not to groan out loud and give myself away. Ms. Devon scans the room. I scribble numbers on the page, and once her eyes slide past me, I text:

What is sticky & brown?

gross. u wnt me 2 answr that?

I smile.

A brown stick.

I imagine I hear Luka groaning at the other end. Ms. Devon stands up and starts down the aisle. I shove my phone in my pocket and scribble yet more numbers on the page. She moves past me and I stare at my textbook, not really seeing it.

The week—which has actually been closer to two weeks if I count all the time I spent in the game last time—has been strange in a lot of ways. Carly and I are still awkward around each other. It feels sort of like that weird, post-breakup phase where you're trying to be friends. Except, I didn't break up with her and I don't understand why she's breaking up with me.

She came to my house yesterday for breakfast, just like she used to. Today she didn't show. I feel like whenever I'm with her now, I'm walking on cracked ice, and one misstep will dunk me.

As if he's tuned to the direction of my thoughts, Luka sends another text.

stay happy. sometimes ppl just need some space

Ms. Devon looks around the room again. I duck my head, pretending I'm working on my math questions.

Instead, I reread Luka's text. I understand the needing-space thing, but I still feel deserted. Dee's still talking to me same as usual, and Kelley's sort of okay. Emily and Sarah smile at me but don't say much.

Jackson's avoiding me altogether. Well, not exactly avoiding, just not going out of his way to hang with me. Of course, if I'm completely honest, I'm not going out of my way to hang with him, either. Too complicated. There are always so many people around him, and I already feel like everyone's staring at me all the time because of my awkwardness with Carly. We've been joined at the hip pretty much forever, and now we're not.

I've seen Jackson in English every morning, and sometimes I catch him with his face turned my way, like he's watching me. But it's impossible to know for sure with his eyes always hidden.

I know I've been watching him. We spent so many hours together in the game—literally days, side by side— that I feel like I've known him a lot longer than I have. Funny, but I've spent more significant time with him than some people I've gone to school with for years.

But not once all week did we end up alone together, not even for a second. People gravitate to him, so he's always surrounded by a crowd. He spends a ton of time with Luka, but no one else in particular. In the caf every day, he stops at different tables and talks with different groups. He's everyone's—and no one's—friend. He's a novelty and he's gorgeous and he's the same in school as he is in the game:

competent, confident, arrogant, cocky. That's pretty much a magnet for a lot of people, guys and girls alike. Charisma. Yeah, he has that in spades, but I guess anyone who moves around as much as he does—being the new guy again and again—would have to develop some special skills. Kind of like being a chameleon.

I wonder who he really is under all that camouflage.

I want him to be the boy who held me in the park, the one who cradled me while I slept in the caves.

Every night this week, I checked the porch roof outside my window, but he didn't come to my house again. I want to talk to him. I want to ask him so many things. He doesn't give me the chance, and while part of me is glad that he's staying away, part of me is hurt in a way I didn't expect.

I keep thinking of the way he kissed my palm, my wrist, and I wonder if he regrets it. If that's why he's staying away.

If we cross paths in the halls, he's perfectly polite, and perfectly distant. He treats me the way he treats everyone else—like an acquaintance. As if he never held me while I freaked out, or watched my back against an alien threat, or bought me a copy of my favorite manga. I feel like he's purposely building a wall between us, brick by brick.

Then I force myself to be honest and admit that I'm doing the same. I don't seek him out. I don't give him an opening. It's safer that way.

But sometimes, when I turn and think he's looking my

way, I see that small, wistful, sort of sad smile and I can't help but think that smile is for me.

When the bell goes, I take my time gathering my stuff, avoiding the mad rush for the door. It rained on Wednesday and Thursday, but today it's sunny and warm, so I decide against going to the caf for lunch. Instead, I head past the gym to the rear doors of the school. There are the sounds of voices and a ball bouncing off the backboard coming from the gym. I pause and glance inside just in time to see Jackson sink a basket. He's going one-on-one with Luka, and they're tossing sarcastic comments back and forth as they play.

They seem to know each other's moves, like they've played before. Often. I watch them for a minute, and then it hits me. That day that Jackson ran with me, I wondered why Luka had his number. Now I think I know. It isn't because of the game. And Jackson isn't hanging with Luka so much just because they have aliens in common. They're *friends*. In typical guy fashion, they probably don't even talk about the game when they're together outside of it.

Eighteen schools. And in his free time Jackson kills aliens. I have a feeling that real friendships are few and far between for him.

Luka sees me, raises a hand in greeting, and grins.

I wave back and then turn away, not sure I want Jackson to notice me.

Though the weather has lured a ton of people outside, they're mostly congregated at the three picnic tables by the side doors of the school or on the grassy hill that slopes down toward the road. I head out past the track to the far end, where the baseball diamond is, and climb to the top row of the bleachers. If I turn my head to the right, I can see our tree and the break in the fence that leads to the path and the street beyond. The street I ran to the day I first got pulled. The street where I'll die if the game kills me.

I turn away and stare at the empty baseball diamond instead. I'm all alone way out here, which is fine because I want to finish the last of *Lord of the Flies*. Then I remember that I told Carly I'd see her at lunch. I don't want her to think I ditched her, so I type a quick text to let her know where I am, just in case.

Closing my eyes, I lean back and tilt my face to the sun, trying to clear my mind and think only about how good the warmth feels.

"Not hungry?"

I gasp and my eyes fly open to find Jackson sitting next to me.

"What are you doing here?"

"You stopped at the gym door but didn't say anything."

"I didn't think you noticed. And I didn't want to disturb your game."

He's quiet for a long minute, and then he says, "I always notice you."

I look away, flustered, and make a show of putting my phone away, then rummaging through my bag for the sandwich I packed this morning. I set the plastic tub on my lap and stare down at it.

"Where's your entourage?" he asks.

"My what?"

"Your friends. The ones you're always with. Deepti, right?"

"She prefers Dee."

He nods. "And Kelley and . . . the blond one. She's in English with us and my Spanish class, but I keep forgetting her name. I want to say Carrie, but that's not right."

"Carly." I shake my head. "Don't tell her you didn't remember her name. She'd freak."

"Why?"

Because she called dibs on you. Because she's a little boy crazy. Because she thinks you're hot. My cheeks flush just thinking about it, because Carly isn't the only one who thinks that. And how can I think it when I know what's behind his glasses? When I know what he is, what he does? And most important, how can I still yearn for his company when he's been blowing hot and cold all week, playing some stupid little game only he knows the rules to? I continue staring at the sandwich container in my lap. I don't want to think about him this way.

After what seems like forever, Jackson says, "She's not for me, Miki."

The way he says that, the intonation he puts on my name, makes my heart speed up. I can't pretend I don't know what he means.

"I, um, haven't seen you much this week."

"I've been in English class every day." That's not what I mean, and he has to know it. He sighs, which tells me he does know. "I'm trying to stay away from you. I'm not a good guy, Miki."

There he goes again with the mysterious warnings. "Are you saying that to convince me, or yourself?"

"I don't need convincing. I live in my skin. I know my motivations, and trust me, they aren't pure."

I cut him a glance through my lashes. "So you're warning me away, for my own good, of course. And yet you follow me out here to be alone with me. You don't think that's kind of a mixed message?"

He smiles a little. "I know I shouldn't be here alone with you, yet here I am. Because I want what I want, not what's best for you. That proves my point. Not a good guy. No mixed message there."

"You don't get to decide what's best for me," I say softly. "And why do you say you're not a good guy? You've saved my life, more than once."

He sighs again. "I have my reasons, and they're selfish ones. Don't imagine I'm good." He shakes his head. "Just don't."

I don't know how to answer that.

He shifts a little closer on the bench, until our shoulders touch. I could explain that away as him wanting to be close so there's no chance of anyone—or anything—overhearing. I'd rather explain it away as him just wanting to be close to me. It feels right sitting here like this with him, which makes no sense because all my *danger* alarms are clanging full blast.

"I need you to answer some questions for me," I say softly, still looking at the plastic tub in my lap. "Before we—" Before we what? Date? Hold hands? Kiss? What am I thinking? What is he thinking? We might not even be on the same page. *I* shouldn't be on that page. Jackson Tate is moody and bossy, cocky and a little scary, and not the sort of boy I would ever in my life think about that way.

Except here I am, thinking about him exactly that way.

And here he is, saying things that make me believe he's doing the same, even though for some reason, he thinks that's not in my best interest.

"It'd be nice if you were less cryptic."

He smiles, a quick flash of white teeth. "See, now you're being cryptic because you're not telling me what you think I'm being cryptic about."

"I—" I press my lips together and shake my head. He's being purposely confusing.

Jackson leans forward and rests his forearms on his thighs, looking straight ahead at the empty baseball diamond. "Ask. I might even answer."

I swivel around on the bench to face him, one leg on either side, the plastic sandwich container balanced on my thigh. "Can I—"

He waits, and when I don't continue, he says, "What?"

"Can I see you without your glasses? I want to look in your eyes while we talk."

His mouth kicks up at the corners in that dark, sexy, dangerous smile. "You've seen me without my glasses. You know what's behind them. Not scared I'm going to suck your life away?"

"If you were planning to kill me, you wouldn't have saved my life in the game."

The smile disappears. "Maybe I'm planning something worse."

I roll my eyes. "Stop with the secretive, self-hating threats. Let's just have a conversation. A normal conversation. It's like you're trying to scare me away."

"I am." He pauses. "You're obsessed with normal. Sometimes being outside the norm is good. It makes you special."

My mouth goes dry because I know he didn't mean that as a generic use of the word *you*. He means me. He thinks I'm special.

"What are we doing here, Jackson?"

The smile comes back. "Having a conversation," he says, purposely misunderstanding me. He turns his face toward me. I don't even try to hide my frustration. "You're gorgeous when you're annoyed, Miki Jones. Your cheeks get all pink"—he brushes the backs of his fingers along my cheek—"and your eyes get sort of squinty."

I laugh, but the sound comes out breathless. "I'm gorgeous when I squint?"

"You're always gorgeous."

I shake my head. I never really think about myself that

way and, until Jackson, I never cared if anyone else did.

He swivels on the bench so he's straddling it, facing me, mirroring my posture. Then he tips his glasses up so they rest high on his forehead and stares at me for a long moment. I stare back, taking my time, really looking at him. His eyes are Drau silver, both human and inhuman at the same time. The Drau's pupils are long and oval, slitted like a reptile's—which makes sense if they come from a planet that's so bright. The slit would allow them to narrow their pupil in a way that protects them from the strength of the light.

But Jackson's pupils are round and human. His lashes are long and spiky and darker than I expected. His eyes are widely spaced, his brows sandy brown and straight, one of them bisected by a scar. From the same Drau attack that scarred his arm? From something else? Without thinking, I reach out and run my finger along the scar. His brows rise. I drop my hand. And my eyes never leave his.

They're exactly as I remember them, frightening and foreign and beautiful.

"Can you do what they do?" I whisper, remembering the way it felt to look in the Drau's eyes, the pain, the sensation of drowning and losing myself, of having my life sucked away.

His expression shuts down. This topic is clearly off the table.

I redirect and come at it from a different angle. "How do they do it? What exactly are they doing?"

"I don't have all the answers, but I'll tell you what I know," he says. *In generic terms. I won't talk about me and what I can or can't do,* he doesn't say. "It's like tuning in to a radio station. They catch your gaze, catch your frequency. The human body works on electrical charges. Action potentials. That's what makes your muscles work. Your nerves. Your brain cells. Everything. The—" He looks around and lowers his voice. "The Drau grab that electricity and drain you dry, like draining a battery. That's why it feels like they're sucking the life out of you. Because they are. By the time they're done, they leave a husk without any spark to fire the engine."

I shudder, remembering exactly how that felt. "Why the eyes?"

"That's a tough one. There's no one I can really ask about this stuff." He pauses. "No, that's not totally true. There's the Committee. I can ask them, but they don't always answer, or if they do, it's sometimes a bit philosophical and hard to grasp, so it's the same as having no one to ask."

"The Committee?" I remember his sardonic tone when he's said stuff before about things being decided by committee. I thought he was kidding. "There's an actual committee?"

"Yeah."

"So, who's on that committee?"

"Committee members."

That's all he offers, and rather than pressing on that topic, I jump back to the one he was willing to talk about.

"So why the eyes?"

"I did some reading. From what I can figure out, it's because the pupil is actually a hole. It's an opening, a doorway the Drau can use to connect to the retina and from there to the optic nerve as a way to draw electrical charge from the body. The optic nerve's a direct bridge to the brain. Makes the whole process pretty easy."

I'm speechless for a second, and this crazy cartoon image of aliens sucking out human brains pops into my head. "And you can do that? Like them?"

His jaw tightens. Despite the way I shifted directions, he still doesn't want to talk about this. Then he surprises me by saying, "It isn't something I do. I tried it once." He looks away and his expression shuts down even more. "The results weren't good."

"Not good for you, or for the being you tried it on?"

He shoots me a startled look. "You pick up on shit, don't you, Miki?" I don't answer because even though that was a question, he wasn't looking for a reply. "It left me amped," he says. "Like I'd sucked back a dozen Red Bulls." I notice that he doesn't say anything about whoever it was he pulled electrical charge from. I want to ask what happened to them, but I hold the question back. Nothing good. I can tell. Just like I can tell that Jackson doesn't want to talk about it.

"Why aren't your eyes blue, like mine? Why are Luka's and Tyrone's eyes blue in the game? Why not the rest of the time?"

"This isn't a conversation. It's an inquisition." But he smiles, and that takes the sting out of his words.

For a couple of minutes, he just sits there looking at me, his gaze traveling over my features like he's memorizing them. Then he leans closer and reaches down. I think he's going to take my wrist and kiss it, the way he did before. My heart skips a beat.

Instead, he takes the plastic container from my lap. He pops open the lid, pulls out half the sandwich, sniffs it suspiciously, and pokes at it with his index finger. "It's green."

Despite our topic of conversation and everything on my mind, I laugh at the look on his face. "That's the homemade avocado spread. The rest is twelve-grain bread, sliced grilled chicken breast, lettuce, and tomatoes."

"You're kidding."

"Hey, take it or leave it. I don't remember inviting you to eat half my lunch."

"You want me to starve?" He doesn't wait for my answer before taking a bite. "Good," he says around a mouthful of sandwich. He sounds surprised.

"I'm so incredibly glad you like it." I roll my eyes as I take the container back and lift the other half of the sandwich. By the time I've finished chewing the first bite, he's already devoured his half.

"You said you've been to eighteen schools. . . . Why?"

"Dad's a road warrior." Before I can ask, he explains, "A consultant. He goes in, cleans up a company's mess, and moves on to the next. He's pretty specialized. He gets transferred a lot. We even lived in Tokyo for six months. That was cool."

His explanation leaves my head spinning, but not just because he's moved around so much.

"What?" he asks.

"The way you said *Dad*. I guess I wasn't thinking of you in terms of having a family."

He gives a short laugh. "You thought I was . . . what? Spawned from an egg?"

"At one point, I considered demon spawn."

Another huff of laughter, rusty and low. The sound shivers through me. "And now?"

Not going there. Instead, I say, "Why didn't your dad just leave you guys at home and travel as he needed? Kelley's dad does a lot of traveling, and he leaves her and her mom and her sister here."

Click. His expression shuts down like I've flipped a switch. I've stumbled on another topic that's off-limits. But again, he surprises me with an answer, albeit one he's clearly edited.

"In the beginning, it was because my parents thought it would be great for our family to experience different places and cultures." His chest expands on a deep breath, then he blows it out. "Eventually it was just because Dad wanted us close."

That isn't the whole story. He's left out a huge chunk. And whatever he's left out is horrifically painful for him. I know enough about suffering to recognize it. I feel sad that he can't share it with me, and hopeful that one day soon, he'll trust me enough to tell me.

I feel around for an innocuous question. "So . . . any siblings?"

He just stares at me, like I've hit him or something. I feel cold, then hot. My instincts scream for me to touch him, to take his hand, to hold it. I ignore that and just sit there waiting.

"No," he finally says, very soft.

"I'm an only, too. I used to wish for a sister. But I always had Carly. Besides, there are some benefits to being an only, right?"

He doesn't say anything. I think again of his eighteen schools and figure he never had the chance to forge close friendships. So maybe being an only child was tougher on him.

The silence stretches, and I feel the need to fill it. "It's weird . . . I had this nightmare a few nights ago and in it, I had a sister. She had green eyes. Her name was Lizzie. But we were in a car accident and she— What?" He's staring at me so intently, I think I must have avocado smeared on my nose or something. I do a quick swipe with the back of my hand.

He's still staring. I stare back. "Your eyes," I murmur, "were you born like that?"

"I was born with an opaque layer over my corneas. My parents took me to a bunch of specialists. No one could figure it out. They weren't cataracts. They weren't anything that anyone had seen before. And because I was able to see as well as anyone else, they decided against surgery. They just left well enough alone. Things didn't change overnight. It was slow and subtle, but by the time I was six, my eyes looked like this. By the time I was seven, my parents figured it was easier for me to wear sunglasses and get a medical note than to try and explain my eyes. Kids can be nasty."

"Adults, too."

"True enough."

"So those diseases you rhymed off for Mr. Shomper. You don't actually have any of them."

"No. I don't have any disease at all."

"Why don't you wear colored contacts to hide the color?"

"I do when I absolutely have to. Like when I got my pic for my driver's license."

"But you don't want to wear them all the time?"

"Can't. They disintegrate within an hour."

I don't know how to word the next question, so I just come out and say it before I chicken out. "So your eyes are Drau, which means somewhere back in your line, you had an ancestor who was one of them."

"Most likely. Does it matter?"

I think about it, then say, "It matters in the scheme of the game. Are there some Drau who are good?" Is that why one of them is part of Jackson's genetic pool, or is that because of a darker reason?

But in the scheme of how I feel about Jackson, no,

it doesn't matter at all.

"Never met a Drau I liked . . . ," Jackson says. "Maybe if they weren't trying to kill me, it'd be different." He takes my partly eaten half a sandwich from me, takes a bite, then hands it back. "Next question."

Which one to ask? I have so many. "If I have alien DNA, why hasn't anyone ever noticed anything weird in my blood work? Or my mom's blood work? I mean, she had a million tests because of her cancer. No one ever said a word. Or is the alien DNA from my dad's side? His mom had eyes like mine."

Jackson holds up his index finger. "You probably get the DNA from both sides. Your strain's pretty strong for it to have come from just one." He holds up a second finger and I realize he's counting off answers to my questions. "Blood tests look at standard stuff. Iron. Red blood cells. White blood cells. Enzymes. Stuff like that. If you go for the average blood tests, they aren't looking for genetic stuff most of the time. The doc has to special order genetic tests. And even then, they don't have tests for every genetic variant."

"So basically you're saying no one will see it because they aren't looking for it."

"And because no one knows what to look for."

"How do you know all this?"

"I've had a while to read up on it. Some of this stuff I don't know for certain. I'm winging it, but it seems to make sense." He shrugs. "Not like I can go to my doctor and ask her to see if there's anything weird about my blood."

I finish the last bite of my sandwich while he speaks. "Good point."

He taps his index finger on the empty plastic container in my lap. "You got anything else to eat?"

I put the tub back in my knapsack and pull out an apple. "I only have one."

"We'll share." He takes the apple from my hand and holds it to my lips. "Bite," he orders softly.

I close my hands around his wrist, holding his hand steady, and I take a bite. He turns the apple and takes a bite from the same spot, his eyes never leaving mine. I look away, flustered.

"You're awfully chatty, Jackson. What happened to the rules?"

He holds the apple out to me. I steady his wrist again and take another bite. His skin is warm under my fingers, and I can feel the tendons of his muscles.

"The rules are in place to keep the soldiers safe. To keep them from being overheard by other people in the real world and sent for a psych eval. To keep them from being overheard by the Drau and killed for a single slipup."

"Yeah. I get that. So why are you breaking them?"

He holds the apple out to me again, but I shake my head. He keeps eating until there's only the core left. And still he doesn't answer. I pull out the plastic tub, open it, and hold it out so he can drop the core inside. I figure he isn't going to answer, so I'm surprised when he says, "They're not written in stone, even though we want the soldiers to think they are."

"You keep saying *soldiers* like we're in a war."

"We are."

I wet my suddenly dry lips. "And you keep saying *we* like you're part of a group separate from the soldiers. . . ."

"I am. And so are you. You're not a soldier, Miki."

There's something in his tone, something dark and frightening.

"What do you mean? Why do you say it like that?"

"Like what?"

"Like I should be afraid?"

"You should be. I keep telling you that."

"Of what? You? Why?"

His mouth tightens in an expression I'm coming to know. It's his stubborn look. He won't answer.

"What else do you have in that bag of tricks?" he asks, looking at my backpack hopefully.

I want to push and poke and drag the answers out of him. Instead, I ask, "Why didn't you get lunch in the caf? I feel kind of bad that you ditched Luka."

"I didn't. He ditched me. He had plans to work on chem with your friend."

"My—" I shake my head. "Carly?" And she never said a word about it to me. I guess she figures it's payback for me failing to share with her.

Jackson reaches for my bag. I let him take it and watch, half amused, half offended, as he unzips the pouch, rummages through, and pulls out a small container. He lifts it to eye level and shakes it.

"Almonds and dried cranberries," I say.

Jackson dips his head and angles a glance at me through his lashes, sending my heart tripping. "I like this," he murmurs.

"What do you like?" I'm breathless, just from the way he's looking at me. "My lunch?"

"*Our* lunch," he corrects with a grin, and I can breathe again. I can even smile. He's so relaxed. So . . . normal. He shakes some cranberries and nuts into his hand, tips his head back, and tosses them in his mouth. Then he holds the container out toward me and asks, "You want some?"

"Sure. Thanks for offering me some of the lunch I packed." My sarcasm seems to go right over his head.

"Miki," he says after a couple of minutes, his expression suddenly serious, his voice very soft. "There are things I put in motion, things I did before—"

I wait, but he just stops and doesn't pick up his train of thought. "Before what?"

Deliberately, he lowers his glasses. "I remember the first time I saw you," he says.

"Lying flat on my back in the lobby, out cold?" But even as I say it, I remember his voice in my head all that afternoon. So he must have seen me before that . . . here at school?

I stare at him, the sun touching his hair, painting it bright and fair, the dark glasses hiding his eyes, his shadow stretching down the rows of seats, and suddenly I can smell the ocean, hear the waves. . . .

"You remember," he says softly.

"No, I—" But I do. I remember something. I just can't place—

"Last summer. You were up to your waist in the water, wearing a dark blue bathing suit. I could see the edge of your tattoo. . . ."

He reaches out and lays the tips of his fingers lightly on my chest, over my heart, over my eagle. I swallow and stare at him, waiting. . . .

"You weren't wearing sunglasses," he continues, letting his hand fall away. "You turned and looked at me. I saw your eyes. I knew you were like me. And then I looked for you until I found you."

"What?"

Then a memory hits me. Mine? His? Both? I'm running on the sand toward the long pier, small in the distance. I veer toward the water, the waves lapping at my feet . . . my ankles . . . my knees. I throw myself in, swallowed by the surf, going under, coming up. I blink the salty sting from my eyes, and there's a boy on the beach, his hair glinting gold, the sun casting his shadow long and lean. I think the corners of his mouth twitch in the hint of a smile. His eyes are shaded by dark glasses. But I know he's looking at me.

And I look straight at him.

A wave takes me and when I come back up, he has his

back to me and he's walking away. He stops by my dad's beach umbrella, his back still toward me, and I see my dad sit forward and tip his head back to look up at the boy, his mouth moving. I lose interest and turn away, diving into the next wave.

"Have you ever been to Atlantic Beach?" I ask. Silly to ask. I know the answer. That hint of a smile . . . I remember the first time I saw him in the lobby, the sense of déjà vu I felt when I saw that smile.

"Once," he says.

"Last summer," I whisper.

"Last summer," he confirms, tipping his glasses back up.

"Why? I mean, why there? Why Atlantic Beach?" During the same week I was there. On the same stretch of beach where I was swimming.

"Why were *you* there?" he asks.

"We always go. We've been going to North Carolina since I was a baby. We rent a cottage every summer for a week." I pause. "Your turn."

He stares out at the empty baseball diamond and takes his time answering. "I'm not sure. I'd say that my parents suggested it, but I'm not certain they did." He turns his face back toward me, his eyes shadowed, his expression troubled. But in usual Jackson fashion, he keeps whatever it is that's bothering him to himself.

"So once you saw me, how did you find me again?"

"Your dad's hat made it easy."

Confused, I just stare at him. Then I remember Dad's ball cap with the Rochester Bass Anglers logo on the front and his name stitched on the back.

"Wait . . . you looked for me . . . you came to Rochester because of me?" The possibility is overwhelming. "I don't understand. I thought your dad was transferred here. I—" Nothing makes sense.

"The Committee has ways of working things out."

Does he mean that the Committee was responsible for his dad's transfer, or that they were responsible for his being in Atlantic Beach?

"That's it? That's all you're going to say? You tell me that you saw me last summer, that you searched until you found me, and I'm supposed to just nod and—" And what? I don't even know what to say.

"Don't ask. Not right now." His voice is low, almost a whisper. "Just let me . . ." He leans in, the wonderful scent of him—citrus shaving cream and warm male skin—luring me closer. I freeze, every cell in my body straining toward him. My lips part. My pulse hammers. I want him to kiss me. I want Jackson Tate to put his strong arms around me and hold me close and put his lips on mine.

He strokes my hair back from my cheek. "Miki . . ."

His eyes fix on me, his pupils dark and dilated, surrounded by swirling silver irises. But something's holding him back. Something is etching regret in his features and making him pull away.

Something he almost told me, and then didn't.

"Jackson," I whisper, not even knowing what I mean to say.

The moment is lost. Maybe I broke it when I spoke his name, or maybe it was gone before that.

He tucks the empty container in my bag, zips it up, and leans away. Then he settles his sunglasses down on the bridge of his nose, hiding his eyes once more. "Bell's gonna go in a second. We'd better head back."

"I can carry my bag," I say as he takes it from me and stands.

"I know." But he makes no move to let me do exactly that.

I clamber down the bleachers after him, and then double my speed to keep up with him as he strides across the field. Easy's gone. Normal's gone. He seems tense and distant, the way he is on a mission, not the way he was sitting beside me on the top level of the bleachers under the midday sun.

"You have a personality disorder," I mutter as we reach the back doors.

He turns, his expression serious, and says, "You. Just being here with you. I need you to know that."

I stare up at him, lost.

"You asked me what I like. I'm answering your question," he clarifies, and the smile he offers is truly savage, dark and edgy and full of promise. "You, Miki. I like you."

CHAPTER **TWENTY-ONE**

I STARE UP AT HIM, MY BREATH COMING TOO FAST, MY thoughts spinning like a tornado.

I think I like you, Miki Jones. Jackson said that to me before, when we were in the underground tunnels. But he didn't mean it the same way he means it now. When he said it then, I laughed and said it back to him because it was light, casual, almost a joke, an exchange between two people who were running high on the rush of adrenaline and the giddy relief of having survived a Drau attack—at least, I was giddily relieved; hard to tell with Jackson.

This time is different. This time he means the words in a completely different way.

I want to take his hand and drag him off somewhere at least semiprivate so I can—

What? Say it back? Ask him to clarify exactly what he means?

I should just grab on to his words and hug them close and let them make me glow from the inside out. But it's hard to bury the part of myself that wants to pepper him with a thousand questions because I need to control even this.

The decision's taken from me when Carly storms over, erupting like a volcano. "You ditched me!"

I stare at her, completely lost.

"You ditched me"—she points at Jackson—"for him! I was supposed to study with Luka, but because I told you I'd meet you in the caf, I went to find you. And waited. And waited!"

"No." I shake my head. "I was at the bleachers. I sent you a text."

"That's a lie!"

I shoot a glance at Jackson. He has his arms crossed over his chest, his expression unreadable. As I look back at Carly, I realize we have an audience. Dee's there, and Kelley. Emily. Maylene. Luka and his friends Dequain and Aaron from the track team, and Aaron's girlfriend, Shareese. A few other people wandering past stop to watch.

There's nothing like a girl fight to grab an audience.

"I did text you." I struggle to keep my tone even. I want to take her arm and lead her away from the growing crowd, but it'll only make things worse if she refuses to budge. Jackson still has my backpack slung over his shoulder. I cross to him and tug at it, but he doesn't let go. With a sigh, I give up that fight, fish out my phone, and turn it to show Carly the text. As I do, I realize I never hit Send. "Oh no. I never sent it!" I show her the message, still there on the phone. "Carly, it was an accident. I meant to send it. I got distracted. You're right to be angry. I'm so sorry."

"I don't need you to tell me I have a right to be angry. And I know all about your distraction," she says, completely ignoring my apology. If anything, she seems even more pissed than she was a minute ago. "I can't believe you! You're dropping all your friends for a guy?"

Could she have shouted that any louder? My cheeks burn with embarrassment and anger. "I'm not dropping anyone." I clench my fists at my sides, frustrated beyond belief.

"Hey, Carly," Jackson says, stepping in front of me. Carly and I were nose to nose, so him putting himself between us means we both have to take a step back. I want to hit him for pushing himself where he has no business being. I want to hug him for stepping in before I say something I will surely regret.

I can't see Jackson's face because he has his back to me and his front to Carly, but when he says her name again, I can hear that he's smiling. And she smiles back, just a little, like she doesn't want to but can't help herself. I know the feeling. Jackson's smile isn't something that can be easily ignored.

"Listen," he says, angling his body so that his back is to the watching crowd. He drops his voice and continues, "We have an assembly this afternoon, right?"

Carly nods. "Yeah . . ."

"I didn't get much lunch," Jackson says, and I have to restrain the urge to punch him in the shoulder. He had more than I did, of *my* lunch. "And Luka and I"—I can see his head turn a little to the left, looking toward Luka for confirmation—"we were thinking of ditching the assembly and heading out for pizza. Come along." An invitation that sounds more like an order. Typical Jackson.

Something twinges inside me at his words. Jealousy? I tamp it down. I'm not sure what Jackson's game is, but I know he's playing one. My guess is that he wants to avoid having either of us embroiled in a public meltdown. Fine with me. I'm not exactly into having an audience.

It's just like him to take over and run the show, and it's actually darkly amusing when I think of how he's the one telling me I can't always control everything.

Looks like Jackson's plan is a success, because from the corner of my eye, I see the track guys wander off. No fight means there's nothing here to see.

I step back and catch a glimpse of Carly's face. She's trying to act cool about this invitation, one eyebrow raised as she looks back and forth between Jackson and Luka.

"Ditch the assembly? What if we get caught?" She doesn't actually sound too worried about that, and I know she isn't. Getting caught ditching assembly isn't anywhere near as bad as getting caught drunk on school property and puking practically in the principal's lap.

Hating the idea of being a public spectacle, and glad

that Carly's no longer bent on having a knock-down-drag-out right here in front of everyone, I edge to the side, my eye on my backpack that's still slung over Jackson's shoulder. Grab my bag. Make my escape. Call Carly later and work things out with a little privacy. Sounds like a plan to me. From this angle, I watch as Jackson turns the full wattage of his smile on Carly. Her eyes widen.

"We better leave before the bell goes," Luka says, and steps forward to throw a casual arm across Carly's shoulders. She tips her head and looks up at him. Their eyes meet and hold and for a second I see a flash of . . . something . . . Interest? In Luka, not Jackson? In both of them? Yet more proof of how painfully far apart Carly and I have drifted. I don't even know which guy she wants.

As I watch the two of them, something tugs at my thoughts, a memory of Carly in my kitchen the day she brought coffees, the day after I first got pulled. We were talking about Luka and she had this expression that was sort of sad. Then she told me to go for it.

When we were little, long before my mom died, Carly gave me her dolls, her cookies, her favorite shirt. It's just her way. And I've done the same for her. Looking at her now, I wonder if she's putting what she thinks I want ahead of what she wants. That would be just like Carly, to hand the boy she likes to me on a platter just because she thinks it'll fix what's broken inside me. But a boy is different from a doll. For one thing, there's his opinion on the matter to take into consideration.

If Carly likes Luka but she's willing to walk away from him for me, it makes me feel even worse about how much we've been fighting lately.

"Pizza it is," Carly says as she shoots me a curious look, like she's trying to figure out what went on between me and Jackson on the bleachers and why he's asking her to ditch school with him. At least she doesn't look furious anymore.

With the expected blowup circumvented, the rest of the audience loses interest and wanders off. Kelley and Dee wave at Carly, then at me, looking back and forth between the two of us. That's another thing I hate about fighting with Carly—the fact that our other friends are invariably trapped in the middle. I'd like to head off with them, but yet another tug at the strap of my bag fails to dislodge it from Jackson's shoulder.

"You driving?" Luka asks Jackson.

"You have a car?"

"No."

"Then I'm driving." Jackson leans over and says something else to Luka, so low I can't hear.

Luka cuts a glance at Carly and says, "Shotgun."

She sends him a sour look and rolls her eyes.

"What?" he asks, all innocent grin and dark, flashing eyes. "My legs are too long to comfortably fit in the back."

Carly's lips twitch, like she can't resist Luka's smile. "Fine," she huffs, but there's no heat in it.

I'm standing there at a loss. Jackson still has my backpack slung over his shoulder, anchored in place by his firm grip on the strap. My repeated tugs on the handle aren't getting him to let go. The three of them head toward the student lot, and I'm stuck following along because I need my bag. Apart from the fact that my books and wallet are in there, my key's in there, too, so I can't go home without it.

In the lot, Luka heads for a black Jeep. It's an older model, matte black with a black soft-top. The tires come up to my thighs, with rims the same matte black as the body.

"Is this an eighty-six? A CJ?" Carly asks.

"You know cars?" Luka asks.

"All my brothers are into Jeeps. They think it's the perfect ride. Can't live with all those guys and not pick up a little bit of info."

"Or a little talent for paintball." Luka grins down at her.

Carly looks up at him through her lashes. "That, too."

"It's a YJ. Eighty-seven," Jackson says. He opens the driver's side door and pushes the seat forward. "In you go," he says to Carly, then tosses the keys to Luka so he can go around and unlock his door.

Carly clambers in, sees me standing there, and shoots me a narrow-eyed look, as if to say, *What are you still doing here?*

Jackson turns to me.

"I need my bag," I say.

"Do you now?" His voice is like warm chocolate.

I press my lips together, trying to figure out what he's playing at. I need to develop a strategy to avoid whatever it is he has planned.

We stand there for a few seconds, then he very deliberately sets my bag on the backseat, basically shoving Carly over to make room for it and trapping her at the same time. He takes a step back and makes a half turn, so I'm between him and the Jeep.

"In you go," he says to me, and smiles. Not a nice smile. One of his wolfish, I'm-the-one-in-charge smiles. And then I get it. He did this on purpose.

"What are you doing?" I whisper, appalled.

His smile doesn't dim. "Helping you and Carly have a nice friendly conversation." He leans close, so his lips are against my ear, sending shivers all the way down to my toes. "I want you happy, Miki, and fighting with your best friend doesn't make you happy."

I gasp and pull back. He wants me happy, and he's trying to offer me a way to get there. Controlling, cocky asshole—who's actually trying to do something incredibly nice. I ought to be furious at being maneuvered into this situation. Except, all he's doing is trying to give me the chance to work things out with my best friend, so how can I be mad at him for that?

I shoot a look at Luka. He's in the passenger seat, staring straight ahead, but I can see that the corner of his mouth is curved up. He was in on it. That must be what Jackson whispered to him. He told Luka to call shotgun so Carly and I would be stuck together in the back. He planned this all along.

Carly starts to push my bag out of the way, no doubt hoping to scramble across the seat and make her escape. Jackson reaches in, sets his palm against the bag, and holds it in place.

"This is not funny!" she says. "You did this on purpose! I can't believe you did this!" I'd think she's accusing Jackson, except she's looking at me.

"We don't like being played," I say, looking at Jackson, then Luka. Carly's gaze shoots to mine and I see a tiny bit of softening there as she realizes this was their ploy, not mine. "Just give me my backpack, and I'll go."

"No," she says, and shakes her head as she heaves a huge sigh. "Get in. They're right. We should talk." She pauses. "Did you really think you sent me that text?"

I nod. "I really did."

She pulls my backpack a little closer to her and reaches over top of it to pat the seat.

I take a deep breath. I'm angry with her. She's angry with me. And it's all just stupid. What are we fighting over? Aliens could decimate our world today, or tomorrow, or the next day. I could die in the game like Richelle.

I could die outside the game, like Mom.

The only thing that's really certain is this moment. The only thing I can control a hundred percent are the choices I make right now.

"Fine," I say, and climb in, making my choice.

Carly reaches into her backpack and pulls out her

cigarettes. So much for being conciliatory. Puffing smoke in my face isn't the best way to start this conversation, and she knows it.

"Not in my car," Jackson says, his voice like steel.

Carly looks at him. I don't turn my head to see his expression, but I can imagine it: hard, implacable. Whatever Carly sees in his face, she tucks the pack of cigarettes away.

Jackson's a careful driver. No rolling stops. The music set to a reasonable volume. Hands in the perfect safe-driving position on the wheel. I'm a little surprised. I would have expected him to be way more cocky. When I mention it, Luka laughs and says, "Insurance is a killer. Even one ticket would bump it into astronomical."

"And I have no intention of losing my wheels because I got cocky." The line sounds practiced, like Jackson's saying what's expected rather than what's true.

"But *cocky* is your middle name," I say sweetly.

Beside me, Carly snorts.

I take that as an opportunity. I already told her I meant to send the text, but I think that showing her again—now that she actually might be willing to look—will cement her belief. I pull out my phone, tilt it so she can see, and say, "I really did think I hit Send. My bad."

She stares at the phone for a long time. Her lips pinch, then relax, and she says, "Your bad."

At least she's talking to me.

We go to a place on Mt. Hope. It's not very busy. Probably because we're past the lunch rush and too early for the dinner rush. Maybe because it's pretty new—slate tiles, bright yellow walls, shiny counters. We head for a booth. Jackson gestures for Carly to slide in. She does and he sits beside her. Luka slides in across from her, which leaves me across from Jackson.

I expect small talk. Sports talk. Something. But Jackson goes in a different direction. He turns his head toward Carly and says, "If the world ended right now, name one thing you'd be proud of and one thing you'd regret."

"What?" She looks as startled as I feel.

"Seriously," he says. "Name one of each. Fast. Before you have too much time to think about it."

"I don't know." She cuts me a glance, clearly confused. "Someone else go first."

Jackson says, "Luka?"

"I'd regret betrayal and be proud of friendship," he says, not losing a beat. "And having some sort of ethics. I'd be proud of that."

"Carly?" Jackson says.

She rolls her eyes. "I don't know. I'd regret not having legs like Stephanie Ling. You know who I mean. She sits in front of you in Spanish. The one who always wears the really short skirts? Which she should, with legs like that."

"Never noticed," Jackson says with a small smile. Chivalry at its best. He's noticed, all right.

"That's the best you can come up with?" Luka asks

Carly, and reaches over to tug gently at the pink streak in her hair.

She presses her lips together and ducks her head so she's looking at him through her lashes.

"Seriously, Carly?" Luka laughs.

"Carly has tons to be proud of," I jump in. "Loyalty. Brains."

"Beauty," she interjects.

"Miki?" Jackson says. "Your turn."

Carly smiles at me, bigger and brighter than she's smiled at me in a while.

I try to smile back. I *mean* to smile back. But suddenly, the smells of melting cheese and tomato sauce and grease wash over me, not appetizing . . . nauseating. The room spins. My focus fades, then snaps back, too sharp.

Luka's talking, then Jackson, but I can't make out the words. I think they're asking questions. Asking me? Asking Carly? I don't know.

I press the tip of my tongue against the backs of my top teeth, breathing through my mouth, trying to ignore the smells. I can't. My stomach churns. My chest rises and falls, too fast. My head spins. There's something wrong. Really wrong.

The world feels too slow. Sounds are too loud, smells too strong, colors too bright.

Then I recognize the sensation and fear uncurls inside me. We're being pulled. I turn my head, expecting Luka's eyes to be blue. He's looking at me questioningly, his brow furrowed. But his eyes are brown.

Not blue.

It takes me a second to process that because my brain feels like its gears are grinding and going nowhere.

If we're not getting pulled, then what's wrong with me?

My breathing speeds up even more, and no matter how hard I try, I can't make it slow down. Terror sinks rows of jagged teeth into me.

Feeling dizzy and sick, weak, trembling, I push to my feet. Anxiety surges and swells. I've had panic attacks before, just after Mom died. There's an edge of panic to whatever's going on here, but that's not it. This is something more. I can't stay here. I have to get away. The yellow walls are too bright, burning my eyes. My jaw aches, my eyes burn, even my skin hurts.

"I have to—" I stumble forward. I need to get out of here.

I hear Carly behind me, her voice coming at me from very far away. "Jackson, move! Miki's sick."

She must be telling Jackson to let her out of the booth. I try to turn my head, to tell her to stay put. Whatever's wrong with me, I don't want it to touch her. But I can't speak, can't move. I'm frozen in place halfway to the door, the fresh air and sunshine just beyond the wide front window. Just beyond my grasp.

I have to get out. I have to get out.

Anxiety flips into full-on panic.

I'm not going to make it.

CHAPTER **TWENTY-TWO**

MY LIMBS PRICKLE WITH THE UNCOMFORTABLE NUMBNESS OF too little blood circulating through them. Terror is a lead ball in my chest, cutting off my airway.

"Deep breath, Miki."

"Jackson?" My fear scales down a notch.

"Deep breath," he says again. He sounds tense. Angry.

I do as he says and take a deep breath, but my chest won't expand all the way. That's when I realize that I'm bent forward at the waist, my back to his front, his arm around me. The backs of my thighs rest against the fronts of his, and I'm sort of sitting on him even though we're both standing.

It's actually not the ideal position for deep breathing, but with my legs numb, it isn't like I have a ton of options.

I don't think they'd hold my weight if I tried to pull away. I flex and release my fingers, and do the same with my toes, drawing blood back into them with a painful surge. Leaning back against him, I let Jackson take most of my weight as I lift one foot to draw a figure eight with my ankle. I switch and do the same on the opposite side. My muscles come back to life with a bright agony that makes me gasp.

"Why is it so dark? Are we back in the cave?" That doesn't make sense. We should have stopped in the lobby first to get scores and weapons. I hope the game isn't changing on me right when I'm getting used to it.

"No." Just that. No explanation of where we are. Typical Jackson. I can feel the leashed energy in his body, but his touch is gentle as he strokes the back of my head, my neck, down to my shoulder. He's still holding me. I don't want him to let me go. "You okay?" he asks.

"I thought I was getting better at being pulled."

"This is different. Better now?"

I think about that, running a quick checklist. The nausea I felt in the pizza place is gone, along with the panic and the dizziness. My limbs feel almost normal now, with just the faint vestiges of prickling dancing along my skin. But I still feel off.

"Better, yeah. I'm not about to hurl. And I think I can stand." I straighten, and I notice the hesitation as he loosens his hold but doesn't fully let me go. His arm stays looped around my waist.

Jackson supports me for another second as I straighten

fully, then lets go and steps away from me. For a guy who swears it's every man for himself, he takes an inordinate interest in my well-being.

"You're taking care of me again," I murmur.

"Again?"

"You've been doing it all along," I say, remembering the first time I was pulled. It was Jackson kneeling by my side as I came to.

"Every man for himself," Jackson whispers, but there's something wrong with the words. They sound off, like he feels pain just saying them.

My eyes adjust to the dimness as I look around, expecting to see the grass, the trees, the boulders. Luka and Tyrone. But nothing is the way it should be. Jackson and I are standing in the flat bottom of what amounts to a giant, narrow bowl lined by row after row of seated figures that extend so high I can't follow them all the way to the top. There's a bit of light here at the bottom of the bowl, but it fades the higher I look. The figures are shadowed, faces and features obscured, but I know they're staring at us. How can they not be? It isn't like there's anything else here to look at.

We're in a stadium. A coliseum.

I feel like I'm on display. I've had to do a hundred kendo competitions in front of judges and crowds, but this isn't like that. There's something about this place, these people, that frightens me. I edge closer to Jackson, until my arm presses against his.

"When are they going to let the lions loose?" I mutter.

"Lions?"

"Haven't you ever watched any shows about gladiators? Lions, tigers, bears . . ."

"That's one of the things I love about you, Miki. You've got balls of steel. And a sense of humor." He pauses. "So I guess that's two things."

His words make me freeze. Things he loves about me? He says that so easily, but I can't quite decipher his tone. There's an undercurrent there I don't understand. Still, heat rushes through me, burning away the last of the chilly numbness in my limbs. I slant him a glance, but he isn't looking at me. He's standing with his thumbs hooked in his belt loops, one hip cocked, his head tipped back as he looks up and up and up. Or maybe his eyes—hidden by those perpetual shades—are closed and he isn't looking at anything at all.

He seems relaxed. Truth, or a pose for my benefit, to make *me* relax? Hard to tell.

Curiosity gets the better of me. I turn full circle and stop dead when I see three figures set apart from the others, equally shadowed, equally eerie. They appear to be sitting on some sort of floating shelf, like three judges or like a commi—

"The Committee?" I whisper, remembering what Jackson said when we were sitting on the bleachers.

"Yes."

He's answering me, and he's not telling me to be quiet, so I figure that it's okay to talk, to ask questions. I cut an uneasy glance at the surrounding audience, which sits eerily still and silent, cloaked in darkness. "Why are we here? Where are Luka and Tyrone?"

"This isn't a mission. Luka and Tyrone weren't subpoenaed."

He's not whispering, so I don't either. "Not a mission? Then what is it? Wait . . . you said subpoenaed. Like a trial? Am I on trial?"

Jackson says, "No—" at the same time as an unfamiliar voice intones, "You may address any questions directly to us."

Us . . . us . . . us . . .

I clap my hands against my ears, but it doesn't relieve the sensation of sound tunneling into my brain, my muscles, my bones. I hear the voice not only through my ears, but I feel the sound of the words vibrating through every receptor on my skin. I taste them on my tongue; I *smell* them. The experience is both terrifying and wondrous. It's a little like Jackson talking inside my head that first day, only amplified by a thousand. A hundred thousand.

"Is—" My entire body cringes from the sound of my own voice. It's like I've been hooked up to a loudspeaker that's aimed directly at my brain. I'm thinking it and saying it and hearing it at a level far above normal, and the sensations gouge my senses like a thousand jagged knives.

"Too much?" the voice asks, and the intensity of the sound playing over my senses lessens.

"Um . . . thanks?" The sensations are softer now,

blossoming inside of me, but muted, not painful like before. I take a second to get used to the weirdness of *inhabiting* my words, then offer the questions I tried to ask the first time. "Is that why I'm here? To ask questions?"

"If you wish." Again, the sound fills my nostrils, bursts on my tongue, shimmers along my touch receptors. Weird, weird, weird.

"If I wish?" I laugh at the absurdity of that, and then stop abruptly at the experience of feeling my laughter in my toes. "Sorry. I don't mean to be rude. This is all just a little overwhelming. And, yes, I wish to ask questions." I've done nothing but wish for answers since the first day. Since the second Jackson started talking in my head.

I'm startled when Jackson reaches for my hand and weaves his fingers with mine, the familiar calluses on his palm rough against my skin. He's holding on to me almost tight enough to hurt, tight enough that I know he has no intention of letting go. I have the strange thought that he isn't holding on to me now to offer support, but because he doesn't want to lose me, like I'm going to float away from him in this strange, dim place, like a balloon, up and up until I disappear in the darkness.

I lift my eyes to the raised figures. "Who are you?"

"You may call us Committee," the voice says.

"But that doesn't answer my question." I don't know where my bravado comes from, but I figure I have nothing to lose. Whatever reason they have for bringing me here, they're the ones in control, the ones calling the shots. Since they said I could ask questions, I might as well go ahead and do exactly that. "I asked who you are, not what I can call you."

If their laughter could be described, then it's warmth and light rushing through my veins, dancing in my limbs. The experience is like nothing I've ever known before.

"You are brave, Miki Jones. And brash. We are everything and nothing. We are the collective consciousness of those who came before. We are the arbiters, the judges, the negotiators, the keepers. We know what was and we guide what will be. We are those who guide you. We have waited for you, though we would not have taken you under ordinary circumstances."

I remember Jackson mentioning something about the Committee waxing philosophical. He wasn't kidding. I take my time figuring out what their words mean. When I can formulate a clarification, I say, "So you're the collective consciousness of those who came before. You mean the aliens who fled their home planet to escape the Drau? The original ones who came to Earth?" My ancestors.

"Yes."

Now I know where Jackson gets his monosyllabic nature. "And by collective consciousness, you mean the thoughts and memories. But you're not really here. You're . . . some sort of memory bank?"

"You are intuitive, Miki Jones. That will stand you in good stead. And you are correct. We ceased to exist in a physical reality centuries ago. We are the memory and the intelligence of those who came before, stored by artificial means, here to protect our adopted planet from the Drau. You, and those like you, are our progeny."

I glance at Jackson. His jaw is tense, his posture stiff. He's too still, like the air before a winter storm. Something's wrong. He doesn't want to be here, but so far, I don't see the threat.

Abruptly, he seems to come to some sort of decision. Reaching up with his free hand to tip his glasses high on his forehead like he did back at the bleachers, he angles a glance at the three figures floating on the shelf. Then he rests both hands on my shoulders and turns me to face him.

"A moment," he says, and though he's looking at me, he's speaking to the Committee.

He stares down at me as if we are alone in this massive, echoing place, eyes crystal gray, swirling and bright, but cold like an endless winter lake. He's locking himself behind his wall. I'm losing him before I ever really had him, and I don't understand.

"Jackson," I whisper, confused and afraid. "What—" My words die. I don't know what to ask. I don't know what's wrong.

But I know with horrible certainty that everything is about to change.

He doesn't take his hands from my shoulders as he leans close so his lips are against my ear.

"Miki," he breathes, my name so soft I barely hear it. He draws me closer, until I'm pressed against him, the warmth and strength of his body flush against mine. "I need you to know something. Listen to me, Miki, and *believe* what I say." His tone is low and intense, his words coming fast and hard, vibrating with tension. "When I saw you that first time . . . your eyes. I knew. You're not like Luka or Tyrone. You're like me. Seeing you, seeing that, it gave me the first hope I'd had in a long time."

Part of me wants to interrupt with a flood of questions. Part of me wants to stay quiet and just listen.

"That hope . . . I had to find you," he says. "And when I did, I made decisions based on what I knew at the time, not what I know now. Not what I *feel* now. I need you to know that. And I need you to know I'm sorry, even though you won't forgive me."

The Committee is silent, giving him the moment he asked for.

I stare at him as he draws back.

"Promise me you'll remember that," he says, his eyes holding mine.

"You're scaring me."

"I know," he says, leaving me zero doubt that whatever this is about, it isn't going to end with sunshine and unicorns. He doesn't tell me not to be afraid. He only says, "Promise."

All I can do is nod.

"Now ask them your questions." He lets me go. He steps away. I look back at the three figures on the shelf who wait, patient and silent, for Jackson and me to finish our exchange.

I've had endless hours of lying awake at night, questions running the wheel of my thoughts, so although I have had no notice, no time to prepare for this meeting, I have so many things to ask.

"I can ask you anything? And you'll answer?" I cut a sidelong glance at Jackson. He's rigid as stone.

"To the best of our ability."

I don't bother with any specific order. I just start asking, figuring I'll shoot the questions out as they come to me. "I want to see what you look like. Can you show me your faces?"

Light comes up like the rising sun, falling across their legs, their torsos, their faces. I gasp. The one on the far right is clearly female. Her hair is dark, as is her skin. She's wearing some sort of white tunic and a heavy gold necklace that lies across her collarbone and upper chest. The only things about her that look anything other than human are her eyes. They're luminescent, as if lit from behind, and I don't have a word for the color—not blue or gray or brown or green, but an incredible mixture of all and none.

Beside her is a man with long, graying blond hair and a thick beard. His shoulders and chest are muscled and broad, his arms enormous. He's draped in shaggy furs. I half expect him to raise a massive hammer and roar that he is Thor, god of thunder. His eyes, like hers, are an eerie color I can't identify. Too bright. Too deep.

On the far left is a thin, bent form wearing a dark robe with a cowl that's pulled up over his head, the edges falling forward to hide his face. At least, I think it's a him. . . .

I glance at Jackson. He's staring at them, his expression giving nothing away.

"What do you see?" I ask, not sure why I do. I just get the feeling that the figures I'm seeing can't be real. They're too convenient, too much like something out of a movie.

"I see three women. One's holding a spindle, one a measuring rod, and one a pair of shears."

"Wha—" I look back toward the three figures and see nothing but the shadowy forms that first appeared on the shelf. "You saw the three Fates," I say to Jackson.

"Because Mr. Shomper was talking about them in English." He shrugs. "Last time, I saw three characters from a game I was playing. What do you see?"

"Cleopatra, Thor, and a monk." I turn back to the three figures, anger and frustration making my tone sharp when I ask, "Why pretend to show me your faces? Why not just say no? How am I supposed to trust any answers you give me now?"

"You saw what you expected to see. We have already told you that we are the collective consciousness of those who came before. We have no true form now."

"What did you look like when you were alive?"

"We looked like you."

"Like me specifically?" Of course not. I hope they'll miss the pinch of sarcasm in my tone.

"Like you. Like humans."

Which explains why the hazy forms on the shelf and those in the endless rows of the stadium appear to have human forms, even though I can't make out details of their features.

"Why teenagers? Why summon a bunch of unskilled kids to fight? To die? Why not adults? Why humans? Why not whatever"—I wave my hand, not sure how to express it—"whatever you are?"

"You are what we are. Our progeny, our hope. There are no others. We were the last of our kind, and you are what we salvaged, the promise for the future."

There are no others. The horror of that assaults me. Complete genocide at the hands of the Drau. I say nothing because there's nothing to say.

"Teenagers are ideal," the Committee continues, smooth and unemotional, oblivious to the magnitude of what they have just imparted. Or maybe not oblivious. Maybe just accepting because there is no changing what has already been.

"Wait," I jump in, my pulse too fast, my palms slick. "You can make us jump through time, forward and back. Why don't you just go back and stop the Drau before they ever came to your planet?"

"You are here. You exist. We do not. We are gone."

I try to understand that. I try to get how they can go back and have Richelle die seven months before she actually died, how they can make her live and fight for seven months after she was killed, but they can't go back and fix things before the Drau destroyed their planet. I shake my head. My brain hurts. It's impossible to make sense of this.

But maybe that's the answer. Maybe this whole getting pulled, jumping through time and space thing is so complicated that despite its advantages it has huge limitations as well. Or maybe their simple explanation, the statement that they are gone, is all it takes. They're *gone*. They don't technically exist. They can't go back.

"Okay," I say, holding up a hand, palm forward. I angle another glance at Jackson, wondering if he's asked all these questions in the past, when he was first pulled, if he understood the answers any better than I do. He's frozen in place, completely unmoving, not looking at me. Why won't he look at me?

I swallow and go back to my original question. "Why teenagers?"

"Children are too young, too small, too weak. Adults have brains that exhibit fully formed neural connections. What you call *getting pulled* is far more difficult for them. Teenagers have valuable adult characteristics, but their brains are not yet fully wired in a set pattern. Adolescence is a time of profound growth and change for the human brain. The prefrontal cortex does not reach maturity until the middle of the third decade of human life."

"You're saying that a teenager's brain is better than an adult's? Don't hear that often."

"For the task at hand, yes. The adult response to a specific stimulus is generally more intellectual, more of a learned response. The teenager's is more instinctual, and that is your strength."

I turn to Jackson. He's watching me, his expression taut and edgy. "On the last mission, you told me to close my eyes right before the flash, but I already knew to do that. You told me to get down, but I was already dropping. I have the same instincts you do."

He nods, and I wonder why he doesn't look happy about it.

"But Luka and Tyrone? They don't have those same instincts?"

I'm asking Jackson, not the Committee. For some reason, I feel like it's essential to hear the answers from him.

"No," he says softly. His answer is enormously important. I've figured out that much, but I haven't figured out *why*.

"Jackson . . ." I want to tell him that whatever it is, I'll forgive him. But I can't make myself say that. The last person I promised to forgive was Mom, and I lied. If there's anything that I've figured out since the first time I got pulled, it's that I'm still angry at her for dying, for leaving me. I haven't forgiven her, and that makes the last thing I ever said to her a lie. I'm not going to lie to Jackson, too.

His lips draw tight at the corners. His eyes swirl, mercury gray. "Ask your questions," he orders. "You might never get this chance again. The Committee isn't always this amenable."

I whirl back to face the three figures on the shelf, silent and patient because they aren't really here. They're the remnants of long-dead ancestors stored in some sort of database. Even though there's only one voice, it isn't only one of them talking in my head. It's a combination of all their thoughts and ideas poured into that one voice.

"Why a game? A deadly game?" I ask, buried emotions bubbling to the surface. I feel cold, then hot, the burn of anger singeing me. "We *die* out there. We don't all come back. What's with the scores and the points? A game trivializes the loss of life." It trivializes Richelle and any others who gave up their lives fighting to keep humanity safe.

"We meant no disrespect. We needed something accessible, something those your age could understand. We frame the battle in terms of a game to help those who are pulled acclimate and quickly come to terms with expectations."

"But there's no training. No buildup. You just throw us out there to die!"

"Not to die. To fight. The more you play, the more adept you become. And you were born knowing how to battle the Drau, part of our legacy to you. It is only a question of you accessing the information."

I think of Richelle, a bubbly cheerleader who was badass, taking top place in all the scores. I think of myself, figuring everything out when I had to, even though guidance was limited. But I'm not convinced.

"You could still train us, do something to offer explanation, have some sort of proper chain of command."

"Because humans do it that way? Does that make it the only way? The best way?"

I don't know what to say to that. It just seems the

commonsense way to me. Train new recruits. Offer information. . . .

Then I remember that Jackson and the others did exactly that when I was first pulled. They told me things. I didn't believe them. Not until I saw it for myself.

As if aware of the turn of my thoughts, the Committee says, "There is no time to convince every human who is pulled, to argue and cajole. Better to show. The Drau have sent reconnaissance teams, the teams you face in the game. We have a few short years at most before they come en masse to strip the planet bare. To annihilate the entire population."

"The entire human population?"

"All humans on the planet will be eradicated or harvested as a food source. Along with all other living species."

My breath leaves me in a rush. "They see us as cattle."

"You are flesh. Muscle and bone. To them you are no different than any other animal on this planet. You are meat. As we were."

I shake my head, thinking it might be time to go vegetarian.

"You said we have a few short years at most. But you think we have even less time than that?"

"Yes. That is why you are training in the field. We send those with special skills to aid those who are new. You have been aided. Now your skills are needed."

I press my fingertips to my temples. "Special skills . . . you mean leaders? Like Jackson?"

"Among others."

The others being those in the other parts of the lobby, the ones Luka and Tyrone can't see.

Could this be any more complicated?

Or any simpler . . .

The game, like any war game, has a hierarchy. There are leaders, who clearly have access to the most information. There are soldiers, who obey orders and are told things on a need-to-know basis. Then there is the Committee, the highest commanders with the most information, shut behind closed doors. How is that any different than any human army?

I glance at Jackson. He's watching me, his expression smooth as stone. That only makes me more afraid. They're giving me information that they don't offer to every soldier. I've wanted answers so badly, and now that I'm getting them, I have the feeling that the price is one I'm going to find too high to pay.

I almost ask what that price is. But then, just in case I'm wrong, I decide not to. Instead, I ask, "But why a video game? I mean, what did you do thirty years ago? Send the troops in to play Pong?"

They're silent. I think I've offended them, stepped over the line. Then the voice says, "A moment, Miki Jones. We are trying to access the answer." A pause. "Ah. Pong. Your question is clear now. There were no Drau here thirty years ago. The first reconnaissance drones came eight years past. They will come in droves within five years at most. And Earth will be no more within a decade of that."

"That fast?" It isn't a question. More an expression of horror. "What happens when they get here?

"They destroy."

I shiver, imagining it. Just last night I saw a trailer on TV for a new video game. It starts with children playing in the sunshine, heads tipping up one by one as a massive dark shadow moves across the sky. Then flames, cries, destruction. The alien ships come and fire on Earth. Everything burns. Everyone dies. I shake my head to clear the image. I need to focus on the here and now. But it won't clear. It lingers and morphs and I see a world burning. Not my world. *Theirs.* They're showing me the truth of the Drau invasion. They're showing me the destruction of their world, pushing horrific images through my thoughts.

It's far worse than anything I could have imagined.

Panting, I press my fists to my forehead, trying to make the images stop, trying to make the death cries fall silent. The heat of the flames sears me. My heart pounds as I watch my ancestors herded into pens. They look like humans, all different shapes and sizes, their cries of fear and pain the same as human cries of fear and pain. They're killed. Cut into manageable-sized portions. My whole body trembles. My lungs scream but the air is too hot and filled with choking ash. I almost fall. Jackson catches my elbow, holding me upright. At his touch, the pain and horror don't disappear, but they ease enough that I can draw a breath.

"Enough." The word slices through the room, through

my thoughts, through the screams, slick as steel. Jackson's voice, barking an order.

And the Committee obeys.

The images, the noise, the terror . . . they all stop, like someone pulled a plug and the projector went dark.

I just stand there, my heart beating so hard it feels like it's jumping into my throat. "You said the Earth will be no more? The world? The whole world? Like that? Like what they did to you?"

"The whole world," the Committee agrees. "Like that."

I must make a sound, or maybe I sway on my feet, because Jackson's there, shoulder to shoulder with me, his arm looping around my waist, offering silent support. I don't look at him. I don't dare. I need to keep it together, keep my emotions locked down. I should step away, rely only on myself. But I can't manage to do it. Instead, I lean on him and keep asking questions, like they haven't just told me the date the world ends.

"The thousand points. Is that truth or rumor? If we get a thousand points, do we get to go free?" Would I want to go free? Or would I want to keep fighting?

"No one on this planet will be free until the Drau threat is neutralized."

I'm breathing too fast, my chest tight, shoulders tense. "Truth or rumor?" I ask again.

There's a hesitation. A split second of silence that's barely enough for me to notice. But I do notice it and I notice Jackson's fists clenched at his sides.

"Truth," the Committee says. "For most."

"But not all?" Or none. Are they lying to me? Why pause if they're not lying?

"Those at the heads of the teams may not leave. They are too few in number and too essential to the scheme."

The heads of the teams. Jackson. I turn and stare at him. I remember sharp and clear how he told me there's only one way out for him. Death? No. I can't bear the thought of Jackson dead.

"They may not leave when they get a thousand points, but can they ever leave?" I pause. "Has anyone ever left? Has anyone reached the thousand points?"

"Enough," Jackson says again, his tone completely different. He sounds . . . resigned, and infinitely sad. He drops his hand from my waist and steps away from me. I feel that wall between us again, the one he builds brick by brick. He's done it with remarkable speed this time, never giving me a chance to knock out even a single block.

He looks up at the Committee and says, "Go."

And to my astonishment, they do. One second, we're surrounded by shadowy, dark figures, and then we're alone in the massive echoing coliseum. The air is too still. The lights too dim. The shadows touch us, creeping across Jackson's determined features.

"I need to do this. Just once," he says, his voice soft, his gaze holding mine. "Just once."

"Do what?" I ask, and something in his eyes makes my breath catch.

CHAPTER **TWENTY-THREE**

WE'RE SEPARATED BY ONLY A SMALL SPACE, AND THEN WE aren't because Jackson steps closer, so close that the faint citrus scent his shaving cream left on his skin lures me. So close that I have to tip my head back to meet his gaze.

Pulse racing, I stand perfectly still as he reaches up to pull the covered elastic from my ponytail. He takes his time, leaving me plenty of opportunity to stop him, to step away. My hair slides down over my shoulders. My breath stops as he takes a thick handful and drags his fingers through to the ends, then lowers his face so his nose traces up the side of my neck to my ear.

"You smell like strawberries," he whispers.

"Shampoo." I barely have enough breath for even that single word. All my senses are filled with him, the feel of his chest against mine, his lips on my skin, the beat of his heart thundering in time with my own.

My breathing turns ragged. I'm grateful for the solid weight of his forearm pressing against my lower back, drawing me closer, holding me up because my legs feel like noodles, my head spinning.

He drags his mouth over the angle of my jaw, my cheek, to my lips.

Fire bursts inside me. My lips part under his. Coming up on my toes, I fist my hands in his hair and kiss him back, sharing the flames that lick at my soul. I breathe as he breathes, liquid heat in my veins.

He kisses me like I am water and he is parched. Like I am air and he is drowning. He kisses me like he is dying and I am his lifeline. He is gentle and rough, taking and giving. In that moment, his kiss is all I know, all I ever want to know.

I come up higher on my toes and my lips cling to his as he pulls away. I'm left shaken and out of my element. I've never been kissed like that. I never imagined such a kiss existed.

I stare at him, stunned. We're both breathless. His pupils are dark and dilated, surrounded only by a thin rim of iridescent gray.

"What was that?" I whisper. I'm cold without his body next to mine. I feel cheated that he's stepped away from me.

"My one chance," he says with a hint of his dark smile.

"For what?"

"To kiss you. To live the moment I've been wanting since the first second I laid eyes on you."

I'm shaken to the core. He's wanted to kiss me all along? Like that?

"Why didn't you?" I ask, thinking of all the times I thought he would kiss me, all the times I wanted him to. All the times he pulled back, stepped away, leaving me disappointed.

"I didn't want to hurt you."

I laugh softly. "Trust me. That didn't hurt."

He drags his fingers back through the shaggy layers of his hair in a totally un-Jackson-like gesture.

"But what I'm going to tell you now will, and I swear to you, I'm sorry for that, Miki." He takes a deep breath and turns away. "You're here because of me." His tone is flat. He doesn't look at me, doesn't touch me now. I feel the absence like a blow to the gut.

"Because of you?" I wrap my arms around myself, my lips still tingling from his kiss, my heart growing wary. "Explain."

"I was first pulled when I was twelve." He spins to face me, his expression icy and cold, and *false*. He's in agony, suffering, I can see it beneath his carefully cultivated veneer.

Images assault me. Bright lights. A truck. The scream of metal on metal. The scent of blood in my nose, the taste metallic and salty on my tongue.

And then I'm broken. Like I was broken in my

nightmare about the car accident. Pinned in place.

Dying.

Such pain, in my body, in my heart.

Not mine. Jackson's. Jackson's pain.

In a snap the images vanish.

"That nightmare you had," he says, turning away once more. "It was mine."

I frown, but I'm not exactly surprised. If anything, I'm more surprised by the fact that what he's saying actually makes sense to me. As if somewhere inside, I knew it all along.

"I saw your nightmare? That night, I dreamed what you dreamed. Did you send it to me on purpose?"

He shakes his head, his posture stiff, his back toward me. I wish he would face me. I wish he would close the yawning distance between us and put his arms around me. "I was thinking of you before I fell asleep. I must have held you in my thoughts and sent you my dreams without meaning to."

"Has that happened to you before?"

Again, he shakes his head. "Not that I know of. Only with you."

"And now, right now, you put your memories of the accident in my head." He doesn't answer. He doesn't need to. I knew he could do that even before I met him, that very first day when I heard him calling my name in my mind. I gather my thoughts, sorting them before I speak. "Your eyes are Drau. And you have their ability to"—I pause, searching for the right words—"to be telepathic, like them. That's how you were going to question the Drau on our last mission. That's how you could speak in my head."

"Yes."

"When you spoke to me that first day, you told me, *Miki! Now!* . . . to save Janice's sister." I tip my head to the side. "What would you have done if I hadn't heard you? If I hadn't run?"

He turns his head and looks at me over his shoulder.

"You would have saved her yourself," I say, confident of that.

He looks away, like he doesn't want to acknowledge the truth. Like he sees himself as some sort of monster.

"Who was the girl in the dream, the one with the green eyes?" I ask, very soft. Because I think I already know, and my heart breaks for him.

"Lizzie was my sister."

I remember so many things in a sudden, painful rush: Jackson's hesitation when I asked if he was an only child. His guarded reply when I asked him if he could do what the Drau did, taking electricity through human eyes. The way he drove, so carefully, obeying all the rules, hands in perfect position on the wheel. The way I woke up from the nightmare, certain that I had killed Lizzie . . . no . . . that was Jackson's certainty. . . .

Lifting my head, I find him in the dimness, standing far away from me, still as stone. Brittle stone. If I go to him, if I touch him, he'll shatter.

I saw it in him right from the start. I kept thinking that Jackson knew something about pain, that he understood my loss. But knowing the truth only makes me wish I'd been wrong. Better that he not know.

"I'm sorry, Jackson." I know from experience that those words don't help, but it's been bred into us to say them when someone dies.

Jackson paces another dozen steps away. I don't like that he feels the need to put even more distance between us. He thinks I'll hate him, that I'll turn from him. Nothing he's telling me would make me do that, yet that's where he thinks these revelations will take us.

Images and words spin through my thoughts, memories of the nightmare and things Jackson said at different times since the moment we met. Things I said. All out of context, but when they come together, they make me wary. More than wary. My stomach knots with dread.

"The shells we terminated," I say. "I didn't just imagine they looked like you, did I? I convinced myself I was seeing things, but I wasn't. Those shells were cloned from Lizzie's DNA."

"Yes."

I close my eyes, lost in the horror of what that must have been like for him, terminating bodies that looked like his dead sister. "How many times have you had to do that?"

"That was the third batch I know of that they made from her DNA."

I shake my head. "But the accident . . . I don't understand.

If she died in the car accident, how did the Drau get her?"

He makes a sharp, cutting gesture. Then he starts to speak, low and fast. "I was dying, impaled by three metal shards, pinned to the seat, bleeding everywhere. I think my legs were crushed. I know I couldn't feel them. Lizzie was hurt. Maybe dying. I don't know. I'll never know. She was part of the game. I wasn't. She kept talking about how she needed to hang on until she got pulled. That she'd make them pull me, too.

"I thought she meant we needed to hang on until paramedics came and got us out, but she was talking about the game. She figured the game would heal us both. I don't think she really thought about what would happen after that.

"I was in and out of consciousness. At some point, we got pulled. We were healed. And I was twelve years old and part of a game I couldn't understand. They left us on the same team. Lizzie watched my ass." He huffs a sharp exhalation out through his nose and shakes his head. "First time out, I was stupid. Cocky. I was a kid. I thought I was invincible.

"My con went orangey red. We were nowhere near finishing the mission, nowhere near getting pulled. I wasn't going to make it through." He swallows, then keeps going, talking even faster. "Lizzie knew I wouldn't make it, so she came up with this genius plan. She stared in my eyes and told me to take what I needed. To make like a Drau and suck some life out of her. Enough that I'd survive. Enough to change the color on my con. She said it was like boosting a car battery. That I just needed a little juice to get me through." His voice breaks, but he keeps going as my heart shatters for him. "She said we were a team. That one of us wouldn't go back without the other."

No team. Every man for himself. Jackson's mantra. The only way he could keep going. My blood thunders in my ears and I'm drenched in horror, knowing what he's going to say next and wishing he wouldn't say it. That it had never happened. If wishes were pennies . . .

"I did it. I was twelve years old and terrified. I didn't want to die. She told me I'd be able to stop. She sounded so sure. I believed her and I did what she said. I looked in her eyes and thought about how I wanted to live, thought about taking what I needed. I can't explain what it felt like. I became a whirlpool, a vortex. My skin sparked. My nerves hummed like transformer wires. I was so amped I was shaking. The next thing I knew, my con was yellow and hers was red and there were Drau everywhere around us, shooting, hunting. A second later, I was on my feet, hunting them."

His gaze locks on mine, his pain stark and bare. "We fought on. We lost three more. And I couldn't take her with me when we were done. I tried. I held her. I looped my harness around us both thinking that would bring her along. It didn't. In the end, I left her lying there, her con bright red. I didn't get a choice." His jaw sets in a tense line, then he goes on. "I left my sister there, but I brought one of *them* back with me. By accident. I thought they were all dead. We shouldn't have made the jump if they weren't. But somehow it was alive and it came along. Back to the real world. I had it by the throat and I wouldn't let go."

I glance at his arm, and though his shirt covers the scars I see them in my mind's eye. I know they're there. He hates himself for that, too, blames himself for bringing a Drau back to the real world. I wonder what happened to it, how he escaped its grasp. He was only a kid. But I don't ask. I feel like if I ask, if I say a single word, he'll shut down and tell me nothing.

"I left her there," he says, "and the Drau took her and they put her on machines and kept her body alive long enough to create an army of shells in her image. And three times now, I've had to go back in and kill my sister all over again."

My legs give way and I'm on my knees, tears streaking down my cheeks. I hold my hand out to him, feeling his pain, aching to heal him. "Jackson," I whisper.

He shakes his head and backs up another step. "No, I'm not done. You think that's the worst of it? It isn't. I didn't just kill my sister, Miki. *I did this to you.* I doomed you to this. I'm the one. I found you. I convinced them to take you. All because I thought it was a way out. I thought I could trade you for my freedom. I convinced them to take you even though they don't usually take kids that have no siblings." He offers an ugly laugh. "How ridiculous is that? They think that if a family loses one child, it'll be easier if they have a second one. A spare." The words are harsh and guttural. "They don't understand humans. Not at all."

I stare at him, trying to understand. "But they took you. They took both of you. Lizzie and you."

Jackson stares at me for a long moment. "I volunteered. Like I had a choice. It was volunteer for the game or die in that car."

I wrap my arms around myself, chilled to the core, my emotions stretching and recoiling like an elastic band. From the euphoria of Jackson's kiss to this, to the tears tracking down my cheeks and the pain in my soul.

"So, I'm in the game because of you?"

"Yes." His beautiful mouth twists. "Hate me now, Miki. I deserve it. I told you my motives were anything but pure." I gasp and flinch when he spins and slams his fist against the wall. He stands there, chest heaving, head bowed. Blood drips from his knuckles. "I'd change it if I could. I'd give my life for you if I could."

He doesn't look at me. I don't know how much time passes. A minute. An hour. Then he says, "And it was for nothing. They'll never let me go. They'll never let either of us go."

I want to go to him. I want to run from him, from this place, from the tangled mess my life has become. I don't know what to think, how to feel. I'm angry and hurt. Betrayed. Appalled. Part of me hates him for what he's consigned me to. Part of me only knows that his pain hurts me, too.

331

He's been doing this for so long. I can't imagine how desperate he was to escape.

My brain is on overload. I can't process everything I've learned.

"Do you remember in the park when you told me not to feel guilty that I was alive when Richelle and Mom and Gram and Sofu were dead? Do you remember that?" I watch as another fat drop of blood slides from his split knuckles and hits the ground.

"You have nothing to feel guilty for," he says, his voice low, vibrating with emotion. "You didn't kill them." He turns to face me then, his eyes blazing. "And you didn't consign the girl you love to this hell."

The girl he loves.

I open my mouth to tell him I hate him for what he's done to me. Or maybe it's to tell him I love him, too. To tell him I forgive him. I do. I forgive him. Don't I?

I need to tell him that maybe he wasn't the one who killed his sister. That maybe the Drau who were attacking them killed her with their weapons.

But the wooziness I recognize too well hits me. I try to push to my feet. I try to speak. Then the world spins into color and light and bright, sharp pain bursting in my head as I make the jump.

CHAPTER **TWENTY-FOUR**

THE RESPAWN IS TERRIBLE. NOT PHYSICALLY—I'M USED TO that part now. But my emotions are tied up in ugly little knots, choking me. I open my eyes to leaves and grass and two familiar boulders; Luka's sitting on one, Tyrone on the other.

"What the hell happened?" Luka asks.

"What do you mean?"

"Something went down at the pizza place. Were you and Jackson pulled before me?"

I don't know what I'm supposed to say, how much I'm allowed to tell him. So I tell him the truth. "I don't know what I'm allowed to tell you."

He stands up and closes the space between us. I have to tilt my head back to meet his eyes. They're blue now, squinting a little as he studies me, his brows drawn in a frown. I look from him to Tyrone and back again.

Fear congeals in my gut. "Where's Jackson?" I ask, my voice a harsh rasp.

Luka rakes his fingers through his dark hair. "I was going to ask you that. He's always here before us."

Panic surges. I slow it down, deep breath, hold, release. Jackson brought me into this to buy his freedom. Maybe it worked. Maybe the Committee accepted the trade. Part of me hates him for that, for sacrificing me like a trussed lamb. But part of me wants that, wants Jackson to be free, safe, away from all this. That's what he wanted. Why he did this to me. But the wiser part of me knows the likelihood is small. Something else is going on here.

"You okay, Miki?" Luka asks.

I want to laugh, or maybe sob. I'm not sure I'll ever be okay again. I open my mouth to tell him that when I get a weird sensation tingling through me, a portent.

"Incoming," I say, not sure how I even know that. I'm already turning before Luka can reply. Two girls I've never seen before stand together, looking at me.

Kendra. Lien. Transfers from another team.

The Committee is talking in my head. I hear them, feel them, the scent of their words tickles my nose, the flavor bursts on my tongue.

I swallow and walk over to the two girls. Transfers, not new recruits. That means they know the score. No explanations needed, just introductions.

"Lien, I'm Miki," I say, offering my hand to the girl on the right. She's about my height with straight dark hair to her shoulders. Her features are delicate and sweet. Her eyes are blue, but we're in the game. No way to know what color they are outside of it, but my guess would be brown. I turn to the other and offer my hand as I incline my head and say, "Hey, Kendra." She's tiny, maybe five feet, with long, blond ringlets and a round face.

Tyrone gets to his feet and crosses the space in two strides. "Wait . . . you know them?"

"Kendra, Lien, that's Tyrone," I say, with a jerk of my head in his direction, "and that's Luka." I look at Tyrone. "I know them now. And I guess you do, too."

Tyrone's watching me with narrowed eyes. I'm torn between telling him about the Committee being all chatty-chat in my head or saying nothing at all. Kendra and Lien are standing close together, shoulders touching, watching the three of us warily.

"They're transfers. From another team," I say.

Tyrone's brows arch high.

"Seriously?" Luka asks. "We've only ever had new recruits." He glances at Lien. "How long have you been in the game?"

"A year," she says.

"Three months," Kendra says.

"Do you know why you were transferred?" Luka asks.

The two girls exchange a look, and Kendra's eyes well with tears. I know what her answer will be even before she says it. "Everyone died. We're all that's left."

The silence is deafening. None of us knows what to say to that. Then I find words, pulling them out from somewhere deep inside. "You're part of our team now. We're in this together."

Lien swallows. Kendra nods, a single tear leaking out to trace down her cheek. On impulse, I grab her hand and then Lien's and squeeze. Human contact. Silent reassurance. The same kind Richelle offered to me that first night in Vegas. The same kind Jackson offered when he brushed his fingers along the back of my hand.

My throat feels thick.

Gear up.

Not the Committee this time. That's Jackson's voice in my head. I close my eyes for a second, not sure how I feel. Glad to hear his voice. Sad that his plan didn't work. I think the words *Where are you?* But there's no answer.

I take a deep breath and face the group.

"So where's Jackson?" Tyrone asks.

"Guess he's sitting this one out."

Tyrone's eyes widen. No one gets to sit one out. We all know that.

"Looks like we're the team now." I look at each of them in turn, meeting their eyes. "Gear up." They all stare at me. "Now," I say, in a near-perfect imitation of Jackson. Then I lead by example and grab my harness, loop it, buckle it down. When I stride to the weapons box, I find something unexpected. There, on the ground, is a kendo sword.

I pick it up and slide it from the sheath. The blade is black, like the blade of Jackson's knife. I push the sword back in and strap the sheath to my back at exactly the right height so I can easily reach back and grab the handle.

When I lift my head, I find that no one has moved. They're all watching me.

"Miki?" Luka asks, and I see the wariness in his eyes.

"Jackson's not coming." Just saying the words makes me feel sick. I've been on exactly two missions and now I've been dropped in as leader. The Committee doesn't know what the hell they're doing. If Jackson hadn't been watching out for me on the other missions, would I have even made it through? I'm no leader. I'm barely a fighter.

What makes you think you get a choice?

He's there, in my head again. Or is it only my memories? Doesn't matter. We're going to be pulled whether I'm ready or not.

Furious, terrified, aware of the futility of fighting any of this, I grab a harness and toss it to Tyrone. He's my responsibility. They all are. "Gear up, or we're going in without."

Maybe that threat gets their attention, or maybe it's my tone, but they do as I say and get their harnesses and weapons on. I glance at my con. Green, with a little map in the corner that has five green triangles.

"Scores," I say, knowing the screen's going to appear before it does. They finish getting their harnesses on and move to the center of the clearing. I couldn't care less about my score because zero points or a thousand, I'm not getting out of this. Maybe none of us are. Maybe the whole thousand points thing is a lie. The Committee was kind of hedgy about that. They never answered me when I asked directly if anyone had ever made it out. But I'm not about to share that info with my team right before we go in.

I follow them to the screen in the center of the clearing for one reason only. I want to see if Jackson's score shows up.

I wait, heart in my throat. There's 3-D Tyrone and Luka. Then 3-D Kendra and Lien. Finally, my picture in its black border.

But 3-D Jackson doesn't come. Disappointment sits like lead in my chest. I bury it and focus on the moment. Kendra and Lien have fairly high scores, better than mine. Good fighters, then. That's a bonus.

Or is it? I remember what Tyrone said about the boy I replaced, about the way he stole points. I hope I don't have to deal with that. Right now, I can barely face dealing with going on a mission at all.

I'd feel intimidated about having the lowest scores if I hadn't already seen that Jackson's sucked, too. Jackson. I close my eyes and take a breath, wishing—

Jump in thirty.

Now I know how Jackson always knew things the rest of us didn't. Direct line to the Committee.

"We jump in thirty," I say.

Luka shoots me a glance. "How do you know that?"

"Does it matter?"

He tips his head, looking at me like he doesn't recognize me. In this moment, I'm not sure I recognize myself.

We respawn in a tight group. Respawn—come back to life in the game. So what's the game now? This, or the life I used to know?

The air is dusty and stale. Information feeds to my brain in a stream, some from my own senses—sights, sounds, smells—and some from the voice of the Committee in my head. We're in Detroit in an abandoned office building that was once beautifully crafted and full of life. The Committee tells me there's a small nest of Drau here, hiding in the vandalized, decaying ruins. It's night. The place is wreathed in shadows.

I look around, getting my bearings. We're in the building's lobby: high ceiling, marble columns, arches. The ceiling above my head is patterned in tiny mosaic tiles. The far end of the lobby has some yellow police tape dangling in an open archway, the adjacent marble stained black like there was a fire here at some point. I take note of that, thinking that we might be moving through some unstable territory.

I glance at my con. It's framed in green. In the corner is the small map with the five green triangles. The rest of the con's screen shows a live feed of the lobby we're standing in. We need to go down. There's no voice in my head telling me that, no indication on my con. I just know. Like Jackson knew, every time. Internal Drau alert system.

Closing my eyes, I try and find him in my thoughts. He isn't there. I feel lost without him. Afraid. I have four people relying on me to get them through this alive, and I don't know that I can even get myself through.

But thinking that way won't help at all. So I lock my emotions away and face the moment, this moment, only this one. I'll face the next one when I have to.

"Stairs," I murmur, and take the lead, thinking as I do that we've been dropped really close. No daylong jog to get to the target like there was in the caves. Not even an hour-long one like there was in Vegas. I don't need to wonder why. I *know*. There's no time for the usual protocols. The situation here is urgent.

The staircase is open and it must have been beautiful once. Now, it's littered with dust and debris, the banisters cracked and broken. I check my con. It shows the stairwell going down into darkness. I follow its lead and take my team into the bowels of the building.

We pass abandoned offices, piled waist high with garbage, glass doors papered over with newsprint. I wait for the sensation that tells me the Drau are near. I reach for it, but find nothing.

We inch along in the darkness. My fear is bitter on my tongue, and the weight of the four other lives depending on me nearly bows me in half.

Wrong. Something's wrong.

I raise one hand, halting our progress, then pull my weapon cylinder free, holding it up so the others can see. I hear a faint swish that tells me at least one of them followed my lead, but I don't look back to make certain.

Careful where I step, I lead them forward, fighting the urge to turn and run. I take a slow look around, trying to spot the source of my unease. I see nothing. Only darkness and shadows. Funny that I find that comforting. It's light we have to be afraid of now.

Behind me, one of them isn't as careful. I hear the snap of wood breaking under the weight of their foot. The sound is painfully loud in the silence.

My heart drums a frantic rhythm. My breath comes in rapid pants. I shake my head as the horrific feeling I recognize from Vegas and the caves washes over me. *Enemy.* The word is a litany in my brain, a poison in my veins, amping up my fear, my pulse, my panic.

Not going there. Not sinking into that mire.

I force my anxiety under control and keep going and going. Closer to the things that want me dead. The things that will take my brain, keep my body alive, use my genetic material to create an army that will help destroy mankind.

Not on my watch. Not happening on my watch.

But the fear inside me burns me now, like alcohol in an open wound.

Trap. Get out. Miki, get out!

Jackson's voice echoes in my thoughts at the same second I'm already screaming, "Get out!"

I spin and shove the girl behind me, little blond Kendra with her angel's face. "Run," I snarl, even though I know it's too late.

Light flares with painful intensity. I blink, knowing I've already failed them, my team, the four lives depending on my decisions. Was this how Jackson felt? No wonder he wanted out. The weight of my responsibility chokes me.

The shriek of metal flays my thoughts. It's the Drau, bending girders, breaking doors. "Get out! Luka, get them out!" I scream, my weapon cylinder in my hand. I fire, spin, fire again. From the corners of my eyes, I catch movement and I hear the sounds of scrambling; then there's a dark flash that tells me Luka didn't listen. He's there, at my back, firing at the bright shapes that flit all around us.

Lights stream past like a subway car rushing through a station. Part of me, the part that's calm and in control, takes stock. My team is at my back. We're in a tight formation in a fairly narrow hallway, firing at the masses of Drau that come at us. Too many for five people. We take some down and they just keep coming, like locusts or a swarm of killer bees.

I step back, pushing my team back in the direction of the stairs. The Drau flash, leaving bright streaks interrupted by milliseconds of darkness. I shoot, step back, shoot again, and finally, finally, we're at the base of the stairs and the Drau are in front of me. I hazard a frantic look up the stairs. There's nothing there. No lights. No Drau.

I've had no practice at this. I've been on exactly two

missions, pretty much flailing my way through both of them, and now I'm the one in charge, the one everyone's depending on to get them out alive.

"Luka." I'm breathing so hard I can barely speak, but I force the words out, making my tone hard and firm. "This is an order. When I say, I need you to get everyone up those stairs. Get them out of the building. Everyone out. You included. Not up for negotiation."

The Drau are holding back, and that makes me more afraid than when they were streaking toward us. They're regrouping. Reformatting. Getting together a fresh plan. So far, the only reason we've done as well as we have is because the hallway was too narrow for them to completely surround us.

I feel it then. The flicker of warning.

"Luka," I snarl. "Now."

I switch my weapon cylinder to my left hand, noting as I do that it melds and conforms to the slightly different shape. With my right hand, I reach back and grab the hilt of the kendo sword. The feel of the grip in my hand is familiar and comforting. This is something I know, something I can control.

I hear the sounds of footsteps on the stairs. Luka doing as I said. They're getting away. They're going to be okay. All I have to do is hold off the Drau, kill enough of them that the damned Committee is satisfied and pulls the others out.

Darts of light shoot past me: the Drau trying to get my

team. With a *kiai* shout I surge forward, my blade cutting a clean sweep. The Drau in front of me freezes, then falls in two parts, the right half going to the right, the left half going to the left. I cleaved it clean in half. The sight sickens me. There's no joy in killing a living thing.

Them or me. I have to remember that.

Panting, I spin and take the next and the next. Shards of light hit me, penetrating with a deep, burning pain. I gasp. I cry out. But I don't fall. I shoot my weapon cylinder. I slash with my blade.

Pain and rage and all the hurts that are part of me surge to the fore, feeding my skill, making me a killing machine. But there are too many. They come too fast. I hack. I shoot. I step back. My foot slips on the stair and I stumble, terror icing my soul.

Footsteps behind me. Before I can turn, a surge of black pulses forward, taking out a Drau that was almost on me.

Jackson. My heart lightens. But when I toss a glance to my left, I see that it's Luka beside me, watching my back. He grabs my elbow, steadying me, and I find my footing again. I'm afraid, so afraid, and I can't tell him that, can't let him see it.

"I told you to go."

"We can't leave the building until the mission's done."

"Can't or won't?"

"Can't. Physically impossible." One more piece of information I didn't know. I have so much to learn. I hope I live long enough to find it all out. "The others are watching the front doors, guarding our escape route," Luka finishes.

There isn't time to say more. A fresh wave of Drau come at us.

I hack until my arm feels like it will fall off, all my competition kendo finesse dissolving into a wretched, desperate attack. I point and shoot until I'm inured to the cries of those who are swallowed by the dark surge.

Them or me. That's my mantra. Them or Luka, and it's my job to keep him safe. My job to get us all out.

I'm dripping sweat as I turn a full circle and find that they're gone. All of them, gone.

I search for the certainty that we're about to be pulled. It isn't there. There's only silence and the harsh drum of my own heartbeat.

"Do we jump in thirty?" Luka asks between rapid gasps.

I shake my head. "No. There's something wrong." I reach back and thrust my sword down into its sheath. I check my con. "Up!"

We run, not aiming for quiet or stealth, our feet pounding on the stairs. We skid around the corner into the dim lobby. The rest of our team looks up from where they're stationed with weapons trained at the double doors.

One thing I've learned about the new girls already. They follow orders and they don't try to steal points. Neither of them hung back when I told them to go. Good to know. The idea of one of my own team not caring if she knifes the others in the back wouldn't sit well with me.

"Trouble?" I ask.

"Nothing," Lien says, shaking her head. "But my gut's telling me it's coming."

I nod in agreement.

Then I hear it. The harsh sounds of a scuffle. A tortured human cry. My head tips back and I look up. All I see is the ceiling, but my certainty is pure and clear. We aren't the only team in the building. And the Drau we took out weren't the only enemy.

The place is riddled with Drau, on every level. What we encountered below was just the tip of the iceberg. I've been on only two missions before this, but I know that the game has changed. This is different, and it's anything but good.

Another cry, more chilling than the last.

I look at my team and find them all watching me, waiting for guidance. "We go up," I say, feeling sick just saying it. Knowing I might be dooming them. "There are other teams up there."

"We've always worked alone," Tyrone says. He looks at Lien. "You ever worked with another team before?"

Lien shakes her head, her face a pale oval in the dim light.

Tyrone and Luka exchange a look.

"Next stage of the Drau invasion?" I ask. The threat ramping up, just like the Committee said. A shudder shakes my spine from my tailbone to my shoulder blades.

"Not a nice thought," Kendra whispers.

"Understatement of the century," Luka says.

"We go up," I say again. "I want to see everyone's cons first."

They hold out their wrists. Kendra's and Lien's are green. Tyrone's is green with just a hint of yellow. Luka's is yellow-green.

"Yours," he says, when I'm done.

"What?"

"Let me see yours." His tone brooks no argument. I hold out my wrist. Mostly yellow with just a touch of green.

He frowns, but he doesn't say anything.

"The second you go orange, you fall back," I say, looking at each of them in turn, remembering what Jackson told me about Richelle and what she ought to have done the night the Drau killed her. "We all get pulled *together* at the end of this. I'm not leaving anyone behind. I don't know what's waiting for us up there, and I don't know if we'll get separated. But my standing order is that if you go orange, it's defensive position all the way. You hang back. You stay alive—" A horrific cry carries down from above us, making the little hairs on my forearms stand on end. "You stay alive," I repeat.

And then we're going up, our feet carrying us toward the death cries that float down from the floors above.

CHAPTER TWENTY-FIVE

THE DRAU RUSH AT US FROM ALL SIDES, FLASHES OF LIGHT and deadly threat. So many of them, like locusts swarming a field. There's no grace to my movements anymore, no vestige of smooth kendo footwork. There's only the leaden weight of my arm as I hack and slash, the sweat dripping in my eyes and down my back. The fear chewing at my soul. Cries echo all around me, and from the corner of my eye, I see someone from another team drop and lie still.

Panting, I aim and shoot at any glowing thing that moves as I sidestep toward the fallen body. I am in the midst of pandemonium. Screams. Howls of agony. The smell of blood and burning flesh. Pressing my back to the wall, I squat and lay my fingers on the side of the girl's throat. I don't see her chest moving. I don't feel a pulse.

Without looking down at her, my gaze scanning back and forth for any threat, I grab her shoulder and roll her onto her back. Her arm flops down and I glance at her con. Red, like Richelle's was red. She's gone.

I want to mourn even though I didn't know her at all. I don't dare take my eyes from any possible threat to look down at her face. I don't know what she looks like. I never will. But I mourn her nonetheless. I mourn all of them. We've been here for hours, or maybe it's been days, moving floor to floor, clearing out the Drau, gathering remnants of the other teams.

My team has their orders. I gave them those orders. Pair up. Stay together. Try to keep each other in sight. That was the best I could do to ensure their safety. I'm working alone. Luka argued about that, but my will prevailed—one of the perks of being the one in charge. Actually, the only perk.

To my right, I catch sight of Luka and Tyrone. They're side by side against the far wall, taking cover behind an overturned metal filing cabinet, shooting out anything that glows and moves. The sight of them gives me hope that we'll somehow get out of here alive.

Retreat isn't an option.

This group of Drau is stronger, faster, and far larger than what we encountered on our previous missions. We can't let them go back and send reports to their mothership, or whatever it is they report back to. We can't let them escalate the threat. I hadn't thought of that until Luka pointed it out, but once he said it, I knew he was right. I

349

think of the people I love: Dad, Carly, Kelley, Dee, Sarah, my aunt Gale, my cousins. So many people counting on us.

I think of Jackson and the fact that I didn't tell him how I feel, didn't tell him how angry I am for what he's done to me. Didn't tell him how much I care.

But I don't dare think of that. It hurts too much. We left it with him thinking I hate him, that I couldn't forgive him. But I think I can. Especially after seeing what I've seen today. The Drau will kill us all—every human on the entire planet—if they get the chance. If I can help make certain that they don't get the chance, then that's what I'll do. My grandfather taught me all about loyalty and bravery and honor. If Sofu were standing here right now, he would fight.

A boy tears across the open space of the empty office and drops down to skid across the floor like he's sliding into first base. A streak of light follows him, and I see the Drau's weapon—fluid and jellylike, metallic, smooth, deadly. My own weapon is deadly, too, cold in my hand. I will it to fire. I shoot. I miss. The Drau's attention shifts to me.

Terror clawing at me, I aim, I fire—

The Drau is pulled into the darkness.

The boy who was running is on the floor at my feet now, panting, his black hair slicked to his skull, his expression grim. He doesn't look at me. He doesn't thank me for saving his life. He doesn't need to. Any second now, the tables could turn and he could be the one saving me. He keeps his gaze on our surroundings, ready to take out any threat while he reaches down and feels for the fallen girl's pulse. I don't say anything, even though I could tell him there's nothing to find. The way he came tearing in this direction, risking so much, tells me that this girl was part of his team. Maybe she was something more to him.

Like Jackson is to me.

I wonder again if he's here somewhere. On another floor of this building, facing the wave of Drau.

Or maybe his trade worked. Maybe the Committee set him free.

I want to believe that because I don't want him anywhere near this. I want him safe. I want him free.

But he's not. In my soul, I know it.

He wouldn't still be talking in my head if he were free.

Beside me, the boy keeps his hand on the dead girl's throat, like he believes that if he just waits long enough, her heart will start to beat again. Another streak of light comes at us. I surge to my feet, aim, shoot. Miss. Something big and solid flies toward me: a broken chunk of desk. It slams against my leg. Pain blossoms, a poisonous flower.

I gasp and stagger, my injured muscles betraying me.

The Drau keeps coming. I bolt forward with a *kiai* shout, taking my weight on my good leg, my gait lumbering and uneven. I'm firing and firing, the recoil slamming my shoulder like a sledgehammer, the force of my will sending black death at the Drau. It's gone, but not before the points of light that spewed from its weapon lodge in my flesh, burning like acid. And not before I hear its tortured scream.

Biting back a groan, I lurch away and sink back to the ground, grateful for the wall at my back protecting me and offering support.

That's when I notice the quiet. I can hear my own panting breaths, melding with those around me.

My team is close enough that I can call to them. *My* team. Like I'm some sort of leader. I remember all the times Jackson told me he didn't want me to be a team player. No. Of course not. He needed me to be a team leader. The thought makes me want to laugh like I did that day on the driveway with Luka. Instead, I focus on what needs to get done. I need to know how many Drau are left on this floor, and how many humans.

"Luka. Tyrone." When they look my way, I jerk my head to the left. "Recon." They move off in that direction.

"Kendra. Lien." I jerk my head to the right, sending them to scout on the far side of the wall.

I push to my feet so I can offer cover to both pairs as they check to see if the floor's clear. My thigh screams in agony. I glance down. No blood. That'll have to do for now. Beside me, the boy with the black hair, the one I saved earlier, struggles to stand. His face is streaked with sweat, or maybe tears. But his features are set with determination. He moves to stand at my side, so we're two instead of one, strangers united by a common foe, a common goal.

"This floor's clear," Tyrone says as he and Luka return.

A minute later, Kendra and Lien offer the same report.

"We go up," I say.

"Which stairs?" Luka asks.

"Were there stairs at that end of the corridor?"

He nods.

I glance at Lien. "And at the end you checked?"

She nods as well.

With the stairs we took to get here, that makes three sets.

"We should split into teams and each take a set," Luka says, his gaze sliding curiously to the silent boy at my side.

"We should stay together," Lien argues, reminding me of the caves and the way I said that to Jackson. I remember the way he acted, like he wanted me to figure out what course we should follow and be the one to make the call. I didn't get it at the time, but I do now. He was getting me ready to take his place. It hurts to think about that, to think about *him*, so I don't.

"Safety in numbers," I murmur. "But if we don't cover all the exits, there's a chance some of them will get out without us noticing." I hate the decision I'm about to make. I hate letting my team fragment into pieces. But in the big scheme of the mission, it's the best choice.

"We split," I say. I look at the black-haired boy. "What's your name?"

"Tom."

I nod. "Miki." I don't bother to introduce the others since we'll be splitting up and the chances of him remembering everyone's name are pretty slim. "Show me your cons." They all hold out their wrists. Everyone's con is now a shade of yellow, some more orangey than others. Their clothes are torn, dust and sweat streaking their faces, eyes shadowed and grim. I figure I look pretty much the same as they do.

Before I can say anything, Luka grabs my wrist and turns it so my con is visible. The little map with the triangles is still in the corner. The live feed of our surroundings still takes up most of the screen. The frame is nowhere near the swirling green it was when we started. It's a dark yellow, shaded by orange.

Luka's eyes meet mine. I don't give him the chance to say a word.

"Luka, Tyrone"—I jerk my head toward the corridor they just checked—"Kendra. Lien"—I nod at the corridor they pronounced clear. "Tom, you're with me." I pause and take a second to meet each of their gazes in turn. "Remember what I said about orange."

"You remember, too," Luka says with a hard look, and then they're gone.

The stairs are a challenge. My injured leg won't take my full weight, so I have to climb one agonizing step at a time with my good leg, dragging my bad one up behind. We encounter nothing on our way up, but as soon as we reach the next floor we're caught in the vortex of the battle. The Drau are so numerous and so bright here that the humans fighting them are merely dark silhouettes that pirouette and surge and dance away.

There's no time, no chance to make a plan. There's only me with a stranger at my back, shooting, turning, shooting again, trying to stay on my feet even though my thigh's screaming in agony with each step I take.

I don't know where Luka and Tyrone are, or Lien and Kendra.

Or Jackson.

I don't even know if he's here. But if he is, if he was sent here to this version of hell, I can only hope he's safe.

Instinct makes me duck. Too late. I arch back, my arms surging up, and pain gouges my back, my spine. I've been hit. I turn. Tom's going down, crumpling to the ground. Light comes at me. Adrenaline slams me like a train.

Grabbing the hilt of my sword, I drag it free of its sheath once more. My attack lacks finesse and any pretense of skill. I hack, I chop—ugly, short movements that get the job done. And still they come. The more I cut down, the more surge forward to take their places.

Their weapons discharge, shards of light piercing me, making me scream, the agony searing clear through my flesh and muscle and bone.

I sink to my knees, and still I fight.

My head jerks up and in that never-ending second, I see the Drau in front of me lift its weapon. I see the flare of the muzzle, burning bright. It fills my vision, fills my mind. I'm frozen, too shocked to even be afraid. I don't want to die here, kneeling on the floor. I don't want to die.

The bright surge comes straight at me and there's nowhere for me to hide.

Then a shadow blocks the light.

"Miki!"

The shadow is Jackson, throwing his body in front of mine, taking the full brunt of the hit in the dead center of his chest.

My heart stops.

Jackson.

He stands there for a second, not moving, not making a sound, and then he crumples to the ground as if his bones have turned to paper.

"Jackson!"

He doesn't answer. He just lies unmoving on the floor in front of me.

A red haze rushes across my vision. Hatred rushes through my heart. With a scream, I come to my feet and shoot and shoot. The lights snuff. Another. Another. I'm like a beast guarding her injured mate, snarling and feral, shooting and hacking at any threat. Until there is nothing left to shoot. Nothing left to kill.

Panting, I stand in a sea of broken chunks of furniture and fallen walls and bodies that lie still and lifeless. The rush of adrenaline that kept me on my feet ebbs. My leg collapses under me. I reach down and feel the swelling through my jeans. I think my femur's broken, and I don't even know when, or how, that happened. Maybe when the chunk of desk hit me.

It doesn't matter. All that matters is Jackson.

I scooch forward, gritting my teeth against the pain.

"Jackson," I say, glancing around, wary of attack. But nothing moves. No people. No Drau. Not a sound. Nothing. "Jackson," I say again, the word broken, my voice broken. But he doesn't answer.

With a groan, I shift so I can reach his head. I turn his face toward me. His glasses are gone, knocked off at some point in this fight. Or maybe he took them off. Maybe he used his Drau eyes against them. Sweat and dirt streak his face. His hair is matted. Blood traces a thin line along his cheek. To me, he is the most beautiful thing I have ever seen.

I reach for his neck and lay my fingers there, holding my breath, willing to give anything if I can just feel a—

Yes. There. Weak and slow, but there, a pulse.

The sound that escapes me is part sob, part cackle.

I grab his wrist and turn it so I can see his con.

Horror congeals in my gut. It's almost red. No, that's not true. No *almost* about it. It's red with maybe the faintest hint of orange clinging at the edge. He's dying. Jackson's dying.

I look around, panicked, ready to cry for help. From whom? Who will help us? I don't even know if there's anyone left alive. Luka? Tyrone? My heart feels like it's been shoved through a meat grinder.

"Jackson," I say again, holding his cheeks between my palms.

His eyelids flutter. Tears blur my vision. Then his eyes open and he's staring up at me.

"Miki," he breathes, and the edge of his mouth curls in a whisper of a smile. "You're okay."

I'm not. I'm not okay. I'll never be okay if he dies here in my arms.

"Don't you die on me. Don't you fricking die on me," I snarl.

"*Tsss* . . . language . . ." His eyelids close. "What . . . makes you . . . think . . . you get a . . . choice?"

My heart stops. "Jackson!" I tap his cheeks. "Jackson!"

His eyelids flutter open again and I stare into his beautiful eyes. Drau eyes, which can steal energy. Eyes that saved him once before.

"Look at me," I order, my voice hard as diamond.

His eyes widen, and he holds my gaze.

"You take what you need. Do you hear me, Jackson Tate? You take what you need."

For a second, I think he doesn't understand what I mean, and then he does. His expression turns to one of horror.

"Never. Miki. Love. You."

My tears come fast and hard. I swipe them away with the back of my hand. "You think you get to do that? You think you get to tell me you love me and then die on me? You think you get to dump me in this game and then take off? You bastard!" His eyes are closed again. My hands slide to his shoulders. I shake him. I can't help it. "Open your eyes! Open them. You look at me. You look at me and tell me you love me. You look at me, Jackson."

His eyes open, and they're clear, free of pain, free of fear. That scares me most of all. He's leaving me. He's accepted that.

And he won't risk killing me like he killed Lizzie. He won't take what he needs to stay alive till we get pulled.

Well, if he won't take, maybe I can give. It isn't stealing energy if I offer it for free.

"I don't forgive you," I grind out. "I don't. You have to grovel. You have to stick around and earn my forgiveness for consigning me to this hell. You look at me, Jackson Tate, and you live. You live to make up for what you did. You owe it to me to live. Do you hear me?" I'm sobbing now, frantic. I drop my head so my cheek rests against his and I whisper, "I love you. I *won't* let you die."

I rear back and grab his cheeks and stare down at him. Something flickers in his eyes. Something dark and dangerous. Predatory. *Yes!*

"You have Drau instincts," I whisper. "Let them out. Let them rule you." I hold his gaze, thinking how badly I need him to live, thinking how I want him to take enough to survive.

"Miki, no—"

He sounds panicked. He tries to jerk away. Too late. I feel it, the pain of the Drau pulling my life away. But not Drau this time, Jackson. And I'm giving it to him freely, though he doesn't want to take it. He's trying to wrench his gaze from mine. But he can't.

Jump in thirty.

The Committee, inside my mind.

Thirty seconds. He only has to live for thirty more seconds. I only have to live for thirty more seconds. And then we'll both be out.

We'll both be safe.

This time.

I come back to myself in the pizza place, standing in the aisle, halfway to the door. The broad plate-glass window stretches in front of me, and beyond it, the sunshine of the fall afternoon. I jerk as something touches my back, and I spin, ready to throw my arms around Jackson.

But it isn't him.

It's Carly.

Somewhere in the recesses of my brain, I remember what happened right before I was pulled by the Committee. It was an eternity ago and only a second ago that I leaped from the booth and dashed to the door. I remember Carly telling Jackson to let her out of the booth.

"You okay?" she asks, sliding her arm around my waist, there for me when I need her, all forgiven.

I look up, over her shoulder, and see Luka standing by the booth. I sag with relief at the sight of him. He made it. He's alive. Carly tightens her hold, keeping me upright.

Tyrone, I mouth to Luka. He gives a short nod. I close my eyes, slapped by relief. They both made it out. *Kendra?*

Lien? Again, he nods.

My gaze skates to the booth, to Jackson.

He's not there.

With a gasp, I take a step forward, breaking from Carly's hold. Frantic, I spin full circle, checking the whole restaurant.

But Jackson's not there.

ACKNOWLEDGMENTS

THESE ACKNOWLEDGMENTS WILL BE HEARTFELT BUT inadequate. I say that up front because a few words of thanks cannot suffice to convey the depth of my gratitude to the many people who have helped me along the way.

First of all, I want to thank Robin Rue, my agent, who listened to my distraught ramblings with patience, didn't so much as blink when I said I wanted to write about aliens, found the perfect home for my manuscript, and promised me we would have fun. She's a woman of her word. I'm having fun, Robin. And a huge thank-you to everyone at Writers' House who works hard on my behalf, with a special shout-out to Beth Miller, who has a heart of gold and steps up when I need her, going so far as to answer my frantic questions on Christmas Eve—I'd say that's beyond the call of duty.

Thank you to the amazing, dedicated team at Katherine Tegen Books, with an adoring special mention of my editor, Sarah Shumway, who fell in love with this story at first sight, worked enthusiastically to help me make it the best it could be, and cheered for it every step of the way. Sarah, you cheer so loud, I can hear you all the way to Canada.

To the friends who inspire and support me, read my early drafts, bounce ideas, hold my hand, and share the highs and the lows, I thank you: Michelle Rowen (whose sage advice started the ball rolling), Nancy Frost, Ann Christopher, Kristi Cook, Lori Devoti, Laura Drewry, Caroline Linden, Sally MacKenzie.

To Lamia A. for a wonderful critique of the early chapters of this story, and for finding the too-adult language in my teen dialogue.

To Aida Aganagic, who loves me enough to walk my dogs with me every day, thus forcing me to actually step away from the computer and get dressed.

To all those in my family who never stopped believing in me and helped me every way they could.

To Henning, for everything, including loading up the kayaks so I can paddle under the endless blue sky, clear my mind completely, and dream up new scenes. To Sheridan and Dylan, for making me laugh, bringing joy and light to every day, and pointing out the flaws in my fight scenes.

And a special thank-you to my readers for opening the door and inviting my stories in.